SILVER FALLS

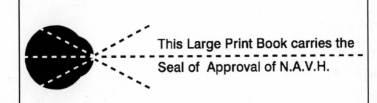

This Large Print Book carries the
Seal of Approval of N.A.V.H.

SILVER FALLS

ANNE STUART

WHEELER PUBLISHING
A part of Gale, Cengage Learning

GALE
CENGAGE Learning

Detroit • New York • San Francisco • New Haven, Conn • Waterville, Maine • London

LIBRARY OF CONGRESS CATALOGING-IN-PUBLICATION DATA

Stuart, Anne (Anne Kristine)
  Silver Falls / by Anne Stuart.
    p. cm.
  ISBN-13: 978-1-4104-1807-4 (alk. paper)
  ISBN-10: 1-4104-1807-3 (alk. paper)
    1. Newlyweds—Fiction. 2. Northwest, Pacific—Fiction. 3.
Large type books. I. Title.
PS3569.T785S55 2009
813'.54—dc22   2009015187

Published in 2009 by arrangement with Harlequin Books S.A.

Printed in the United States of America
1 2 3 4 5 6 7 13 12 11 10 09

ACKNOWLEDGMENTS

It sometimes takes a village to write a book, and I had the best possible people to help.

First I need to thank Lynda Ward, who's always there when I need her.

Sally Fifield, who has the most disturbing imagination possible (and if I find it creepy you know it's got to be bad).

Jenny Crusie and Lani Diane Rich spent hours in Campfire helping me clarify where it was going, and every single form of writing software that works on Macs gave me added help, including Scrivener, Save the Cat, Writer's Dream Kit and Wordist.

And above all, a special thanks to my Baby Boy Editor, Adam Wilson, who was incredibly patient, incredibly detailed and pretty damned funny.

PROLOGUE

Jessica Barrowman shivered in her pretty blue dress. She should have brought her raincoat, but it would have covered up the new dress, and she wanted him to see it. He'd told her he loved to see her in blue — it matched the color of her eyes — and ever since, she'd worn nothing but, so much so that her roommate had even remarked on it.

Jessica had smiled and said nothing. It felt kind of weird to be the other woman, but there was something exciting about the whole secrecy thing. Sneaking around, meeting at out-of-the-way motels, quickies in the back of the car, even going down on him in his office. He liked to wrap her long, silken hair around his body, and when she once talked about cutting it he'd gotten so angry he'd walked away from her and ignored her for three weeks.

The worst three weeks of her life.

But he'd come back, and she'd been blissfully happy. There was something so delicious about an older man, not one of the
stupid boys she'd dated. He couldn't care
less about football, or rap music, or drinking beer or playing video games.

He was from a different world — he was
sophisticated, elegant, wise. He drank
whiskey, and wine, for heaven's sake. And
he'd never, ever try to shove her around like
her last boyfriend.

There were times when she wished she
could tell her roommate, Janice, about him.
Times when she wanted to tell the whole
campus. She'd almost called his wife once,
but then thought better of it. She'd made
him really mad once, and it had almost
scared her. Well, she knew better than to be
scared, but still . . . She couldn't stand the
thought of not seeing him for another three
weeks.

He had a special present, he said. For their
three-month anniversary, and she'd bought
this new dress on purpose. If Janice had
been in the room she would have told her.
He was going to tell her he was leaving his
wife. She was sure of it. He'd brought her a
promise ring, since they couldn't be engaged
until after the divorce, but she knew he
loved her. Knew he'd do anything for her.

8

She hadn't liked climbing up the stupid mountain in her new shoes. She was wearing the blue enamel barrettes he'd given her, and she didn't want to meet him when she was sweaty and out of breath. So she'd started up earlier, with her raincoat and boots, dumping them in the bushes just before she came to the clearing where they'd first declared their love.

He was already there, waiting for her. He looked at her and smiled, that sweet, lovely smile of his, and she went up and kissed him.

He kissed her back, holding her hands in his for a moment. "Turn around," he said, his voice husky with promise. "I want this to be a surprise."

She turned, and felt his hands on her shoulders, and she shivered in anticipatory delight. His fingers stroked the sides of her neck, and she made a little sound of pleasure. And then they tightened for a moment.

It was his favorite kind of sex play, and she was very tolerant. He'd never used it as foreplay before, but she didn't object, leaning back against him. "Don't you want to be inside me first?" she whispered, her voice slightly muffled by the pressure of his fingers.

"Later," he said, his lips brushing her ear. "Later." And his fingers tightened.

Sometimes he liked it when she fought back. Except this time he was scaring her — she didn't give a shit whether he liked it or not — and she clawed at his hands, trying to yank them away.

Gloves. Why the fuck was he wearing gloves? She couldn't breathe . . . the pain was hard, burning, and she kicked back at him, as hard as she could, but he didn't seem to notice.

Things were getting darker, the sound of the falls roaring in her ears, blackness all around, and she thought, I'm dying, and his lips brushed her ear again.

"I love you, Jessica," he whispered.

But by then it was too late, and she heard nothing more.

He looked down at her. Poor thing, she was covered in mud. He was going to get filthy himself, but he couldn't leave her like this. She had to know how much he loved her, how much he appreciated her sacrifice.

He stripped off his clothes, everything but his boots. He turned her over, arranged her carefully, and pushed his hard penis into her unyielding flesh. This was always the best part. It always ended too quickly, but he wept tears of gratitude as he came.

He pulled away from her, removed the condom and tossed it over the falls. He leaned over and kissed her slack mouth, closed her eyelids and kissed them as well. He unfastened her blue enamel barrettes, letting her hair fall free about her face. And then he rolled her over the edge of the cliff, watching as she danced down the waterfall, her blond hair trailing her body like a wedding veil.

This had been a mistake — his self-control had been off. He liked to wait a safe amount of time between them. The buildup and the anticipation was almost as delicious as the act itself.

But something had driven him to move quickly. She'd become possessive too fast. It was why he seldom picked women from his hometown.

So he'd made his move sooner than he liked. Regret was a foolish emotion, and he rather liked the fact that he never felt any. Needs were acceptable. Emotions were weak.

Now he should be fine. Calm and collected. And no one would ever guess what had happened up at Silver Falls.

There'd be no more Jessica, not unless he was very very careful. No, he could wait.

But then, he'd always been a careful man.

11

She was number thirty-seven, and no one had even begun to suspect. Even though his quest was almost over, he didn't have to stop indulging his particular appetites.

He pulled his clothes on. He'd have to burn them. He always burned his clothes, which saddened him. He would have liked to have kept a whole closetful, for souvenirs.

He had to make do with the barrettes. He held them to his face, sniffing them appreciatively. They smelled like the shampoo she used. And then he put them in his pocket and turned.

He saw her coat and boots at the last minute, and for a moment he was annoyed. It could have complicated things if he'd missed them, and for a moment he hated her.

But that moment passed. He threw the coat and boots after her, into the deep, churning water. She was long gone, and the clothing disappeared as well, and he found he could smile again. He could forgive her.

Lovely Jessica. He'd miss her.

And he started down the mountain, whistling softly.

1

It was raining again. Of course it was, Rachel thought, peering up through the window at the gray, listless sky as her husband's black BMW pulled into their driveway. In Silver Falls, Washington, it was either raining, about to rain or just had finished raining. Even on an otherwise still night you could hear the rush of the thundering falls up on Silver Mountain, the roar of the water leaching into your brain until you felt as if you were drowning.

It was little wonder she had this sense of impending doom. There were any number of scientific studies proving the depressing effect of sunless days on human nature. She was used to the hot, sunny climates where she and her daughter had lived during the past ten years. She was simply having a hard time with rain, and gloom and shadows. She'd adapt. Everyone was moving to the Pacific Northwest — she'd grow to love it sooner or later.

She smoothed the discreet black shift down over her full hips, her hands restless. David wasn't going to be happy with her — she'd missed another appointment with the lawyer, she'd failed to meet him at his office and she'd let Sophie spend the night with friends on a school night rather than attend Stephen Henry's reading. David wouldn't argue with her, of course. Not David. He would look terribly disappointed, and that was far more effective than any number of screaming tantrums.

The thought of mild-mannered David throwing a tantrum was enough to make her grin. He pulled the BMW to a stop exactly two and a half feet from the garage, opened the door and stuck out his black umbrella, unfurling it before he stepped out of the car into the light mist. He caught Rachel's smile, and he smiled back, though his expression was tinged with that damnable, omnipresent disappointment.

"You missed our three-o'clock meeting at the lawyer's," he greeted her, clinking cheekbones with her in a ritual sign of affection. "I thought you were going to make sure you got there."

Guilt annoyed her, but she felt it anyway. "I'm so sorry, David," she said, trying to

14

sound penitent. "I just got caught up in work." Which was a lie. She'd looked up at the faint glow of her watch in the darkroom, saw that she had plenty of time to get to their appointment and then promptly ignored it.

"This is the third time, Rachel," he said with utmost patience. "Are you having second thoughts about letting me adopt Sophie? It was your idea in the first place."

That wasn't exactly how Rachel remembered it, but she didn't bother correcting him. Being married meant making compromises, being tactful, something she could always work on.

"Don't be ridiculous," she said. "There's nothing I want more than for us to be a family. I just get . . . distracted."

He reached out and brushed an affectionate hand through her tangled red hair. "Always a dreamer, aren't you, Rachel?" he said, some of the disapproval vanishing. "Your daughter's more responsible than you are."

She took an instinctive step backward, trying to push her wild hair back into a semblance of order. David was a lovely man, but he had an unfortunate tendency to be ever so slightly patronizing. "I'm perfectly responsible when it's important," she said, keeping the edge out of her voice.

"And my adopting Sophie isn't important?" The disappointment was back in full, and Rachel bit back an instinctive retort. He hated it when she was bitchy, and she hated it as well. For Sophie's sake, most of all.

But then, Sophie wasn't there at the moment. "You know it is, David. But there isn't any hurry, is there? We've only been married four months, and I don't know about you but I'm planning to stay married for the next fifty years. There's no need to rush into anything." She tried her most winning smile, the smile that had first caught his eyes six months ago in San Francisco, even if it was a little tight around the edges.

"Of course not," David said easily. That was what she'd first loved about him. His ability to take things in stride, including her temper. "Are you ready to go? We're running late as it is. You know how my father likes to have his audience gathered before he launches into a reading."

"I know," she said, glumly, unable to summon up much more enthusiasm. David's father, Stephen Henry Middleton, professor emeritus of Silver Falls College, self-styled poet laureate of the Pacific Northwest, should have been a welcome part of the

16

package. She hadn't known any kind of father for the past thirteen years, not since she'd been kicked out of the house for being seventeen and pregnant, and Stephen Henry was born to be a patriarch. He doted on an unappreciative Sophie and managed just the right amount of decorous flirting with his daughter-in-law. Maybe it was Sophie's hidden dislike that tipped her off. Her daughter always had had far better instincts than she had.

"I'm ready," she said, plastering on her best smile.

David took a spotless white linen handkerchief from his elegant suit, reached up and wiped her lipstick off her mouth. "There," he said with a sigh of satisfaction. "That's much better. Aren't you going to change your shoes?"

She'd loved that bright slash of color on her mouth, but marriage was give and take, and she knew David didn't like makeup. She must have done it subconsciously, just to annoy him. She really had to stop doing things like that or she'd never settle in.

She looked down at her shoes. She was still wearing the two-inch heels that put her a good three inches taller than David's blond head. They were the brightly colored espadrilles she'd picked up in Mexico, with straps around the ankles that made her strong legs look sexy. She sighed. "Sorry, I forget," she said, kicking them off and going in search of the ballet slippers he preferred. He followed her, shoes in his hand. "Sorry," she said again, grabbing the plain black flats. She had a weakness for shoes, and she always left them all over the place, and David was always picking them up. He moved past her, placing them in the labeled cubby hole of the custom closet that both delighted and intimidated her with its strict organization, then held out his arm.

"Where's Sophie?"

"I told her she could spend the night at Kristen Bannister's. You know what a math wonk she is — she promised to help Kristen understand the bizarre properties of God knows what, and I knew we wouldn't want to be late."

Just the faintest flash of impatience on David's handsome face, gone almost as it appeared. "There are times I think you married me for the math program here in town."

"Of course not. Just because her gift for math makes me feel like the village idiot doesn't mean I'd run off with the first man who had access to an accelerated math program. I had no idea the local high school was so good."

"I told you," he pointed out. "When you were having trouble helping her. Home-schooling can only take you so far."

"I married you for *you*, David," she said firmly. "How can you doubt it?"

"I don't," he said, looking happier. "It's just that my father adores Sophie and he doesn't see her often enough."

But Sophie didn't adore his father. "Schoolwork comes first, don't you agree?"

"Of course." As a college professor he couldn't very well say anything else. "We'll have to bring her over for dinner some time this week to make up for it."

"Of course," Rachel said. Sophie would go if she asked her to. But Rachel hadn't lived thirty years, half of them on her own, without learning how to get what she wanted. After all, she was doing this for Sophie, giving her a sane life away from the nomadic travels that had suddenly turned tragic, giving her access to the kind of school that would nurture her extraordinary gift. Sophie had better things to do than cater to the overweening vanity of an aging academic.

Then again, Rachel had better things to do herself, and yet she was going off, the perfect faculty wife in the perfect little college town where it never stopped raining

19

and she felt like she was slowly suffocating. . . .

"Are you all right?" David said, his voice soft with concern. "You clutched my arm."

"Just a hand cramp, darling. I've been working too hard."

He smiled at her fondly. "I love it that you've kept up with your photography, but you know you don't have to. I make more than enough for both of us."

They'd had this discussion before, and they'd probably be still arguing about it on their deathbeds, seventy happy years from now. She shoved her hair back from her face. "It's not about the money, David. It's who I am."

He led her out into the damp night, closing the door of the house behind him and double locking the door. He'd left no lights on — he was religious about saving electricity. "And what you are is perfect," he said. "Do you mind us taking your car? Mine still smells from that run-in with a dead deer."

"Of course. Do you want me to take your car and get it washed tomorrow?"

He shook his head. "You know how silly I am . . . It's my baby, and I hate to have anyone else touch it, even you, darling. I'll see to it. I can use the Range Rover until then."

David loved his Range Rover with an Anglophile's passion, and it seldom saw the light of day. It usually sat in state in David's immaculate garage.

She said nothing. David had his life arranged to perfection, and who was she to argue? So she merely smiled indulgently, tucked her perfect little evening bag under her perfect arm, and got in the car with her perfect husband. It was going to be a long night.

Caleb Middleton ducked beneath the tarp that covered what should have been the hallway in his house and headed into the half-finished bathroom. He expected that the plumbing would have died, but he turned the faucet and rust-colored water dribbled out, slowly at first, then turning into a steady stream. He turned on the shower — no hot water, of course, but the gravity-fed pump was working — and he stripped off his muddy clothes and shoes and stepped in.

He didn't close his eyes. He could still see her body, trapped in the branches. He'd called the police, anonymously, but Maggie Bannister wouldn't have any trouble tracking his cell phone. And then the questions would begin, and he'd lie, and no one would believe him. Maggie had always kept a distrustful eye on him when she was a simple beat cop — now that she was the sheriff she'd be even more likely to think the worst of him.

There was even a musty towel in the open shelves under the sink. He pulled it out, to find that something had eaten a large hole in it. It didn't matter. He dried himself and pulled on clean clothes, then picked up the muddy ones and wrapped them in the towel. If it ever stopped raining long enough he'd burn them. Otherwise he'd bury them and forget about it. If he could.

In the years he'd been gone his half-finished house hadn't been abandoned — there was a pile of firewood and kindling by the woodstove, dozens of empty beer bottles and an ashtray full of roaches. Teenagers must have used the place for a makeout spot. He didn't mind — he would have done the same. Had done the same.

He walked across the rough floors to the front of the living room and looked down over the town of Silver Falls. The clouds hung low, but he could see the outlines of the college campus where his brother and father worked, the streets of the small town laid out in perfect order. The waterfall was up behind him, and he could hear it roaring down over the steady sound of rain. After years in the deserts of Iraq and Afghanistan he should have welcomed the rain.

It smelled like death to him. Death and decay and despair. They were part of his everyday life, and yet here, in a peaceful little town, death was stronger than in the war zones where he worked.

He was here to face death, and the questions that had always plagued him, questions that he'd avoided finding the answers to. But that had changed — he couldn't hide from the ugly truth any more. Starting with the dead woman caught in the branches at the bottom of the falls.

Maybe he shouldn't have called the cops, but he couldn't just leave her there. He stared out at the curtain of rain that separated his half-finished house from the rest of the world. He'd need to get his generator up and running, he'd need to replace the wind-shredded tarp that flapped in the wind. He'd need to do any number of things before he headed back down the mountain to find his father and brother.

And this time he wasn't going to leave until he found the truth. Even if it was as bad as it could possibly be, as horrifying as he'd always feared, he'd face it. You could only run for so long, and now that there was a new member in his happy little family, he couldn't wait any longer. David had done the unthinkable and gotten married. His father had written him in one of his cryptic letters.

And Caleb could no longer pretend that something very bad wasn't going on in this gloomy, tight-assed little town.

Sophie Chapman shoved her blond hair back and made a face at her best friend Kristen. At least there were a few good things about this rain-soaked, godforsaken place, and Kristen was right there at the top of the list. In her thirteen years, Sophie had been in more countries than most people saw in a lifetime, and she had an easy time of making friends. She and Kristen had been soul mates from the moment they met at Silver Falls Union High School, and they'd been almost inseparable ever since. Sophie was the math whiz, Kristen was the brilliant writer — they complemented each other's skills perfectly. Kristen's mother, the sheriff of this gloomy town, was down-to-earth, no-nonsense and surprisingly easygoing, and she got along very well with Sophie's mother. If not for Maggie, all Rachel would have was David, and a little bit of him went a long way.

She loved her mother, but sometimes she was just particularly brainless, like when it came to choosing a husband. Yes, losing Tessa had been hard. Sophie still missed her, still grieved for her and the awful way she'd died, but she was far too practical to let it turn her into a drama queen. Bad things happened, bad people existed. You just had to do your best to avoid both of them.

It was getting a little harder to avoid her stepfather. Not that he was evil, of course. He went out of his way to dote on her, giving her little presents that she really didn't want. She was very good at sussing people out, though, and there was something about him that didn't compute.

She didn't waste time thinking about it. He made her mother happy, gave her the normal life that she must have always wanted. For some reason Sophie had thought they were having a wonderful time, traveling the world, getting by on the money Rachel made from her photographs. Sometimes, when she sold stuff to a travel magazine, they could stay in nice hotels and eat steak. Sometimes it was youth hostels and granola. It didn't matter — it was all a grand adventure, and Sophie had loved it.

Apparently Rachel hadn't. David Middleton had shown up a few weeks after Tessa was found, and her mother had fallen for him like a stone. Rachel, who usually kept her distance from men on the make, had dropped all her usual defenses and jumped straight into marriage with a stranger.

She'd always loved her mother's impulsiveness — now she wasn't so sure. There was no way she could tell her mother she found David a little creepy. He watched her too much, paid too much attention to her, trying to be her friend. The last person she wanted to be friends with was the man who slept with her mother. Rachel was so certain this was the answer to all their problems: a safe life in a sweet little town in the Pacific Northwest — what could be better?

Sophie could think of a number of places, but she'd taken one look at her mother's face and kept her mouth shut. Besides, it was natural that she'd be jealous of the first real rival for her mother's attention, according to the guidance counselor.

So here she was, making the best of things, and Kristen was definitely one of the best.

"You want to see if my mother will give us a ride to the mall?" Kristen suggested lazily, stretched out on her bedroom floor. "She should be off-duty soon, and we've done

26

our homework."

Sophie had never been particularly fond of malls, and Silver Falls's pathetic version of it was even less enticing. However, Kristen looked hopeful, so she nodded, agreeable as always. "As long as we don't have to meet any boys."

"You are such a party pooper," Kristen said cheerfully. "I think Crash has got a game tonight."

Crash being Kristen's current crush, a singularly thickheaded soccer player on the junior varsity. Sophie wasn't particularly impressed with the crop of young men Silver Falls had produced. But then, she wasn't interested in falling in love, not yet. Not until she was sure her mother had made the right decision.

"Kristen?" Sheriff Bannister's voice called from the kitchen. "I need you girls to come down here."

Sophie knew that tone of voice. She'd heard it before, when Tessa had died, and she recognized it now with a certain sick dread. For a moment she froze.

"I wonder what's up with Mom?" Kristen said, clueless. "She doesn't sound like she's going to want to take us to the mall."

"If I were you I wouldn't even ask," Sophie said, climbing off the bed and following her friend down the stairs in the shabby old split level.

Mrs. Bannister had a grim look on her face, and she was still wearing her uniform, and Sophie knew what was coming before she even opened her mouth. "Girls, there's been a murder."

And Sophie had the feeling that things weren't going to be right again for a long time.

Stephen Henry Middleton was being called upon to read. The old ham never missed an opportunity, Rachel thought, scooping up a tray of empty glasses and heading for the kitchen. The only way she survived these cocktail parties was to make herself busy — drinking wasn't an option. She had too great a tendency to say what she really thought when she had a drink, and being honest in the sacred halls of Silver Falls College was definitely frowned upon.

She put her butt against the swinging door into the kitchen and backed out of the room before David could see her. Stephen Henry wouldn't notice. Stephen Henry never noticed anyone but himself.

Sure enough, his sonorous tones began to spread throughout the downstairs of the old house, and Rachel set the tray down, then made a dash for the porch door. The rain had stopped for the moment, the air was cool and damp, and she slipped outside, closing the door behind her very quietly. A little fresh air would do wonders, and this party, in honor of Stephen Henry's fifteenth collection of self-published poems, would go on until the old man had read every single last one to his adoring crowd. No one would notice she was missing.

Her stomach rumbled. She was on a diet — hell, she was always on a diet. With her bone structure she didn't dare eat as much as she wanted, and she'd gotten through the day with a green salad with lemon juice, a fat-free yogurt, and a thin slice of gluten-free bread. A healthy mind in a healthy body, David used to say, but right then Rachel didn't feel like either. She felt like pancakes and bacon and scrambled eggs and real maple syrup. She'd sell her soul for an IHOP.

The polite smattering of applause drifted out from the house, followed by the faint sounds of Stephen Henry. Even from a wheelchair he managed to project, and the occasional word would leak into the night outside. She was going to have to study her inscribed copy "— to darling Rachel, the loveliest daughter-in-law a poet could ever have —" because Stephen Henry was bound to quiz her, and a simple "I loved all of it" would never work.

Maybe she had time to drive out to the interstate for a Happy Meal or something, she thought, leaning against the damp brick and breathing in the cool night air. She wasn't eating enough to keep a bird alive, though David would smell a Big Mac on her breath and look troubled. David was a strict vegetarian, so strict he wouldn't even kiss her when she ate meat. And she'd been eating a lot of meat lately. Maybe Stephen Henry had something fattening in his kitchen cabinets, though she doubted it. Maybe . . .

"What are you doing, skulking around in the dark?"

The voice came out of nowhere, and she barely managed to stifle a shriek as a tall figure emerged from the shadows. She hadn't bothered to turn on the porch light, and she couldn't see him clearly — she only knew she'd never met him before.

He moved closer, and his face came into the light. Not a kind face — it was thin, with sharp cheekbones, hooded eyes and cool twist to the mouth. "You're not sneaking a cigarette," he said, "and as far as I can tell I'm the only one out prowling tonight,

30

so you couldn't be meeting a lover." He looked at her, a long, assessing stare, and Rachel couldn't rid herself of the thought that he was sizing her up and decided she wasn't lover-material. "So why are you lurking outside Stephen Henry's house? It is still his house, isn't it?"

"They'll have to use a crowbar to get him out," she muttered. Even though the poet laureate of Silver Falls College had retired ten years ago, he always found an excuse not to vacate the impressive faculty housing that had always been his as dean of students. No matter how hard everyone, including his son, tried.

The stranger laughed. "That sounds like him. So why are you hiding out here?"

"He's doing a reading," she said gloomily.

He laughed again, and she got the impression he didn't laugh often. "I don't blame you. He goes on forever." He paused, and Stephen Henry's velvety tones seeped out of the old house. "You must be new here. Who are you, one of the faculty wives?"

"Why wouldn't I be on the faculty myself?" she shot back, annoyed.

"Because you're dressed too appropriately. Faculty can do what they want, the wives and husbands have to toe the line."

"Then who are you? A faculty husband?

31

I've never seen you before."

He just looked at her. "Do I look like the kind of man who toes the line?" he said. He didn't wait for her answer. "Is your husband in there? He isn't going to like it that you skipped out on the old man."

"He's used to it." She didn't bother asking him how he knew she was married. She wore a ring, and he was the kind of man who noticed everything.

She heard the phone ring inside the house, while her father-in-law simply raised his voice to be heard over it. A moment later even Stephen Henry shut up, and there was dead silence, followed by a buzz of conversation.

"Sounds like there's something more exciting than a poetry reading going on," the stranger said in a lazy voice. "Don't you think you ought to go in and find your husband?"

"What's this obsession with my husband?"

He leaned back against the iron fencing. "What's this lack of interest in him on your part?" he said. "Why are you trading barbs with a stranger in the dark?"

Because she felt alive for the first time in months. She was annoyed, stimulated, irritated and bizarrely happy. "I'm not," she said, plastering the good wife smile on her face and turning toward the door. "I'm going to find him."

The touch of his hand was electrifying. It was light, just a brush against her arm, but the message was clear. "Don't go back in," he said. "If he made you wear that dress then he doesn't deserve you."

She looked at him as he stood in the shadows, apart from the well-regulated life she'd chosen. Chosen for her daughter, chosen for herself. If she were a different woman, she'd simply go with him, leaving everything behind, the proper black dress, the safe life, the perfect family she'd created. But she was doing this for Sophie, she reminded herself, who'd lived through enough chaos. She didn't have a choice.

She pulled away from him, more sharply than she needed to. "I think I'd better find out what's going on. Are you coming in?"

Only the ghost of a smile. "I think I'll stay here for the time being. I don't think anyone will be particularly happy to see me."

She stared at him a moment longer. There was something she was missing, something important. . . .

The kitchen door opened suddenly, and David stood there, looking distressed. "I thought I'd find you out here," he said. "You need to come in. Another girl's been murdered."

She froze, forgetting about the stranger behind her. "Another? David, what are you talking about? I haven't heard about any murders."

He looked nervous, her sensitive husband. "I didn't see the point of mentioning it, given what you and Sophie had just been through. Anyway, it's not something we talk about here, particularly since the last one was years ago. We thought . . ." He peered into the darkness, and his voice sharpened. "Who's that with you?"

She looked back, and the stranger moved into the bright light. She couldn't very well introduce him, since he hadn't given his name.

"Hello, David," the man said.

Her husband turned pale. "Shit," he said. The first time Rachel had ever heard him curse. "What are *you* doing here?"

"Haven't you heard the story about the prodigal son?" His face was expressionless. "Is this your wife?"

"It is," David said, putting a possessive hand on her. Another anomaly — he seldom touched her in front of other people.

"Are you going to introduce us?" There was just the faint taunt in his voice. Whoever the stranger was, David wasn't happy to see him. And David was always unfailingly polite.

"I don't think so."

The man laughed. "You can't keep her away from me forever. You know that."

"I can try."

"What the hell is going on?" Rachel said. "Why are you two having a pissing contest?"

"Old habits die hard," the stranger murmured. "Are you going to invite me in?"

"Now isn't a good time, Caleb," David said stiffly.

"Is it ever?"

The damp night air had turned to rain once more, and Rachel had had enough. "My name is Rachel Chapman," she said, seriously annoyed. "And of course you're invited in."

"Rachel Chapman Middleton," David corrected her.

The smile the stranger sent David was nothing short of a triumphant smirk, and he moved into the house, pushing David out of the way. David fell back, and there was no reading the strained expression on his face.

"Don't you think you could give the old man a break?" he said. "Just go away. Go back to whatever disaster zone you've been haunting and leave us alone, for God's sake."

"Who's there?" Stephen Henry's deep voice could be heard through the closed door.

"Might as well face the music, David," the stranger, Caleb, said. "You want to do it together?"

"I better warn him." David pushed past him, shoving the kitchen door open. Leaving Rachel alone in the kitchen with the stranger who was no stranger at all.

He gave her a faint, quizzical smile. "You'll have to excuse me. I have some old acquaintances to renew."

She was tempted to stay put, or even better, go take her car and drive home. This was supposed to be a safe place, where murder couldn't happen. But It had happened, apparently more than once, and she needed to get to Sophie, fast.

But Sophie was at Maggie Bannister's house — the safest possible place. She needed to calm down, not rush into anything and end up freaking Sophie out.

She could be reasonable, wait for David. In the meantime she wanted to know who was the man who managed to rattle her unflappable husband.

She followed him into the living room

where Stephen Henry had been holding forth. Half the guests had already departed in the wake of the horrifying news, and the ones who remained were looking even more stunned at the sight of the newcomer.

Stephen Henry looked up, his long silver mane pushed back from his face in artistic disarray. His faded blue eyes focused on the newcomer, and to Rachel's astonishment, a smile wreathed his face.

"My long-lost son," he said. "Welcome home, Caleb. We've missed you."

2

With a superhuman effort Rachel shut her mouth, waiting, watching, when she wanted nothing more than to go up to her sulky husband, shake him and say "why the hell did you tell me you were an only child?" In fact, when he'd come into their shattered lives he'd said that was one thing he had in common with Sophie — he knew what it was like to grow up alone. He'd lied. And she really hated liars.

She moved across the room and sat down on one of the uncomfortable antique sofas that Stephen Henry preferred, since he didn't have to sit on them. The other guests were disappearing rapidly, and David was still too caught up in whatever was going on between him and his long-lost brother to realize how much shit he was in with his perfect faculty wife.

"You don't look particularly pleased by the return of your brother, David," Stephen

Henry said with a slight smirk. "Don't tell me you two are fighting already."

"Oh, we're not fighting," Caleb said easily, and he seemed oddly amused by the tension in the room. "I just surprised him."

"Is that true, David?"

Rachel watched as her husband swallowed some of the cold-eyed anger that was so unlike him. He managed a stiff smile. "Of course. Why wouldn't I be happy that Caleb has come back to town?"

"Maybe because he's already putting moves on your wife? You never could hold a girlfriend, could you, David?" Stephen Henry said with his usual malice. "They all seemed to prefer your brother. And you did it on purpose, didn't you, Caleb, you naughty boy? Always the troublemaker. That's one thing I've cherished about you."

"Have you?" Caleb said, his low, husky voice at odds with his father's plummy tones. "I always had the impression that you preferred David."

"Oh, I've never played favorites," the old man said airily. "You both know that. It's your own sibling rivalry that's gotten you in trouble. How long are you staying this time? One day? Two?"

Caleb glanced at his brother. "I thought I'd stick around this time. I have a few

39

things to work out, a few answers I need. I told the bureau that I was taking an extended leave."

"What would the wars do without you?" David said, sarcastic.

"Rachel, my elder son is a reporter," Stephen Henry said. "What you might call a war correspondent — he's always been drawn to death and disaster, and he happened to find the perfect profession — one that allows him to wallow in it. It always followed him like a plague when he was younger, and I must admit life has been a great deal more peaceful with him off somewhere. But of course I welcome both my sons with a full heart."

At least he didn't say "fruit of my loins," which Rachel half expected. But since she was finally being addressed directly she decided not to continue with their polite bantering.

"Why is this the first time I've heard of your other son's existence? You have no photos. David's never mentioned him."

"Hush, child," Stephen Henry said. "You'll hurt his feelings."

"I doubt it," Caleb said.

"The truth is, Caleb never really held still long enough for photographs. And he and David never did get along." He turned to his younger son. "I would hope you'd both make more of an effort. I'm an old man — I deserve better than watching my two children fight each other."

David said nothing, an odd, distant look in his pale blue eyes.

"I don't have a problem with David," Caleb said, sounding innocent.

"Then keep your hands off his wife," Stephen Henry said.

Caleb shot her a quizzical glance. "I've barely touched her."

"Barely?" David echoed, suddenly alert. "Listen, you son of a bitch —"

"That's your mother you're calling a bitch, my boy," Stephen Henry said. "Rachel, dear, would you be kind enough to get me a Scotch and water? You know how I like it — just a splash of Perrier to make me feel virtuous. And get one for the two boys as well. Not the best Scotch — they don't deserve it. The Glenfiddich will do."

"I don't want a drink," David said.

"You'll both drink and be civilized about it. Rachel?"

"I really need to get home to Sophie," she said, desperate to get out of there.

"But David told me Sophie wasn't home. In fact, she's with the chief of police. I don't think we need to worry about her, do you?"

41

Yes, she did, but she wasn't going to argue. She rose, reluctantly. Stephen Henry always had the tendency to treat her like "the little woman," a fact which annoyed her no end, but right then she welcomed a relief from the tension. "Certainly," she said in a dulcet voice.

"And take your time," Stephen Henry called after her as she pushed the kitchen door open. "I need to make a few things clear to my obstreperous sons."

The Glenfiddich was out on the counter, and she took down three cut-crystal glasses from the cupboard. Stephen Henry had already given her detailed instructions on how he liked his Scotch, and David drank it the same way. She could only assume the unwanted prodigal son would be satisfied with the same thing, and she splashed the whiskey and Perrier into each glass. And then she took out one more glass, poured two fingers of whiskey into it and downed it, neat, smothering the choking feeling. She'd never been much of a drinker — in her wild youth it had been weed, but she'd given that up when she'd gotten pregnant and had never been interested in finding something to take its place. But right then she needed a drink, and badly.

"You always let him treat you like a servant?"

Caleb had come through the swinging door, as silent as the grave, she thought, then shook herself. "I don't think your brother is going to be happy to find you in here with me."

"I have no intention of letting him find me. I told him I was going out for a smoke — David won't even notice. The old man is busy reading him the riot act. He doesn't understand why the two of us can't be friends, and I'm not about to let him know exactly what kind of dark secrets lie between us. My father's happier in his ignorance."

"David doesn't have dark secrets," she said, putting her empty glass in the sink.

"Then why didn't you know he had a brother?" Caleb reached past her for one of the glasses of whiskey, and his arm brushed hers, probably no more than the cloth of his denim shirt, but she felt it. "I'm sure he'll fill you in on all the morbid details tonight. Just make sure you don't have nightmares."

"Nightmares?"

His smile was cool and wry. "No, I think you're too practical to have nightmares. That's why you married David, isn't it? It was the practical thing to do."

"Go to hell," she said, picking the glass

43

out of the sink and reaching for the whiskey bottle again.

He raised his eyebrows. "I'm sorry, did I hit a little too close to the bone? My brother's not one for passionate love matches . . . unless he's changed in the last five years. He's a very calculating fellow."

"I'll have you know that your brother is a very passionate man," she said, pouring another generous dollop of the whiskey into her glass. Lying, of course. It was David's calm, unemotional demeanor that had first drawn her to him in a time of emotional chaos, when Tessa had been killed. Passion was one thing she could happily do without.

"Really? I never would have imagined it. Why don't you tell me all about it? We can go for a drive, get to know each other, and you can give me all the details about your sex life. Does he go down on you?"

She stared at him, shocked, the glass untouched in her hand.

"No? That's a shame. I would." He reached over and took the other two glasses. "Don't worry about these — I can be a butler as well as you can be a maid. Why don't you put that glass down and go home before you're too sauced to drive? I'll make sure David gets back eventually."

"Eventually?" In fact, the thought of getting the hell out of there was incredibly powerful. She couldn't think, not with that man watching her, not with her husband and father-in-law in the other room, arguing in soft voices.

"We have a lot of time to catch up on," Caleb said. "I promise you we aren't going to kill each other. At least, not tonight."

She looked at him for a long moment. It was hard to believe the two of them were related. David was fair, with a pale complexion and soft blue eyes, and he was no more than average height with a slight tendency to thicken up around the middle. He exercised conscientiously, and lectured Rachel on nutrition and health. She hadn't had a candy bar in four months.

Whereas Caleb Middleton was taller, around six feet, and lean, almost skinny. His hair was long and black, his eyes a shade of brown so dark they were almost black. And that narrow, clever, mocking face was a polar opposite of David's pleasant expression.

"So what are you thinking about so intently? Did you already forget where you parked the car?"

"I'm thinking you don't look anything like your father or your brother," she said.

His eyes crinkled with amusement. "You

45

got me there. I'm adopted. My mother thought she couldn't have children so she bought me. And then, lo and behold, she gave birth to David. Clearly she hadn't needed to bother with me at all."

"Is that your excuse?"

"Excuse for what?" He looked genuinely perplexed.

"For being an asshole. You were a poor, unwanted child who was passed over for the real son, and therefore you go out of your way to make everyone's life miserable."

He seemed more amused than offended. "Oh, I wasn't unwanted. There were times when I think my mother preferred me, and Stephen Henry still has a soft spot for me in that selfish organ he calls a heart. I think I preferred David to be the Golden Boy. That way I could fly beneath the radar, do what I wanted, and most people never even noticed."

"When you walked into your father's living room the remaining guests looked at you like you were a ghost. I think they noticed," she said.

"So they get to gossip about my return and the murdered girl, and wonder whether there's any connection." His voice was light, contemplative.

"A connection?" Rachel echoed, horrified.

"Why in God's name could there be a connection?"

His smile was cool and dismissive. "It's not that hard to figure out, Mrs. Middleton. Most of the people of Silver Falls would like to think of me as a murderer. Feel free to add yourself to that list if you want to."

She just stared at him. "That's nothing to joke about."

"No, it isn't. If I were a sensitive soul I wouldn't have mentioned it, but I think you'd better learn the lay of the land. If there's a murder, I'm your man." He shrugged. "Go home, Mrs. Middleton. I've already told you enough." He took the whiskey glass out of her hand, poured it down the sink.

"Good idea," she said. "I need to go find Sophie. This is going to be difficult for her."

The kitchen door was pushed open, and David stood there, an unreadable expression on his face. "Sheriff Bannister is here, and she wants to talk to all of us."

"Thank God," Rachel said, brushing past the two brothers and rushing into the living room.

Maggie Bannister, a sensible woman in sensible shoes, squatted beside Stephen Henry's wheelchair, taking notes, a patient expression on her broad, leathery face.

She looked up when Rachel rushed into the room, and rose to her full five feet two inches. "Don't worry, Rachel, Sophie's just fine."

"Thank God she was over at your house," Rachel said. "Does she know?"

"I've told both girls. I gather you went through something like this in the past."

There was a sick, sour feeling in the pit of her stomach, churning with the bite of the whiskey she'd downed. "Her best friend in San Francisco. I don't want her to experience that kind of trauma again."

"Considering her best friend is *my* daughter, I can promise you she won't," Maggie drawled. "This was a college student, name of Jessica Barrowman. Looks like she was raped and murdered and thrown over the falls sometime today, and her body was found a few hours ago. We'll know more once the medical examiner has a look. But since our local black sheep has chosen today to return, I thought I'd ask him and his family a few questions."

Rachel looked behind her, at Caleb Middleton's cool, impassive face. Not the face of a murderer, surely. Not the face of a monster who could do that to someone not much more than a child.

"I don't need you here, Rachel." Her brisk

48

voice was kind. "Why don't you go on home and the boys will be along soon."

"The boys?"

Maggie smiled briefly. "Sorry, I'm fifteen years older and I've known them all their lives. We've got the rotten kid and the good one." Her pale gray eyes drifted impartially over David and his brother. "I just need to ask them a few questions and they'll be done."

"I want to see Sophie."

Maggie shook her head. "She's in bed already, Rachel, and she's got Kristen for support. That daughter of yours has got a good head on her shoulders. She's not the type to fall apart."

No, I am, Rachel thought. "I still . . ."

"Let it be, Rachel. If you go in all fussed up then she'll start worrying. I know thirteen-year-old girls — I've had three of them. Just go on like normal and tomorrow you two can talk."

She was an adult, Rachel reminded herself. She'd learned to follow her head, not her heart, which only led to disaster. The smart thing to do *was* let Sophie sleep.

"Go on home now and let me do my work." Maggie had perfected the voice of authority.

And without looking at her lying husband,

her newfound, troubling brother-in-law, or their egocentric father, she left.

This was not what he'd expected. All his carefully laid plans, his fanatical attention to details, were about to be upended by the unexpected return of his nemesis.

And he was already putting moves on Rachel.

Like always. Caleb wanted everything he had, and he destroyed without conscience. From Murph, the stray mutt he'd bought for a dollar at a school fair, to Libba, with her pale, pale skin and her beautiful curtain of blond hair. Caleb had taken them and destroyed them, and if he wasn't careful he would do the same with Rachel.

And Sophie. The thought of him going anywhere near the girl made him shake with anger, and it took all his effort to calm himself. He had to be very careful. Thoughtful and measured. Emotions led to mistakes, and he hadn't made a mistake in decades.

Why had he shown up now, on today of all days? He had to suspect something — thirty-five years of being a scapegoat would have gotten him thinking, and his brother was smart enough. Why now?

He took a deep, calming breath. Caleb's unexpected return could be put to good use, if he just stopped to think about it for long enough. There were clues, hints that had led to him all along, from Murph's distorted body to Libba's accident and eventual disappearance. If he was careful enough, clever enough, all would work out as it should.

It would require perfect timing, detailed planning. And above all, supreme self-control. Caleb wouldn't like that, had always liked to get under his skin, and he hadn't changed. He would go after Rachel, do his best to steal her away, fill her head full of lies.

But Rachel would never believe those lies. Rachel was his shining beacon, his hope for the future. She was the normal, happy life that fulfilled him and brought him to completion. She had brought him life, and most of all, she had brought him Sophie. During the last few months he had found a kind of transcendent peace insulating him from everything, making him feel powerful and untouchable, knowing that everything was finally as it should be. He'd made a brief miscalculation with Jessica, a slip of his usual self-control. Not enough to put him in any danger, but the timing was unfortunate.

And then there was Sophie. She was a different matter. Caleb had never liked young girls, and Sophie was years younger than any of those who had died. With any luck, Caleb wouldn't even notice Rachel's pure young daughter, never suspect his brother's patience.

He would wait. Caleb would leave, bored, and then all his detailed plans would come to fruition, with no interference from his despised older brother.

If Caleb didn't leave, well, he'd already made arrangements for that eventuality. With so many clues leading straight to Caleb's door Maggie Bannister wouldn't be able to catch her breath.

No, there was no need to overreact. What was his favorite prayer? All would be well, all manner of things would be well.

And he started to whistle once more.

3

Rachel drove home through the light rain, her hands gripping the steering wheel, Caleb Middleton's words ringing in her ears. She'd never been the nervous type — a woman alone with a child in tow couldn't afford to be hesitant and she'd always believed she could deal with any disaster.

And she had. Floods, uprisings, being stranded, being followed. She'd met those dangers and more and been secure in her ability to deal with everything. Everything but a brutal murder in their tight-knit community in San Francisco, a murder which had struck too close to home.

Thank God David had showed up when he did. An English professor on sabbatical, a sane, calm oasis in the aftermath of Tessa's murder. He radiated safety and normalcy, the kind of man who'd provide the life she'd selfishly denied Sophie. For years they'd traveled the world, and she never realized that she was depriving her daughter of any chance at stability. Sure, she'd given Sophie the richness of adventure, but in the end it had been irresponsible. It wasn't until they landed in San Francisco for a while that she realized her darling daughter was a freaking genius when it came to math. At the age of thirteen she was working on college-level stuff, and Rachel had always despised math.

But in a sheltered academic community like Silver Falls, there'd be the right kind of program, the individual study, and having a professor for a stepfather would ensure Sophie got everything she needed.

And she was happy — Rachel was sure of it. Sure enough that she wasn't about to give even the slightest hint that she was having second thoughts. Because she wasn't. She'd made her choice, the best for Sophie, and she'd happily live with it. Regret was for idiots.

Of course, she'd assumed San Francisco was a safe haven as well. There would never be a murder in David's world — he was much too organized to let that happen. She would bring Sophie into that world and give them both time to heal.

She told herself it was just really bad timing. If David's brother had appeared even six months later she'd be all settled into her normal, constricting new life and his stupid dark hints wouldn't have bothered her. They would have rolled off her back like all this fucking rain.

And she'd promised to stop saying *fuck.* David hated that word, hated to hear it coming from anyone, particularly his new wife. All her arguments about the expressiveness of good old Anglo-Saxon went over his head, and he'd even gone so far as to suggest a jar where she stuck a dollar every time she used the word.

One look at her face and he'd backed down at that idea, but he still fussed, and she remained hamstrung. The first few months in this tiny college town, in her new life, had been easy, the novelty of it enough to keep her going. But as time passed the elegant prairie-style house had begun to feel like a prison, and the word *fuck* had come up with increasing frequency.

But Sophie said she liked it here. She liked the school, even though she sniffed at the uniforms. And she loved her friends, particularly Kristen Bannister. And she was thriving with the specialized math program, though that was no surprise. Sophie had always been infinitely adaptable, equally at home in Africa or Kansas.

No, Rachel thought, so long as Sophie was okay she could grin and bear it. David was a kind man, an honest man, and she'd learned long ago that sex wasn't all that it was cracked up to be. Fortunately David performed his husbandly duties with increasing infrequency, even going so far as to suggest they have separate bedrooms since she tended to thrash about in her sleep.

No, everything was absolutely fine in her young marriage. It was just a normal time of adjustment, and the horrifying murder the result of a lover's quarrel, nothing to do with her. She and David were fine. But they certainly didn't need Caleb Middleton reappearing to make things worse.

She pulled into the driveway and stared up at the house. When she'd first seen it she'd been charmed — it was a Frank Lloyd Wright knockoff, all angles and planes and soothing to the eyes. There was a wing to the right that held her studio and the family room, and one to the left for the five bedrooms, one of which had been turned into David's office. It was a house for a large, rambunctious family. Unfortunately it had never held one. And all those stained-glass windows kept the occasional ray of sunshine from penetrating, and the empty halls echoed. Even her studio seemed haunted.

She sat for a long moment, the car still running. Maggie said Sophie was already asleep, but she could drive over there, pick her up and head straight out of town, never looking back. In a few days they could be continents away from this place, in the sun, free from this prison of rain and sorrow.

She turned off the car, shaking her head. It hadn't been a good idea to have that drink — alcohol made her paranoid. Sophie was fine, she'd gotten through Tessa's horrific murder and she'd get through the death of a stranger. Tomorrow, in the dubious light of day, everything would seem much better. She wouldn't have this crazy, irrational urge to throw Sophie into the car and get the hell out of here.

She'd always been too impulsive. Impulsive when she'd run away with Jared, impulsive when she'd refused her rigid parents' generous offer of a lifetime of servitude and her child put up for adoption. And she'd been impulsive when she'd decided to marry a man she barely knew, simply because he was safe and gentle. She wasn't going to compound that by taking off at the drop of a hat.

She locked the doors behind her, for once going through the ritual of double locks that David preferred, and leaned her head against the solid door.

So it had been a lousy, shitty day. Things would look better in the morning. They always did. She and Sophie would talk, and if Sophie even hinted at doubts, they'd be out of there before the sun set.

But for now, for this night, all she could do was sleep on it. And hope she'd have the answers when she woke up.

Caleb couldn't sleep. By the time he drove back up the winding muddy road to his ruined house he was still feeling jangled, like he'd had a triple espresso with chocolate on the side.

He'd bought the place on a whim years ago — the abandoned project of a failed architect who thought he was the reincarnation of Frank Lloyd Wright. He'd built his own house in town, then started this one halfway up the mountain, where he'd gone bankrupt and shot himself. Since no one was willing to buy a half-finished monstrosity halfway up a mountain with a history like that, Caleb got it cheap.

He turned on the two lights he'd bought earlier that day. He'd gotten the electricity turned back on, but expecting anything like internet service was a lost cause. He wasn't going to be there that long.

Longer than he'd ever been before, though. He'd never spent more than two nights in this godforsaken little town, and he didn't like the fact that right now he was trapped, thanks to the red-haired amazon who'd been idiot enough to marry his brother.

Stephen Henry had sent him the wedding announcement, and he'd freaked, moving so fast that he'd missed the part about her daughter. How the hell could she have let herself and her daughter be drawn into such an infernal mess? And why the hell did he have to come and clean it up?

Because nobody else would. Nobody else had the faintest idea what was going on, and if he tried to tell them they wouldn't believe him. They never had, and years ago he'd given up trying. He was committed to seeing this through, and he'd do just that. He couldn't live with another death on his conscience.

The wife was interesting. All wrong for David — he couldn't figure out why the hell they'd ended up with each other. David went for the same willowy blondes that Caleb had preferred, and Rachel was neither willowy nor blonde. She had curves — ripe, lush, sensual curves that even that dull black dress couldn't disguise. Her hair was a blazing red, not a subdued auburn, and her mouth was stubborn, her eyes defiant. Not David's type at all. David liked his women docile and compliant. Rachel Middleton was a volcano about to erupt.

Why had he chosen her? That was just one of the questions he needed to have answered. What had made him choose a totally unlikely woman and bring her back to Silver Falls? Maggie Bannister had mentioned something about Rachel's daughter being involved in an earlier murder, and his instinctive alarm system went into full mode. One murdered girl was unfortunate. Two was just too damned coincidental, and he never believed in coincidence.

He went to the tiny fridge and pulled out a beer, twisting the cap off. It went flying, rolling across the floor and landing in the middle of the stained plywood. Any other man would have taken that part of the sub-floor up and replaced it, replaced the reminder of the man who'd bled out there, in the ruins of his dream. Caleb liked it.

It kept things in perspective. At one point that could have been him. But it wasn't, and it never would be. He'd never stay in this goddamn town long enough for the darkness to reach him. He'd find out what he needed to know, the truth he'd been avoiding for most of his life, and then he'd move on.

He was going to have to find a way to get to his brother, and the new wife looked like she was going to be the perfect venue. She had a temper, passion running deep — exactly the wrong kind of woman for someone like David. There must be a reason for such a colossal mismatch. She was unhappy, afraid she'd made the wrong choice but too stubborn to admit it. That would make her vulnerable, though she'd do her damnedest to hide it, but she was tough — he could see it in the back of her clear blue eyes. Funny that he'd noticed they were blue. Most of the time he'd been with her had been in the shadows.

It would be no kindness to leave her alone. The truth always came with a heavy cost, but in the end it was worth it. He'd pay that cost, and so would she. She'd hate him, but she'd be alive. And in the end she just might be grateful. At least he'd make sure the two of them were safe before he left.

He started a fire in the woodstove to take some of the damp chill from the air. There were enough construction scraps still lying around to keep him warm for a month or more. Though if he had to stay that long he'd probably just end up in a pool of blood like the architect.

He shook out his sleeping bag, putting it near the fire. He was going to need to order a mattress. The one he'd left behind had been eaten by mice and christened by half the teenage population of Silver Falls. He was someone who could sleep anywhere — on rock-hard ground, in hammocks, on trains or boats, the desert or a snow cave. But there were ghosts in this house, ghosts in his soul when he came home, and he needed all the help he could get.

He drained the last of his beer, put it on its side and sent it rolling away from him, then stretched out on the sleeping bag. It had been a hell of a day, and it was only just beginning. He was going to see that drowned face in his dreams, in his nightmares, and it would haunt him, like so many others.

He closed his eyes, listening to the crackle of the fire, the pounding of the rain overhead, the whipping of the tarp in the wind.

But he didn't see the dead girl. All he could see was Rachel Middleton. Who didn't realize she was dancing on the edge of a precipice. Or that the one person who could help her would just as likely shove her off.

■ ■ ■ ■

Rachel dreamed about the black sheep. She tossed in the king-size bed, restless, troubled, and she could hear his voice in the back of her mind, low, raspy, so unlike David's carefully modulated pitch.

The covers were too hot, pressing down on her skin, and she kicked them off as she rolled onto her back, then onto her stomach again. The air felt stagnant, decaying, and opening the window would only make it worse. It was too cold for an air conditioner, but the thick air felt like a weight pressing down on her chest.

She heard the sound, the tiny scratching noise at the door of her bedroom, and she was instantly awake, wary, as light began to filter into her bedroom. She could barely see his silhouette as he closed the door behind him, closed himself inside, with her. And her pulse began to quicken. Not in anticipation. David's matrimonial visits were brief and pleasant, but a far cry from the desperate passion she'd searched for when she was younger.

Desperate passion led to heartbreak and betrayal. She was much better off with the safety and comfort David provided, and she lay back, waiting for him.

He moved forward, and the faint light from the adjoining bathroom illuminated his face. He looked distracted. Different. Odd.

"Do you need something, David?" she asked, swinging her legs over the side of the bed. She was wearing flannel boxers and a tank for nightclothes, not the silky lingerie he'd requested for his visits to her bedroom. And she hadn't showered since this afternoon — he wouldn't like that, either.

"I need you," he said, and grabbed her. His hands were rough, almost desperate, and he yanked her into his arms, kissing her, his mouth grinding against her, his hips pressing up against her body with urgency.

She pushed against him, trying to slow him down, but he was stronger than she realized, and he shoved her back on the bed, landing on top of her with a graceless thud. "Please," he panted, pulling at her clothes. "Please."

There was no way she could deny him. No real reason to. He was desperate, fumbling at his own clothes, and she tried to put her hands on his, to slow him down, to calm him, but he shoved them away.

"David," she said in a calming voice.

"Don't talk! Don't say anything!" He

couldn't seem to manage her clothes, so she lifted her hips and pulled the boxers off herself, tossing them on the floor, and then leaned back, spreading her legs for him.

He was on her like a crazy person, yanking his trousers down, slamming his hips up against hers, and she lifted, waiting for him.

He was barely erect. Again. She reached down, to try to help him, but he shoved her hand away, grinding at her in desperation, his flaccid penis rubbing up against her.

She could have used her mouth to help him, but he didn't like that. When they made love he liked to be the one in charge, the giver of pleasure. That had all disappeared in his current panic. He kept pounding at her, trying to shove his way in, but it was useless. With a hoarse cry he rolled off her, lying on his back, beside her, panting.

She turned to him. "David," she said, putting her hand on his shoulder, not sure what to say, not sure what had happened. "It'll get better."

He shuddered, scrambling away from her. "Don't touch me," he said in a choked whisper. "Don't touch me, don't talk, don't say anything." He stumbled toward the door, his trousers down around his hips, and a moment later he was gone. The door slammed shut behind him, leaving Rachel alone in the dark.

She got off the bed, found her discarded boxers and pulled them back on, then grabbed the silk kimono she'd bought in Kyoto a decade ago and went after him. His bedroom door was locked, but she could hear him beyond the thick panel, hear the choking noise that sounded like muffled sobs, and it broke her heart.

Or it should have. "David," she said through the wood. "Let me in."

"Go away."

"We need to talk, sweetie. Don't be upset. You were in too much of a hurry. We can try again."

"Go away! Go away, go away, go away!" His voice rose to a shrill shriek. He'd moved, coming up to the door and pounding on it so hard it shook in the frame. "Get away from me!"

She backed away. Somewhere in the distance she could hear the walnut-encased clock strike three, and the rain beat a steady counterpoint to the throbbing of her heart. This was the third time he'd come to her, unable to perform, but he'd never been so frantic before.

She headed back to her bedroom, rubbing at her wrist. She'd have bruises in the morning, she thought absently. And she suddenly felt dirty. She closed her door behind her, then, at the last minute she locked it, before heading into the bathroom. She turned on the hot water, then began to pull off her clothes.

There were too many mirrors in the bathroom — she always hated the unexpected views she'd get of her less than perfect body, and she tried to avoid it, but it was close to impossible. She pulled the tank over her head, and then paused.

There was blood on her mouth. A smear of blood over her lips, and she realized he'd done it when he'd been trying to kiss her.

No wonder he'd freaked out. David had a horror of blood — whenever he had some drawn for a medical test he fainted. The one time she'd scraped her knuckles grating cheese he'd left the kitchen in a blind panic.

She grabbed some toilet paper and dabbed at her lip. David's sensitivity was one of the things she loved about him.

But right now she was feeling more than a little annoyed. He was the one who'd made her bleed — he had no right running off like a scared little girl.

"Fuck it," she said out loud, savoring the forbidden word, and climbed into the shower. Tomorrow morning she'd be solicitous and caring. Tomorrow her split lip would be almost healed and he'd come to her bed and finish what he'd started. For now, she was going to savor her solitude.

4

Sophie dumped her school books in her locker just as Kristen caught up with her. "How was the guidance counselor?"

Sophie made a face. "She asked me if I masturbated."

"Eww," Kristen said. "I always thought she was a perv. Did you tell her you and I turned tricks every weekend down at the roadhouse?"

Sophie laughed. "If I'd thought of it, I would have. She wouldn't believe I wasn't having a full-blown meltdown, so I had to placate her with a few tears."

"Speaking of which, why *aren't you* having a full-blown meltdown? Your best friend was murdered six months ago, and now another girl's been killed, and you seem to be taking it in stride. Don't you care? I'd be having hysterics."

Sophie looked at her. "I thought you knew me better than that. I don't have hysterics."

She shoved her locker shut, hoisting her backpack over her shoulder. "There's nothing I can do about it. It creeps me out that someone was murdered, it reminds me of Tessa. But that happened in San Francisco — there's no connection. I'm mostly worried about my mom freaking out. She goes into full protect mode and she's just as likely to throw me in a car and start driving without thinking it through."

"Wouldn't that be a good thing? I thought you didn't like it here."

"I like it here well enough," she said with a shrug. "And my mom's really happy. She's so in love with David that she's not thinking clearly. She worships the ground he walks on."

"That doesn't sound like your mother," Kristen said doubtfully.

"She does it in her own way," Sophie muttered. "At least she doesn't hang on him. But there's no other reason she would have just thrown everything away and married him. We had a wonderful life when we were traveling. I thought she loved it as much as I did."

"Maybe she was ready to settle down."

"I guess. But why did she have to pick David?" She couldn't keep the dislike out of her voice.

"I still don't understand why he bothers you so much. I've always thought he was pretty cute. Are you sure you're not doing that jealous thing? Most daughters don't want to see their mothers remarried. They don't want to share."

"She was never married in the first place. And I'd be happy to share her. Just not with David Middleton," Sophie said firmly.

"And you don't have any solid reason why you don't like him?"

"Nope. But as long as my mother thinks I'm happy, I'm going to try not to worry about it. As long as I can keep my distance, I'll be fine."

Kristen looked at her admiringly. "You have such a Zenlike calm. How long did you spend in India?"

Sophie laughed. "Three months. I think I get it more from the six months in Nepal. Mom says I was born with an old soul. My mother's always been impulsive — one of us has to be the calm one. So to get back to your original question, yes, the murder bothers me. Yes, I still mourn Tessa. But flailing around doesn't help. Okay?"

"Okay," Kristen said, easygoing. "Wanna come home with me?"

Sophie shook her head. "My mother's going to need to fuss for a while. I'll call you later."

"Good luck, man. You're going to need it."

Sophie started toward the door just as the final bell rang. For a moment she was alone, and she closed her eyes, and thought of Tessa, the last time she'd seen her, happy and full of life. And of the photo in the newspaper of her corpse, the one she wasn't supposed to have seen.

She let the pain dance in her heart for a moment, and then she pushed it away. Her mother was waiting for her, and she had enough to worry about. Plastering a calm smile on her face, she headed out into the early afternoon rain.

Rachel had pulled her Volvo up outside the high school, her fingers drumming on the steering wheel. It had taken all her self-control not to run over to the school and snatch Sophie out of it, but for once she controlled her impulse. The more emotional a fuss she made, the harder it would be for Sophie. Going through Tessa's disappearance and murder had been horrible enough. It was just nasty that their lives had to brush up against something like that again.

She left the motor running — if she didn't

the windows would fog up and it would take forever for them to clear, and she wanted to grab Sophie and get her home as quickly as possible.

Sophie came out of the redbrick building with Kristen, her pale blond hair barely contained in turtle-shell barrettes. She looked normal enough, and Rachel wondered whether she was imagining the shadows in her eyes.

"Hi, babe," Rachel said as Sophie slid into the front seat of the car, dumping her books on the floor.

"I know about the murder. How are you doing?"

"Maggie said she'd told you. I wanted to come over but she said you were already asleep." She still couldn't rid herself of her guilt.

"You saw Chief Bannister last night? Why did she talk to you?"

"Not to me. To David and his father. And his brother."

"David's got a brother?" Sophie looked less than thrilled. "Is he as boring as David?"

"Behave yourself, babe," Rachel said. "David isn't boring."

"You taught me never to lie — you're setting a bad example. David is very nice but

73

he's boring as hell. So is his creepy father."
She managed a ghost of her usual grin. "At
least I've got Kristen and the math program
— they're more than enough to offset two
old men. Or is it three? Tell me about my
new uncle. Is he the killer? Is that why Chief
Bannister was questioning him?"

"God, Sophie!" Rachel shuddered. "Don't
be so ghoulish. No one suspects anyone. It
was probably a lovers' quarrel — that's the
usual reason women are murdered. That's
even what happened with Tessa. She was
seeing someone and not telling anyone
about it."

"Except me," Sophie said, any attempt at
lightness vanishing. "She told me about
him. I should have said something."

"I've told you a hundred times that it isn't
your fault, angel," Rachel said firmly. "The
man who killed Tessa was some kind of
monster. A young girl is no match for
someone like that."

"I would be," she said in a quiet voice. "I
would be now."

"There are no monsters in Silver Falls."

"Then who killed that college student?"

"I don't know, but whoever it is, he must
have moved on."

"If you say so," Sophie said breezily, but
Rachel wasn't fooled for a moment.

"I wish you'd called me last night."

"No need, Ma. I told you, I'm fine. So tell me about David's boring brother. How come we never heard of him before?"

"He's not boring. It might be better if he was. He's the black sheep of the family."

Sophie immediately brightened. "Cool. Is he staying with us? What's brought him back home?"

"God, no! I don't know where he's staying. As for why he's back, maybe it's just bad timing."

"I wanna meet him. Is he a hottie? Most black sheep are."

Rachel snorted with laughter. "And just how many black sheep have you known, baby girl?"

"Only in books . . . But they sound delicious. Unless he's an old goat like Stephen Henry." She shuddered dramatically.

Rachel grinned. "He's not like your grandfather."

"Not my grandfather."

"You'll probably find Caleb Middleton fascinating. He has that cynical, world-weary air that susceptible females find romantic, and you'll probably be no exception."

"Cool," Sophie said again. "How about you? Are you susceptible?"

"Hardly. I'm a married woman. Besides, I've always kept clear of bad boys — I'm too smart and too stubborn for them."

"I don't know, I think a bad boy might be just what you need. David's awfully tame. I know he's your true love and all that, but don't you wish you had a little more excitement in your life?"

"I've had more than enough excitement to last me. Tame is good in a husband and father."

"*Not* my father," Sophie said. "You're not going to let him adopt me, right?"

"I promised I'd wait until you were more comfortable with the idea. But you're happy here, aren't you, baby? You're glad we're not wandering the globe anymore? You like David?" Sophie was the only human being on this earth who could make her feel anxious. She wanted so desperately to make it right for her daughter that she would have done anything, married anyone to give her the normal home life and the opportunities she deserved.

"Of course, Ma," Sophie said cheerfully. "I'm just yanking your chain. David's great, and he never tries to boss me around or be too chummy. And even if Stephen Henry's a pain in the butt he's nice enough. You did great, Ma. You love David and he adores you. So it's all good."

She sounded like she meant it. It would be nice if Sophie took to David the way she'd probably react to Caleb, but the truth of the matter was, David was boring. Good, solid, dependable. Far from perfect — he was a little vain, with just the barest trace of a control freak that he mostly managed to keep under control.

No, Sophie would find Caleb much more interesting. After all, she was her mother's daughter.

"Uh . . . Ma? Don't you want to get home?"

Rachel jerked. "Sorry, babe. I was just thinking too much. Yeah, let's go home. I think I need chocolate."

"Sounds good to me," Sophie said cheerfully. And only a mother would have recognized the strain beneath her young voice.

By the time they got back to the house the day had turned unseasonably warm, almost muggy, and the omnipresent clouds only magnified the sense of impending doom. The air was thick, and Rachel could practically feel the mold forming on her skin. How did people live like this?

She turned on every light as she walked through the house, making a mental note to go out and buy hundred-watt lightbulbs to replace David's muted lighting. Sophie headed into the family room at the back of the house to work on her homework. It was as far from David's library/office as possible in the spread-out house, the only room that had a television, and Sophie had claimed it for her own. Apart from the studio, it was the only room where Rachel really felt comfortable. That would change, of course, once she lived here longer. She'd talk David into brighter colors, more comfortable furniture. In the meantime she'd have to make do with music livening the place up.

She pulled a bottle of water from the fridge, reached over and turned on the radio, loud. David preferred new-age music so bland that it was practically Muzak. Rachel found an oldies station and turned it up full blast. How could bad things be threatening when the Beach Boys were singing "Wouldn't it Be Nice?"? She could close her eyes and almost imagine she was in the bright Southern California sunshine, Sophie beside her, surrounded by the crash of the waves, the smell of suntan oil and hot dogs. Here she was, thirty years old and she'd never learned to surf. It would take an earthquake to move David from this town where he'd lived his entire life — if she intended to stay married to him then surfing, and any other kind of adventure, would be out of the question.

And what kind of thought was that — *if* she stayed married? She wasn't a quitter. She'd made a commitment, a choice for her daughter's future. She wasn't going to change her mind and go chasing after lost chances. She'd had plenty of years to follow her heart. It was time to follow her head.

Sure enough, the Beach Boys finished and Aretha came on, singing "Chain of Fools." Maybe if she listened long enough she'd find the answers to all her problems.

And why the hell did she have problems? She had a daughter she adored, a kind husband, a new life. So she was just the tiniest bit bored. So what? She'd spent most of her life being much too impulsive, grabbing Sophie and heading out for new adventures. It was past time to grow up, do the sensible thing. And she'd done it. She was hardly going to renege now. Besides, she'd always hated whiners — was she becoming one herself?

Neil Diamond was next, and she reached over and turned it off. There was a limit, and Neil Diamond was way past it. She was heading for the refrigerator when the sound of Sophie's bright voice filtered into the kitchen.

Who could she be talking to? David never came home early, and Rachel had yet to meet anyone in this buttoned-up town who was likely to just drop in unannounced with the possible exception of Maggie, and she was kind of busy right now. The sound of the deep voice, answering her daughter, was enough to send panic lancing through her.

She slammed out of the kitchen, practically skidding into the family room where Sophie sat on the floor, legs crossed, her books scattered around her, her laptop spread out on the coffee table as she carried on an easy conversation with Caleb Middleton.

"What the hell are you doing here?" she demanded, not caring how she sounded.

Caleb was lounging in a chair, his long legs stretched out in front of him, and he simply looked up at her. "Meeting my niece. You didn't tell me what a charming daughter you have."

"In the kitchen. Now." She could barely keep the anger out of her voice.

"Ma!" Sophie protested. "We were having a good time."

Caleb got to his feet in a leisurely manner designed to infuriate her. "We'll continue our conversation later, Sophie."

"The hell you will," Rachel muttered, herding him into the kitchen. She switched on the radio again so Sophie couldn't overhear her. "I want you to stay away from my daughter."

He cocked his head, looking at her quizzically. "Why would you think I'd be any particular danger to her?" he said, entirely reasonable. "She's too young for me. How old are you?"

"Stop that!"

"Stop what?" He leaned back against the counter, watching her with that unsettling stillness. "What's got you so wound up?"

"There's a murderer on the loose — why shouldn't I be wound up?"

"What's that got to do with me?"

"Oh, I don't know, maybe because you said it did," she snapped.

"When did I say that?"

"Last night. In your father's kitchen."

"I was trying to bait you. Look at it this way — I'd only just arrived in town. I wasn't here long enough to find someone annoying to murder. Time, however, has fixed that." His look at her was pointed.

"That supposed to make me nervous?"

"You don't strike me as someone who's easily frightened."

"You're right. You come to town and a

81

young woman dies. I find that an uncomfortable coincidence."

"Maybe it's no coincidence," he said, his voice expressionless.

She stared at him. "What do you mean by that?"

"Haven't you heard about me, Rachel? I'm the bad seed of Silver Falls. The kind of kid who boosted cars and stole my brother's girlfriends. The kind of kid who killed his mother and put his father in a wheelchair."

She wasn't going to panic. "Exactly how much of that is true?"

He looked at her. "Some of it. It'll be up to you to figure out what's what. In the meantime, you need to be careful. Things are going to get worse before they get better. Maybe you should pack Sophie up, go on a little vacation until things settle down."

"Things aren't *un*settled, and we're not going anywhere," she said, trying to hide how tempting that was. "Sophie and I are both very happy here. She loves the school, loves her new life. The math program here is extraordinary, and she's a gifted child."

"There are other programs. Tell me, does she love my brother? David has never been the paternal type."

"They get along very well. Sophie doesn't need a father, she simply needs a structured, ordinary life and a chance to use her brain. I've dragged her all around the world, never gave her a chance to have a normal life, a normal home. She's got that now and I'm not about to throw it away on a whim."

"Normal home? Honey, you struck out on that one," he drawled. "And what about you? You don't strike me as a structured, ordinary woman."

"I can be," she said firmly. "I can be anything my daughter needs me to be."

"How about gone?"

"Why are you trying to get rid of us?"

He looked at her for a long moment, his deep brown eyes shadowed. And then he blinked. "Just a momentary lapse on my part, sweetheart. People will tell you I seldom do the right thing — it goes against my nature. Stay here if you want. Just keep an eye on your daughter."

"I always do. Which is why I don't want you anywhere near her."

"Trust me, I'm the least of your worries. I could tell you something interesting about Jessica Barrowman."

"Who's Jessica Barrowman?"

"The murder victim." His voice was flat.

"I thought you hadn't been here long enough to know her?"

"I'm a fast learner," he said. "I've been

here long enough to find out a few things about the murder. Jessica Barrowman was young, thin, with long straight blond hair down her back. Just like your daughter. You might consider getting Sophie a haircut and a perm."

Her stomach lurched in sudden panic. "You son of a bitch —"

He caught her arm as she charged him, spinning her around until it was trapped behind her back. Their bodies were pressed together for a long, endless moment as they looked at each other, the tension crackling between the two of them.

Rachel didn't move. His grip on her arm was like iron, his body was warm and hard against hers, and she could feel his heart beating, fast. Her own heart was racing — with fury, she told herself. His grip loosened on her arm, releasing her, but she didn't move, and neither did he.

Why now, she thought. Why, after all this time, did this man have to show up now? Why couldn't she have met him five years ago and gotten him out of her system then, when she was free to do so? Why did he have to appear now, with a hidden agenda, and she couldn't decide whether she wanted to shove him away or move closer, so close that they could practically melt together, so close that she could close her eyes and their breathing would be perfectly in sync, so close her eyes and his mouth would cover hers and she'd kiss him back and realize it wasn't worth the trouble, it never was.

But why did it have to be now that she was uncharacteristically tempted?

She stepped back, and he let her go without any show of reluctance. "Does my brother know you're not happy?"

"I'm perfectly happy in my marriage," she said, ignoring the debacle in her bed last night.

"Are you?" He looked past her, his eyes narrowing for a moment, and then suddenly he moved closer. "I could change your mind . . ."

David walked into the kitchen, just as Caleb reached for her, and she waited for his explosion.

None came. "What are you doing here, Caleb?" David said, sounding only slightly distracted.

Caleb's smile was easy, just barely taunting. "It's been a long time. I wanted to see what you were up to."

"What do you mean by that?"

"You've got a new family. A lovely new daughter. It's only logical that I'd want to meet her and get to know her mother better. Why, I bet Rachel doesn't know anything about our childhood. I could tell her stories that would probably shock the hell out of her."

"No, thank you," Rachel said, moving to stand by her husband. "I know all I need to know about David, and I don't really need to know anything at all about you."

"Don't be rude, Rachel," David admonished. "You'll find that Caleb likes to stir things up whenever he can. He likes to play the bad boy, but in the end he's really quite harmless."

"Am I, David?" Caleb's smile was far from reassuring. "You might be surprised."

Whatever had happened to upset David seemed well past, and he looked at his brother with fond benevolence. "I've known you for thirty-five years, Caleb. I doubt you could surprise me anymore." He leaned over and kissed Rachel on the cheek. "We're going over to my father's for dinner, sweetheart. That way you don't have to cook."

Shit, that was all she needed. Another interminable evening with Stephen Henry. "Sorry, can't do it. It's a school night and Sophie's got a lot of work to do. You'll have to take my apologies."

"Father will be so disappointed. You know how fond he is of Sophie," David said.

"Sorry, but rules are rules. Sophie can't go out on school nights, even for family reunions." She could see David was about to protest, and she forestalled him. "Last night was different — part of her school credit is from tutoring other students."

"That's all right, Rachel," Caleb said. "The fatted calf can wait until the weekend. The prodigal son has no intention of going anywhere soon."

"What about your job?" David said.

"Leave of absence. For the next few weeks I'm going to immerse myself in the old town. I want to find out just what's been going on for the last twenty years."

"Twenty years?" Rachel echoed, startled.

"I took off when I was seventeen. I've been back a few times since then, but only for a matter of days. I'm afraid the town of Silver Falls has never made me feel particularly welcome."

"What happened when you were seventeen?"

"He stole a car," David said. "Again. He got drunk, stole a car and ran my parents off the road. Stephen Henry has been in a wheelchair ever since and my mother died."

There was a moment of shocked silence, and then Caleb spoke, sounding singularly unconcerned. "I hate to be picky, but I

87

should point out that they were my parents as well."

"You didn't even stay for the funeral," David said.

"I couldn't very well — you'd been so helpful with the police that I had no choice but to disappear for a few years. Fortunately Stephen Henry cleared things up and the charges were dropped."

"He always had a soft spot for you. He was probably more than happy to lie for you."

"Lie?" Caleb echoed. "There are no lies in our happy little family."

"Father's waiting for us," David said, the edge creeping back. He turned to Rachel. "I really think you and Sophie should come with us. If for no other reason than it would be safer. There's a murderer loose."

She shook her head. "We'll lock the doors and we'll be fine. Give my love to Stephen Henry."

"I might think twice about that," Caleb murmured. "The old man is a lecher." He ignored David's sputtered protest. "You know he is, so don't argue. Let's go. And Rachel's right — she might very well be safer here." He looked at her, and all his mockery vanished. "Keep an eye on your daughter. If you're not going to leave town, then watch her like a hawk."

"Leave? Why would Rachel leave?" David sounded oddly frantic.

"Maybe because there's a serial killer on the loose, and if she took her daughter on a vacation until he's caught it would be easier for her?" Caleb suggested.

"She can't leave . . . Rachel isn't the kind of woman who runs away."

Rachel was feeling exactly like that kind of woman. She managed to nod convincingly.

"Even if there's a serial killer at work?" Caleb said.

"What makes you think Rachel would be the target?" David said.

Caleb turned to look at him. "Who knows what goes on in the mind of a serial killer?"

"One death doesn't make for a serial killer. Do you think I can't take care of my own family?" David snapped, and she could hear the edge of panic in his voice.

"I'm sure you can." He changed the subject. "Shall we go visit our patriarch? He wants us to bond." Caleb's tone of voice made it patently clear that that was a vain hope.

But David surprised her. "I'd like that," he said, his animosity vanishing. "It's been too long."

Caleb looked equally surprised but not particularly gratified. "If you say so."

"We'll miss you," David said to Rachel. And then, to her astonishment, he pulled her into his arms, mashing his mouth against hers, trying to shove his tongue past her lips.

David never used his tongue. He seldom kissed her, and then it was very chaste. At that moment he had one hand on her butt, squeezing so hard it hurt, and another clamped on her breast. She forced herself to remain still, resisting the impulse to shove him away, to wipe her arm across her mouth. When he finally released her she managed a smile by sheer force of will.

"Don't be gone too long, darling," she said in what she hoped was an encouraging voice. It sounded dubious at best.

Caleb was watching them, a faint, disbelieving expression on his face. He saw far too much, and Rachel was half-tempted to grab David and plant another kiss on him, just to show the man.

She didn't move until they were out the door, and then she crossed the room to lock it behind them. Leaving her alone with her daughter, and her doubts.

5

Another cool, rainy day, Rachel thought the next afternoon, closing the door on her darkroom. She just couldn't face choosing to work in even more darkness — the persistent gloom of Silver Falls was hard enough. She'd actually gotten on the internet to check out weather patterns — maybe this was just an unusually rainy period. Surely the Pacific Northwest wasn't always so wretched, or people wouldn't be moving there.

The research was far from promising. The rest of the state, even some of the rainiest areas, averaged far less rainfall than this tiny little college town. Silver Falls consistently averaged twice the yearly rainfall of Seattle and Portland combined, and this year was ostensibly drier than usual. It was no wonder nothing ever seemed to dry out and it felt like mold was growing everywhere. It probably was.

She poured herself a cup of coffee and stared out toward Silver Mountain, shrouded with clouds as it always was. She and Sophie had planned to hike there on the next clear day, but that day hadn't come.

It had taken all of Rachel's resolve not to keep Sophie home that morning. Sophie, of course, had shrugged off the murder relatively well, thanks to the invulnerability of youth, but Caleb's words kept echoing in her ear. The victim had been young and slender, with long, straight blond hair. She'd scoured the *Silver Falls Sentinel* for the gruesome details — Jessica Barrowman had been a student at the college, just eighteen years old. Her face haunted her.

She looked too much like Tessa.

She and Sophie had arrived back on the west coast after two years in Spain, and the cool, foggy atmosphere of San Francisco had been a welcome change from the sun and heat and bright blue sky. It had been easy enough to find a community — she had enough connections from her photography friends and it had been easy to find a place to live and a job, and Sophie ended up at the local alternative school in the Fillmore District just outside of Japantown. Sophie settled in quickly, aided by her usual ability to make friends, the closest one being Tessa Montgomery, a girl three years older than she, just sixteen, and almost a clone. They were always being mistaken for sisters as they wandered around the big, fascinating city.

But then Tessa had a boyfriend. A mysterious one she met in Golden Gate Park. He was older, she said, and rich, and romantic, and sexy, and he was going to wait until she was old enough to get married but Tessa didn't want to. She'd spilled all this to Sophie, her best friend, and Sophie had been taught by her mother not to gossip and not to repeat secrets.

It wasn't until Tessa didn't come home one day that Sophie finally told Rachel about Tessa's secret lover. And when Tessa's body had been found six days later Sophie had been inconsolable.

Rachel wasn't sure how they would have gotten through that time if it weren't for David. She couldn't even remember how she'd met him — one day he was just there, calm and friendly, a college professor on sabbatical, doing research. He had a sublet nearby, and his quiet, gentle manner was the perfect antidote to the anger and despair that filled her community. Even Sophie liked him. She was more like her old self when he was there, able to laugh at his admittedly pathetic attempts at a joke.

One thing Rachel liked about him was that he never pressured her for sex — he was an exquisite gentleman. In fact, she was the one who finally instigated them going to bed together, and it was . . . pleasant. No fireworks or earth moving, but very nice, despite David's almost virginal shyness. And the next morning he'd asked her to marry him.

She might have said no, until she looked at Sophie. Unlike her amazon mother, Sophie had never been particularly sturdy, and she was looking almost frail, her pale skin translucent, and on impulse Rachel had said yes, anything to get Sophie out of the city that was now synonymous with death. The accelerated math program had been the icing on the cake, clearly this was meant to be.

The sun had been shining the day they'd arrived in Silver Falls, Washington. As far as she could tell it hadn't been seen since.

And now this safe place seemed suddenly dangerous. Tessa and Jessica looked too much alike. They'd both been molested and strangled. Though Tessa's body had been found in the Bay, and Jessica had been tossed over the waterfall at the head of the mountain that loomed over the small town like a gargoyle.

If that wasn't bad enough, Jessica wasn't the first. There had been others. The *Sentinel* printed the timeline, and Rachel read it over with grim fascination. The first was more than twenty years ago — just before David's mother had been killed. The next was four years later, then a stretch of safety for seven years before another young, blond woman had died. And since then, nothing. Until a few days ago. Around the time when Caleb Middleton had returned to town.

It had to be coincidental. Didn't it? Except hadn't he himself said it wasn't?

Suddenly the house felt oppressive, smothering. There was only a light mist today — liquid sunshine, David used to say playfully. For the next seven hours Sophie was safe at school. She had clear orders not to leave until Rachel picked her up, and she had no choice but trust Sophie's good sense. Sophie was far from docile — there were times it was clear she thought Rachel was the fragile one, but in fact the two of them were alike. Strong-minded and not prey to bullshit. But she also loved her mother enough not to worry her by failing to follow orders. At least, she hoped so.

Rachel shoved two of her cameras into the gypsy bag, grabbed her raincoat and headed out the door. She was tempted to drive until she found sunshine, but the likelihood of getting back in time to pick up Sophie was remote. For now she just needed to get away from everything and everyone, into the dark, forbidding woods that surrounded the town. It wasn't like she was in any danger. The local victims had all been a decade younger than she was, with long, straight blond hair and no curves. No one was going to have any interest in a curvy redhead with a temper.

She headed east, toward Silver Mountain. She was wearing her hiking shoes — she could climb up to the falls and look out over the valley. Maybe from that height she'd see sunshine somewhere in the distance.

By the time she parked her car at the start of the trail the rain was coming down a little more enthusiastically, pelting the thick canopy of leaves overhead. She had no intention of letting it slow her down. In the four months they'd been living there she'd learned that if she waited for a sunny day she'd never leave the house. The ground was slippery beneath her feet, but she moved carefully. She'd hiked all over the world, with Sophie strapped to her back and her cameras in her hands. This puny little mountain wasn't going to be any kind of challenge.

There was something oddly liberating about climbing. Even with the muddy terrain beneath her feet and the wet branches slapping at her, her spirits began to rise. The water from Silver River was rushing down the hill, and she realized she'd never seen the waterfall that gave the town its name. She had more than enough time to make it up there and be back to pick up Sophie.

The rain came down more heavily, and she pulled up the hood of her rain slicker. "Do your worst," she said out loud, looking up at the dark, angry sky. A crack of thunder was her answer, and she froze.

Maybe climbing in a thunderstorm might not be the smartest thing she could possibly do, but once she set a course she wasn't likely to turn back, whether she'd made the right decision or not. She was no quitter, even when things got a little rough. Besides, she hadn't seen much of thunder and lightning during the constant rainstorms, and for all she knew it was just God with a twisted sense of humor. She waited, but there was no sound but the heavy beating of the rain on the lush, overgrown greenery surrounding her, and the rush of wind through the trees, echoed by the roar of the waterfall up ahead.

In the end she almost gave up. Each rise looked like it would be the last one, but the mountain reached higher and higher. Her hiking shoes were caked with mud, her jacket turned out to be water resistant, not waterproof, and the wind picked up, lashing rain into her face and eyes. She kept climbing, trying to follow the omnipresent sound of rushing water, but it seemed to come from all around her. It had been too long since she'd climbed — she was out of shape, but she was damned if she was going to let this weak-ass mountain get the better of her.

But it was getting late, and not even pride would keep her from getting back to Sophie on time. She'd almost given up hope of finding the actual falls when she suddenly came upon a clearing in the dense undergrowth. The heavy torrent of rain had slowed to a sullen mist, and as she moved to the steep bank she pushed the hood off her head. The thunder of the waterfall had been muffled by the jacket, and she moved closer to the steep edge, peering into the dark, foamy water.

The pounding noise would drown out any sound a woman could make. A scream would be swallowed up in the rush of the river, and she shivered, taking a step back.

She didn't want to think about it, think about the poor girl caught in the branches of the Silver River. Old folk songs were slipping around in her head. "I met her on the mountain, there I took her life." Had Jessica Barrowman met her murderer on this mountain, expecting a lover's tryst and finding only death? Was that what had happened to Tessa?

What drove men to seduce women only to kill them? What strange, twisted need did that meet? Was it Freudian, reaching back into the womb? Maybe they felt abandoned by their mothers. Or maybe they had gender issues or were acting out their fears. Or maybe, just maybe they were sick fucks who got off on pain and suffering. In the long run she was better off not knowing. She could happily live the rest of her life without ever understanding the inner workings of a killer's mind. She had no intention of getting any closer to one than reading about it in the newspaper.

Mist was rising, swirling from the water as it sluiced down the hillside, and for a moment she thought she could see something, a ghost, a memory, and she took a step closer, blindly. The earth crumbled beneath her feet, and she was falling, the mud slick beneath her, the water coming up to meet her, and she tried to scream —

The hands on her were rough, yanking her back from the precipice, strong arms around her, and she fought, kicking back until they released her. She went sprawling in the mud, sliding backward until she ended up against a tree, the wind knocked out of her, and all she could think was that she was going to die.

She looked up as she struggled for breath, staring at the dark, hooded figure that loomed over her, his face obscured. He reached down for her, and she tried to say something, tried to scream. It didn't matter that he'd just saved her — he was going to throw her over into the deadly falls and when his hand caught her arm, she lunged at him, trying to fight him off.

He shoved her, and she fell back onto the muddy ground. Her breath came back with a sudden burning tear at her lungs, and she tried to get up again.

"Don't make me hit you," Caleb Middleton's cool, laconic voice came from beneath the rain hood. "I'm trying to save your goddamned life and I don't appreciate being attacked for my efforts."

She managed to get to her feet, ignoring the searing pain in her chest. He stood between her and the falls, and she wondered whether she dared try to rush him again, to tip him over into the deadly water. She'd do anything to stay alive for Sophie's sake, and she eyed him warily.

"Don't even think about it," he said. "You try to shove me over the falls and I'll take you with me." He shoved the hood off his head, and he looked annoyed, not deadly. "In case you didn't notice I just saved your life. You might at least stop looking at me like I'm a monster. Believe it or not, I'm one of the good guys. At least for the moment."

She was just beginning to breathe naturally, and common sense came back in a rush. Of course he didn't want to kill her — he had the perfect chance and instead he'd pulled her back. Besides, what possible reason would he have to want to hurt her?

Unless of course he was a serial killer. And in that case, she was a sturdy redhead in her thirties, not a young, willowy blonde, and therefore safe.

"So, have you decided? Do you want to keep sitting in the mud or do you want to go somewhere and get dried off?"

"Where?" She didn't trust him, but they were at a standstill.

"My place. It's not far —"

"You live up here?"

"On the rare occasion when I'm in the States, yes. Where else would I live? My brother isn't about to welcome me with open arms and Stephen Henry and I do best with a polite distance between us. I'd offer you my hand but you'd probably bite it. Get to your feet on your own and you can come and get warm."

"I'm not going anywhere with you."

"Spoken like a redhead," he said. "Though, right now you looked more like a drowned kitten than a mother lion. If you try to walk down the mountain in your condition you're likely to fall and twist your ankle. Even if you kept upright you wouldn't make it to your daughter's school by three o'clock, and I'm sure that's what you had in mind. If you come back to my place and dry off I'll give you a ride to your car and you'll be there in time."

She tried to ignore the sudden ice in the pit of her stomach. "How do you know when my daughter gets out of school?"

"I grew up here, remember? School has always let out at three. And you better move quick — I'm not going to stand out here forever, waiting for you to make up your mind."

He was right — it was late. As usual, time had gotten away from her. Rachel scrambled to her feet with as much dignity as she could muster, keeping a wary eye on him in case he made any sudden moves.

"I'd appreciate a lift into town," she said. "I can dry off there."

"We can argue about it once we're out of the rain. I don't suppose you want to hold on to me while we climb down there? It's a little rough."

"I'll follow you," she said, wary. "If you tell me how you happened to be up here just as I was about to fall into the water."

"I could say it was fate, but the fact is you're about as delicate a climber as a grizzly bear, and I could see the bushes moving as you thrashed your way up here. I came out to see who was tearing up the hillside — hell, maybe I'd catch the killer at work. You're just lucky I was curious, or you might be floating down the stream like an elderly Ophelia."

"Elderly?" she said, furious.

"Ophelia was around Juliet's age — fifteen or sixteen. I believe you're well past that."

"Fuck you. Maybe I'll push you into the falls just for the hell of it. Even if you aren't the serial killer, you're no great gift to society. My husband would probably thank me."

"Yes," he said, amused. "He probably

would." He spread his arms out. "Give it your best shot."

The last thing she wanted to do was put her hands on him. "I'm not going to bother. Sooner or later some irate husband will blow a hole in you."

"The only married woman I'm interested in is you."

She froze. He was looking at her out of those sharp, dark eyes, and illogical as it was, she believed him. She just wasn't sure why.

The rain had stopped, at least for the moment, and she looked at the path she'd used. If she hurried, she might make it in time, without subjecting herself to any more time in Caleb Middleton's uncomfortable presence.

But she couldn't put Sophie at risk. "Stop talking and show me where your car is," she said, keeping her voice clipped and unemotional.

The faint hint of a smile played at the corner of his mouth. "Yes, ma'am. Follow me." He disappeared into the woods, and she hesitated. He disturbed her, on every level, and willingly putting herself in his company felt like a very bad idea. The only thing worse was having Sophie get tired of waiting and walk home.

She started after him, pushing past the wet branches, following him down the steep, muddy path. She slid once, landing on her butt, and he glanced back at her but didn't slow down. She got to her feet once more and hurried on, trying to keep him in sight without getting too close.

Her first image of the house was the bright blue of the tarp covering the half-finished roof. The trees had grown up all around it, and she could see lines and angles, oddly familiar. It was more of a ruin than a half-finished house, and yet she couldn't rid herself of a feeling that she'd been there before.

"Lovely," she said in an undertone. "Do you even have a telephone?" Maybe she could call home when she got there, see if David could pick Sophie up. Except then she'd have to explain where she was, and who she was with. That, or lie, and neither of those choices was acceptable. There was nothing wrong with what she was doing — she just didn't feel like having to explain it to David.

"Of course I do."

"Where's your car?" she said when she reached the level ground. She stared up at the house. There was a long series of rickety-looking steps leading up to the front door, and there were two wings spreading out from either side. Eerily like David's house, which she still couldn't think of as her own.

He was already halfway up the steps. "Around back. It's a rental, and I'm not about to let a mud rat in it. Come inside, Rachel. I promise I won't strangle you."

She didn't move. "Don't you think that's a little tasteless?"

"I've never been troubled by matters of taste, and if my intended victim were a yappy broad like you the first thing I'd do is shut you up. Either come in and clean off or get down the mountain on your own. I'm getting tired of all this."

"You're a son of a bitch, aren't you?"

"Yes." He kept climbing the stairs, and she had two choices. Make it on her own, and go with him.

He was arrogant, dangerous, rude and much too good-looking for her peace of mind. She liked gentle men like David, not bastards like his brother.

She looked up at the half-finished, prairie-style house, and she had the odd feeling that she was at the point of no return.

She put her foot on the first step and began climbing.

He whistled beneath his breath as he drove

into the garage and closed the door behind him. The women of his household were gone — Sophie was at school, Rachel had gone looking for his brother. He'd known she would — women couldn't keep away from Caleb once he decided to lure them, and he'd been watching Rachel with those dark eyes of his.

David had driven by the parking area at the base of Silver Mountain, just to be sure. Rachel's Volvo was parked there, the car he'd given her for a wedding present. He couldn't help it — he chuckled. She was so easy to manipulate, so transparent. His brother would probably have her on her back in record time.

An ordinary man would have been disturbed. Not David. He'd known almost immediately that he'd made a mistake in marrying Rachel. She'd seemed the answer to everything — she calmed him when his needs flared, and he thought she'd be perfect. By the time Sophie reached the right age he might even have moved past his darkest desires. He'd been having a harder time controlling them recently. He'd never felt the need to strike only six months apart. He could keep Rachel as the perfect wife, the perfect cover. And he could watch Sophie grow into the young woman she was meant to be. And when that happened, maybe this strange cycle, that had lasted more than twenty years, would come to an end. Something would happen to Rachel, and he could live out his life with Sophie, serene and brilliant.

In the meantime, Rachel was proving a sore disappointment. He kept hoping he could train her, but she ignored his hints, and he understood human nature well enough to know that she wouldn't respond well to direct orders. There was nothing he could do about it, except get rid of her in as timely a manner as possible.

But first he had to make absolutely certain that Sophie would be his.

He knew that she wanted him. Her careful way of avoiding him, of never meeting his gaze, of being studiously distant and polite, simply covered the same longing he felt for her. He had to be very delicate about it. She was young and shy, despite what her mother said. Her friend had been easier — older, more self-assured. He could bless Tessa for bringing him to Sophie. This was who he'd been waiting for, the one to make him complete. Not her mother. And it had all been sheer luck. He'd found Tessa, and she'd been perfect for a time, and when he'd finished he should have been able to go back to his normal life.

But he couldn't keep away from the funeral, and the moment he saw Sophie, he knew she was meant for him.

For a short while he'd hoped he could be like other men. That Rachel would be the answer until Sophie came of age.

But his needs were growing stronger.

He opened the trunk of the car and took a step back, assailed by the stench. Rotting flesh. He should have dumped her weeks ago, but for some reason the chance never came up. He had to admit that a certain part of him enjoyed knowing she was back there, wrapped in a tarp. He liked driving Rachel around, telling her about the bloated deer corpse he'd accidentally run over. She'd believed him, the silly cow. Because she adored him.

He took the cans of air freshener and sprayed them liberally through the trunk. He should have gone up to Costco and bought a case — it was taking forever to get rid of the smell. But then, someone might have noticed, and he was a very careful man.

He closed the trunk again, then opened the back door of the garage to release some of the lingering odor. It was getting close to three o'clock — if she wasn't back to the car then he'd be able to pick up Sophie. He always liked those moments. She would sit beside him in the car, her hands clasped in her lap, her long legs beneath the school uniform deliberately enticing him. Maybe he'd take her for a drive, talk to her about how depressed her mother had been. He'd explain that Rachel had been hiding it from her daughter, but that she was indeed a deeply troubled woman.

He needed to be careful, though. Sophie was smart as a whip, and devoted to her mother.

There was no hurry. At least, he hoped not. He was making very sure that all his bases were covered, now that Caleb was back in town. And if he was lucky, he could ride this for another few years.

But he wasn't quite sure if he could tolerate Rachel that long. She seemed to accept his departure from their marriage bed with good grace, and she hadn't minded when he'd withdrawn more and more.

Maybe she'd behave herself, learn her place, preparing her daughter.

Otherwise, one slip and the falls could take her. And no one would ever know he'd been the one to push.

6

"This place is a death trap," Rachel said, standing in the middle of what should have been the living room, oblivious to the ancient bloodstain on the plywood beneath her.

Caleb stripped off his rain-soaked slicker and hung it on one of the nails, turning to her. "An interesting way of looking at things. Why do you say that?"

"I nearly fell through one of the steps." She was making no effort to divest herself of her muddy clothes. "Are you going to drive me down to town?"

"I should have warned you about that one. Upkeep on this place isn't a high priority."

"I can see that." She looked around her, and he could practically read her mind. The place was a disaster — a half-constructed architect's dream that had suffered the indignities of rain, wind and abandonment for the last fifteen years. He'd tacked fresh tarps on the western side of the frame to keep the wind from blowing through, but he hadn't gotten around to replacing the shredded blue fabric that covered the roof, and there were pools of rain water at regular intervals on the warped floor. "So why does this place look familiar?" she said suddenly pushing back the hood of her raincoat.

"Good eye. It was designed and built by the architect who did David's house. And yours."

He could see her shoulders relax slightly. A mistake on her part, but she didn't realize the mess she'd gotten herself in. "Yes, I can see that now," she said. "Why didn't he finish it?"

Caleb shrugged. "He went bankrupt and killed himself. That's his blood you're standing on."

She looked down at the dark stain, and to her credit she didn't leap away with a squeal. "And you left it there?"

"It's a helpful reminder of knowing your limitations. Hubris and all — you can't reach too high or the gods will smite you."

"In your case I'm not sure it sank in," she said, moving past the stain to look out the framing that should have held a window. "You don't seem particularly meek and humble."

112

"No, that's never been my particular character defect." He moved closer to her, carefully, so as not to startle her. "You can see your house quite clearly if there's no rain."

"Which means never," she said gloomily. "Why did you buy a house just like David's?"

"Maybe you should ask him. Maybe the question is . . . why did he buy a house like mine."

She turned her head to look at him. She was a tall woman, almost his height, and her eyes were clear and bright. "Why are you here?"

For one brief, crazy moment he considered telling her the truth. She wouldn't believe him, of course. No one ever had, though his mother had suspected the truth. And he couldn't risk her telling David.

So he lied. "I haven't seen my father in years. I thought it was about time."

"And David?"

"He's visited me occasionally when I've been on assignment. He's more sentimental than I am — he's always made sure our brotherly connection remains strong. I last saw him in Tunisia."

"I didn't realize David traveled that much." She unzipped her coat. He had a

113

good fire going in the woodstove, and despite the gaping windows, the room was warm.

"There are a lot of things about David you don't know. Why don't I get you some clean clothes and you can change? If your daughter sees you like that she's going to worry."

She looked down at her muddy clothes, considering. "Mud dries."

"During the rainy season? You're more optimistic than I would have thought," Caleb said.

"What do you mean, rainy season? Does the sun ever shine in this misbegotten place?"

"It's been known to happen," he said. "We've got four distinct seasons. Less rain. More rain. A lot more rain. And the deluge."

"Nevertheless . . ."

He ignored her, disappearing into the far room, returning with his baggiest pair of jeans and an oversized flannel shirt. "Here."

She made no move to take them, so he simply dumped them in her arms. "The bathroom's behind that door. It even locks."

"I really need to get back down to my car."

"You have time."

"Then I have time to get to my own house and change my clothes."

"But again, I'm not putting you in my car in that condition," he said, all breezy sweetness that he didn't expect to fool her for one moment.

It didn't. She made a low noise, somewhere between a snarl and a growl, and stomped off away from him, slamming the bathroom door behind her.

He found himself grinning. She was a firecracker, red hair and all, a fighter. This would be so much easier with a frail flower, but Rachel wasn't the type to wilt.

Once more he considered telling her the truth. He could tell her what kind of danger she was in, but she wouldn't believe him. For the moment she was safe. And what he had told her was the simple truth. The women had all been the same physical type — thin, average height, long, straight blond hair. A far cry from Rachel Middleton's Amazonian proportions.

Sophie was a different matter, but she was way too young. In a couple of years or so she might be at risk, making him doubly grateful he'd finally chosen to face his worst fears. If he'd put it off, if she'd died, he'd never forgive himself.

In a way he was already at that point. He couldn't remember a time when he hadn't had suspicions, doubts, but the truth of it was unacceptable even to a hard-core cynic like himself. But maybe, just maybe, the girl on the mountain wouldn't have died if he'd come sooner. Maybe Libba, maybe even Sophie's friend Tessa.

There were times when the real monsters were those who stood by and said nothing while evil erupted. And any silence would make him the monster everyone had always believed him to be.

He'd told Rachel to leave, warned her as best he could. He'd keep trying, if only to save the tattered remnants of his conscience, as ripped and shredded as the tarp that had once covered the roof of this haunted house. But if she wouldn't leave, she could at least help him, willingly or not.

Taking David's wife was the surest way of doing what he had to do.

The jeans barely fit, and she knew he'd chosen extra-baggy ones, not like the lean-fitting ones he wore. Asshole. She dumped her mud-encrusted pants and shirt on the floor, pulled his clothes on, grumbling beneath her breath. To her amazement he had warm water in the rust-stained sink. She washed some of the mud from her face, then paused, staring back at her reflection.

She could barely recognize herself. Her

hair had gotten loose, and it was a tangled mess around her face. A kind soul might say it was sensual, David would have said it was messy. The last thing she wanted was for the black sheep to think she was sensual.

She was pretty damned safe on that account. He was a talker, nothing more. She hadn't bothered with makeup, and her pale face looked oddly vulnerable, her eyes wary. But she was never vulnerable — she couldn't afford to be. He'd given her a blue flannel shirt, by accident, of course, but it made the blue in her eyes stand out.

She didn't look like the woman she was used to seeing in the mirror. No light sprinkling of freckles across her nose, no color in her cheeks, a sober expression on her face when she used to laugh, loud and often. What had happened to her? Had she started to mold in the dark, dank climate?

She should take Sophie and head for the sun. Just a vacation, a trip to see friends, she'd tell David. She'd stay away long enough to see things clearly, and if . . . make that when . . . she came back she'd have a better sense of who she was. She'd lost that over the last few months, and she couldn't figure out why. It wasn't as if David was an overbearing, macho pig like his adopted brother.

She pushed open the door, and he was standing with his back to her, staring out at the downpour. He turned, a couple of beers in his hands.

"I'm driving," she said, but he put one in her hand anyway.

"So am I. One beer won't hurt you. Unless you don't like beer. I'm afraid I'm fresh out of chardonnay."

"I like beer," she said, and took a healthy slug.

"So, have a seat," he said.

"Where?"

"I've got a bed in the other room. . . ."

She slammed the half-empty beer bottle down on the broken table. "I'm out of here."

"Calm down, princess. Just a suggestion. There's always the floor."

He meant for sitting, of course. But she couldn't rid herself of the feeling that he was thinking more than that.

And it didn't make sense. She had no illusions about herself — she wasn't the kind of woman that men chased. Her relationships, after her first disastrous one, had been comfortable, friend-driven, with sex as almost an afterthought, which was why she'd gotten along so well with David when he'd showed up, solicitous and caring, while they were dealing with the aftermath of Tessa's hideous murder.

She didn't have the slightest doubt that Caleb's interest had to do with his relationship with his brother and absolutely nothing to do with her. And it was perfectly reasonable that she would find that annoying. It wasn't that she was interested in him. She simply didn't like being manipulated.

"The beer doesn't taste that bad."

She looked up. "What?"

"You're making a face like you're sucking on a lemon."

She looked at him through the mottled light. He had electricity up there. A bare incandescent bulb hung from the ceiling, the light glaring, throwing strange shadows on everything. "You know, Caleb, that's not exactly the right thing to say to a woman while you're trying to come on like the big bad wolf," she said, tipping the bottle back.

She'd managed to startle him enough, and he laughed. "If I'm the big bad wolf then who are you? Little Red Riding Hood?"

"No, honey. I'm the practical pig, and you sure as hell aren't going to blow my house down."

For a moment he didn't move. And then suddenly he was closer, moving in on her in a way that was threatening, arousing, annoying. "I could try," he said, his voice soft

119

and low.

"Give it up, Caleb. You aren't going to convince me you want me so you may as well stop it." She moved away from him, dropping down to sit cross-legged on the floor. "So what have you got against your brother?"

He stayed where he was, looking down at her with an odd expression in his dark eyes. "Why do you find it hard to believe I'm attracted to you?"

"Why do you answer a question with another question." She took another swig of the beer. She shouldn't be sitting here, trading words with him, she should be in the car, being driven down the muddy road, or hightailing it down there on her own. She would, in just a couple of minutes. In the meantime this was a dangerous game, enticing after so many months of well-behaved safety.

He took a seat across from her, far enough away to give her a false sense of security. And she knew it was false. "Tell me about Tessa," he said.

It took all the fun out of a risky encounter. "How do you know about Tessa. And why do you want to know?"

"I'm a reporter. I don't betray my sources. Don't you think it's odd that there have been two similar murders in your vicinity in the last six months?"

Again that unsettling knowledge, that thought. "If you know Tessa was murdered six months ago, then I don't really need to tell you anything," she said, trying to hide her sudden panic.

"Sophie told me."

She freaked. "Keep away from my daughter!"

"Oh, please!" he said, rolling his eyes. "I like women, not children. She's a good kid, smart like her mother. Maybe smarter than her mother — she knows who she can trust."

"God, don't tell me she trusts you! I'm going to have to explain a few things to her once I get down from here."

He didn't rise to the bait. "Look me in the eye and tell me you really think I'm a danger to your daughter."

She didn't bother. He had hypnotic eyes — it was one of the dangers about him, along with his long, lean body and his sinful mouth. Not to mention his history.

"I suspect you're a danger to everyone you come in contact with," she said, draining the beer.

For a moment he looked startled. "Sometimes," he said finally.

A stray shiver ran across her back. "I'm

121

ready to go home now."

"You still haven't told me about Tessa."

She rose, leaving her empty bottle behind. "She died. As far as the police could figure out she was the random victim of a serial killer, one who's been active all over the Northwest. They grow the biggest crazies out here, you know. Ted Bundy and the Green River Killer and probably others. My theory is all this rain drives you crazy."

"How did she die?"

"None of your *fucking* business!" She automatically clapped her hands over mouth. *"Damn!"*

"You don't swear? What kind of Mormon are you?" He'd risen himself, taller than she was, dangerous though she wasn't quite sure why.

"I promised I'd stop saying *fuck,*" she said. "It's an ugly word."

"It's a great word in the right circumstances. It can, for instance, indicate a very enjoyable way to spend an afternoon. I suppose you promised my brother? He's an English professor — he should understand."

"It's overused."

"That doesn't mean it doesn't have its place."

"Jesus Fucking Christ!" Rachel exploded.

"Are you always this much of a pain in the ass?"

"Why do you suppose they drove me out of town?" he replied. "Oh, sorry, that was answering a question with a question." He moved closer, and she decided to stand her ground. A mistake.

"Yes," he said, so close she could practically touch him. "Yes, I'm always such a pain in the ass, yes, I actually do want you, and as for what I've got against my brother, it would take too long to tell you and you wouldn't believe me."

"Try me," she said. Big mistake.

"I was waiting for the offer." He moved so fast she didn't have time to react. He cupped her face, pulling her closer, and kissed her.

Her arms were free to fight him, and she punched him in the stomach, but he didn't flinch, merely moved closer, one arm imprisoning her, trapping her hands between their bodies. "I'm just trying to prove my point," he murmured, and kissed her again, his mouth hard on hers.

She clamped her jaw together, freezing, since he had her in too strong a hold to shove him away. His hand cupped her neck, his fingers brushing against the side of her face, a calming, gentle touch that slowly

123

began to leach the fury from her body. She could feel his heart beat through the layers of clothing that separated them, and her own heart beat a counterpoint to his. He lifted his head, looking down at her stubborn face. "Kiss me back and I'll let you go," he said softly.

"Fuck off."

He kissed her anyway, and she remained stonily still, as his other hand trailed up her back to the perfect, sensitive spot just beneath her shoulder blades, and she felt her treacherous body soften.

Oh, the hell with it. She kissed him back. She opened her mouth, slid her arms around his waist, pulling him closer still, and kissed him, with all the hunger and need that had been locked in her body for months, years. She kissed him because she couldn't have him, kissed him because he showed up too late, kissed him until she felt his cock swell against her belly and the fierce need became his own as well.

And then she shoved him away, wiped her mouth with the sleeve of the flannel shirt, his flannel shirt, and said, "Ready to drive me home?"

He looked shocked, which was a triumph in itself. "Where did that come from?"

She wished she could come up with a

snappy answer. From her inner Barbie, from her repressed romantic side, from her self-destructive nature. Instead she shrugged. "I just thought I'd give you a taste of what you're missing."

He was still staring at her like he was seeing her for the first time, which he probably was. Up until now she was part of some game-playing agenda, and an unsavory one at that. She had no idea what he was trying to prove, but she wasn't about to play.

"You can drive me home or I'll take your car," she said in her most practical voice. He'd have no idea that beneath her blasé exterior her heart was pounding, her palms were damp and she was more turned on than she had been in fourteen years. Not since Sophie's father. Of course he had ditched her once he found out she was pregnant and she'd been on her own. She ought to know better.

She crossed her arms, partly to hide the trembling, and arched an eyebrow. "Sooner rather than later would be good," she said in an even tone.

He moved then, and for a moment she thought he was going to touch her again. She wasn't sure what she'd do if he did, but at the last minute he seemed to think better of it. "I'll get my keys," he said, his voice equally expressionless.

They went down the outer steps in silence. The rain was coming down harder now, and the rough wood was slick enough that she held on to the rickety railing, being careful to avoid the weak step as she went. He moved past her, around the back of the foundation, and she followed him, only to come face-to-face with the most ramshackle, ancient Jeep she'd ever seen.

"I thought you had a rental car that you didn't want to get muddy," she said, glaring at him.

"I lied. The doors don't work — you'll have to climb in over the side."

Great, she thought. His baggy pants were too tight on her generous butt, and she'd probably split them as she scrambled into the car. Tossing her own clothes in back, she reached for the top of the door, ready to hoist herself in, when she felt his hands on her waist, lifting her, swinging her over into the front seat of the Jeep.

It happened so fast she didn't have time to protest. She landed in a heap, righting herself before he climbed in the driver's side with insulting ease. "No seat belts," he said. "If we start going off the road you'll have to hold on to me."

"Yeah, right." She glanced at her watch.

Twenty to three, and they were three-quarters of the way up Silver Mountain. "You wanna step on it? I don't want to be late."

The Jeep started forward with a leap, tossing her back against the seat. A moment later they were careening down the narrow dirt road at breakneck speeds and she was clutching the cracked leather of the seat, holding on for dear life and trying to remember some kind of prayer to ward off certain death.

They all escaped her — she was stuck with muttering "oh God oh God oh God" beneath her breath. Caleb was having too much fun, taking the switchback curves with abandon, and she wondered what the hell Sophie would do if she was left without a mother and no legal tie to David.

Caleb glanced at her every few moments, waiting to see her reaction, but she gritted her teeth and said nothing. By the time they reached her parked car, she was ready to scream, and when he slammed to a stop he turned and looked at her.

"Fast enough for you?"

Hitting him again wouldn't be a good idea — it would give him an excuse to touch her and she still hadn't recovered from their kiss. "Fine, thank you." She slung one leg

127

over the side of the door, planning to use the back of the seat for leverage, when he put his hands on her butt and shoved.

She landed on her feet, a good thing, because another car had just pulled up beside hers. A black BMW, with David behind the wheel.

"Oh, fuck," Rachel whispered.

"Watch your language, Mrs. Middleton," Caleb cautioned. "You don't want him to know you feel guilty."

She turned on him. "I don't! I don't have anything to feel guilty for."

"Except kissing me." He looked up. "Hey, David," he said in a louder voice. "I'm returning your wife. Reluctantly, I must admit. She got caught up at the falls."

She expected David's usual look of sad disappointment as he climbed out of the car, but oddly enough he looked quite sunny. "What were you doing up there, Rachel? It's a rotten day for hiking. Don't tell me you're as morbid as the rest of this town."

"I'd never seen the falls, and I was hoping to get some pictures. But you're right — a rotten day. I slipped in the mud and almost went over. Fortunately Caleb was there to catch me."

"Fortunate indeed," David said. "I was

worried when you didn't come home. Sophie's school closed early and I thought I'd better make sure you got the message. Clearly you didn't."

All thought of Caleb and guilt vanished in her sudden panic. "Where is she? What happened? Is she all right?"

"Of course she is. She went home with Kristen — if she's not safe in the home of the police chief I don't know where she would be. I'm afraid they've found another body."

The air around them suddenly seemed to freeze, like a slow-motion horror movie, and it felt like someone punched her in the chest, hard. "Who?" she managed to choke out.

"They don't know — apparently she'd been dead for a while. They found her body downriver, but Chief Bannister says they're thinking she may have gone over the falls as well." He looked past at her at Caleb, an odd expression playing around his mouth. "Have you seen anyone up there the last day or so, Caleb? Anyone suspicious?"

"No." The word was short, sharp, and she glanced back at Caleb. He looked stricken, guilty, an odd expression for him, a far cry from his usual mockery. A moment later that expression was gone, and he shrugged.

"Not a safe town for young women, is it? I think your wife and her daughter should take a nice long vacation until Maggie Bannister finds out who's doing this."

David's eyebrows snapped together. "Don't be ridiculous, Caleb. There's evil everywhere, and you, more than anyone, would know it. They stay here, where I can protect them."

"I'll be the one who decides where I stay!" Rachel snapped. "You two can argue all you want — I'm going to get my daughter."

David moved in front of her. "Rachel, she's fine —" he began, but she shoved past him, heading for her Volvo. He said something else, but she didn't listen, she simply jumped in the car and sped off, one thing and one thing only on her mind. She had to find her baby and make certain she was safe. And then, if she had even an ounce of brain left her in head, they were getting the hell out of town.

7

Caleb looked into his baby brother's guile-less, pale blue eyes and just managed to meet his smile. "I didn't touch her, I swear."

"Of course you didn't, Caleb. I trust you with my life." There was no edge to the simple statement, no malice or hidden sub-text. "It's just that you're so damned roman-tic, and always have been. The bad boy always gets the girl." His smile was disarm-ing. "But Rachel's got a good head on her shoulders. I'm sure even if you do your best to tempt her she'll be able to resist. She doesn't have much of a sexual appetite."

"Do you think I wouldn't consider that a challenge?"

"You and I both know you'd never go out of your way to take what's mine. The prob-lem is it comes to you naturally. Every girl I ever liked was head-over-heels in love with you. Even that stupid mutt I found liked you better than me."

131

"I remember," Caleb said softly.

David looked sorrowful. "Such a sad, sad day. Who in the world could have done such a thing to a poor, helpless animal, no matter how stupid he was." He gave a small shudder of distress. "I just don't understand human nature, Caleb. Do you?"

Caleb didn't blink. It had been twenty-six years since he'd found the only dog he'd ever owned hanging from a tree down by the river. He'd had enough time to get over it. The knot of grief was familiar, even welcome. "I think I understand it better than you think, David."

He hadn't expected his words to rattle his brother, and they didn't. "Even my own mother preferred you, ridiculous as that is. She gave birth to me — you should have been less important to her."

"David, she loved you."

David smiled sweetly. "Of course she did. And I loved her. She just didn't love me enough."

Caleb felt the grief come again, tinged with the old anger, but he squashed it down. To do what he came to do he'd have to be cool and collected, as cool as his brother was. "Did you want to talk to me about something, David? You could come up back to the house . . ."

"That monstrosity? No, thank you. I just wanted to make sure my wife was all right. And that she heard about the body they found."

"And why is that?"

David blinked. "So she'll be careful, of course. Because just when you think you have all the answers, you find out you're quite wrong."

"He's changing his style, isn't he?" Caleb leaned back against his Jeep. "He never used to kill so close together. There was always at least a year between each death. And he never killed twice in the same place. He's getting sloppy."

"Yes, he is," David agreed, as calm and measured as always. "But who can guess what's in the mind of a sociopath?"

"You think that's it? He's a sociopath?"

"I've done a great deal of research on the matter, and that's the only conclusion I could come up with. He's simply without conscience. How else could he commit such atrocities?" David moved back to his car, a wistful expression on his face. "Do keep away from Rachel, won't you? I'd hate to see anything happen to her."

It took all Caleb's self-control not to lunge for his brother's car. But he'd spent years in war zones, or even worse, newsrooms, and he knew how to bluff and to watch his ass.

"You have my word on it, David," Caleb said, as the rain began to sprinkle down once more. "No one's going to hurt Rachel or her daughter. No one."

David simply smiled. "Come for dinner tonight. We need to spend time together, and this way it'll keep her mind off the new murder."

"So we can be like a normal, happy family?"

"We are a normal, happy family, Caleb. Haven't you noticed? All we needed was for you to come home again. And you did."

"If you say so," Caleb said. "What makes you think Rachel wants anything to do with me? Maybe she has other plans."

David shook his head. "Rachel wants whatever I want. And she would never leave. She knows it would distress me, and she has very fond feelings for me. And besides, if she left I'd simply go with her."

Caleb should have expected it, but the ice at the pit of his stomach was like a lump. "Stay here with me, David," he said, suddenly urgent. "We can fight this together. We can stop this."

David shook his head, stepping back into his car. "Too late, big brother. Years too late. Come to dinner. I don't think Sophie will be there — my wife doesn't trust you around her. Which is silly — you never liked the young, innocent ones." There was a pause. "I do."

He gave his brother an angelic smile. "We'll see you about seven." And he pulled out into the road, heading off at his usual, decorous pace.

Caleb stood motionless, watching his brother drive away. When he realized belatedly that his hand was clenched in a fist, and he consciously relaxed it, taking a deep, calming breath. He'd waited too long, turned his back on the truth for too many years. There was blood on his hands, blood on his conscience.

Because he'd left.

But that time was past. He'd meant it — no one else was going to be hurt. No one. The only kind of penance he could pay was to keep it from happening again.

And he would. No matter how bloody the price.

David Middleton whistled a tuneless little song beneath his breath as he drove back into town, a feeling of well-being coursing through his body. He'd felt much better since he'd given up eating meat — a body free from animal pollutants was much more attuned to the dark beauty of life.

He glanced in his rearview mirror. Caleb was still standing there, and David knew he should feel sorrow and regret. Caleb so wanted to help.

But Caleb didn't understand that his baby brother didn't need help. He wasn't delusional, or even terribly dangerous. He did what he had to do, what gave him pleasure, and he was very, very careful. He never hurt them if he could help it — fast and efficient was his code and his pride.

Caleb wouldn't understand his fascination. Nor would he appreciate that he never had sex with them until they were already dead. He considered it quite kind of him — he'd studied enough to know that the most exquisite pleasure would be at the point of death, not afterward. But he spared them that. Just a few moments of blind panic, and then it was over for them. And then he could enjoy himself.

He always came at them from the back. He'd tried it once, strangling her while he was facing her, and it had been quite unsettling. So much so, that he hadn't been able to have sex. In the end, though, that had been a blessing. No one connected that death with the other victims of the serial killer who preyed on young women.

136

The one thing that bothered him was that they hadn't come up with a proper name for him. The Green River Killer, the Hillside Strangler, the Zodiac Killer. All of those had a certain ring to them.

Then again, Ted Bundy had never had any particular name, and he was the best of the best. And despite the commonly held belief that Bundy was brilliant, in fact, his IQ was a pathetic 124. If a man of middling intelligence could get away with his hobby for such a long time then David, with his own far more impressive 140, should have no trouble at all.

He whistled as he drove through the soft mist, watching it swirl across the rain-dark road like a woman's long flow of hair. His older brother thought he'd made a mistake, but he'd always known exactly what he was doing. Even his recent overeagerness, his increased appetites, all played into a master plan. It was always foolish to underestimate him. They all had over the years. It worked to his advantage so well that it no longer offended him. Things were unfolding just as he had ordained, and by the time Caleb realized he'd been set up it would be too late.

He switched on the radio. The college station was playing the Mozart requiem, presumably in honor of the latest victim, a decomposed body found floating down-stream from the falls. He whistled along as he drove, at peace with the world.

The sound of the police siren broke through Rachel's panic, and she took her foot off the gas pedal, slowing to a guilty stop, cursing beneath her breath. All she could think about was getting to Sophie — she must have been going sixty in a thirty-mile-an-hour speed zone. She clutched the steering wheel tightly, knowing the drill, only to look up to meet Maggie Bannister's stern face.

"Do you know how fast — ?"

"Oh, shit, Maggie! Where's Sophie? And what the hell are you doing making traffic stops when there's been a second murder?"

Maggie grimaced. "Sophie's fine. You don't think I'd let her be in any danger, do you? She and Kristen are both at the station, playing on their computers. It's you I'm worried about. I knew you'd panic, given your history. And considering how fast you were driving . . ."

"Oh, *fuck* my driving. I need to see Sophie."

"I told you, she's fine," Maggie said grimly. "She knows you're coming for her, and she's taking all this mess a hell of a lot more calmly than you are. I should have your ass for speeding."

"Screw that."

"I can't do that. This is my new job."

"What?"

"Second dead body. Presumably another murder, though we won't know for certain until the autopsy. But it ties in with the killings in other parts of the country. So far we have the FBI coming in and taking over, treating me like a secretary, so chances are we've got bigger fish as well. There have even been suspicious cases outside the country."

Rachel stared at her, her mouth dry, her heart racing. "So they think this is a full-blown serial killer?"

Maggie nodded. "Which is good news. It means that it's a stranger, not anyone we know. Some FBI asshole named Johnson has taken over the case, and he's not interested in my opinions — I'm on traffic duty until they decide the killer's moved on."

"How do we know that? David said a new girl had just been found."

"David told you that, did he? And where were you when he passed on that information?" Maggie said in her brusque, even voice.

Rachel stared at her. "Does it matter?"

Maggie was a master of implacability. "I'm

curious about everything. I may be off the case but that doesn't mean I'm letting go. This is my town, my people, and I'm looking out for them."

"But you can't think David had anything to do with it?"

"I told you, I'm just curious. I want to see how the news spreads. David told you, and then you told . . . anyone?"

"I had just come down the mountain from his brother's house. He told us both, and then I took off." She tried to tell herself that didn't sound damning.

"You mind me asking, as a friend, what you were doing with our local bad boy? Caleb's not the kind of man young wives should hang around with. Particularly if they're married to his brother. Those two had a rivalry going on that would put World War Two to shame. Any fool could see that it was mainly one-sided. One brother just couldn't stand it when the other one got attention."

"It's no big deal. I'd climbed up the falls and I didn't have time to get back down without catching a ride. Fortunately Caleb was up there. Whose side?"

"Huh? Oh, who was the competitive one? I think I'll leave you time to figure it out. If I were you I wouldn't jump to any conclusions." She took a step back. "You know, I ought to give you one hell of a ticket, but I figure you've got extenuating circumstances. Just don't do it again." Maggie's voice was stern.

"Yes, ma'am. Do you want me to bring Kristen with us when I pick up Sophie?"

For a moment Maggie hesitated. "Sure," she said finally. "Just keep a close eye on them. If this is the same man who's killed young women all through the Northwest then presumably he's long gone. But you can't be too careful."

"How could he be long gone if there's a new body?"

"She'd been dead for a while, though she only recently hit the water. We're not even sure who she is. If the FBI knows, they're not telling. I don't know where she's been stashed all this time but she sure didn't smell pretty."

"Oh, God," Rachel said faintly.

"Yeah." Maggie's voice was grim. "I'll be by as soon as I get off work. Just don't leave them alone. You stay with them, okay?"

"Okay," Rachel said. "I'll feed them dinner."

"I get off at five — I can pick her up then. And why don't you let me take Sophie back with me? You know how good they are together. They can give each other support."

"I couldn't ask that of you."

"I'm offering. In fact, I'm insisting. Kristen's a bit of a drama queen, and Sophie calms her down. So don't you worry about dinner. I'll get pizza and we'll watch some dumb teenage comedy and everything will be fine." Maggie's eyes narrowed. "I'm worried about you. I think you need a break without having to worry about Sophie."

"Easier said than done." She wanted to deny that she needed help — she'd been on her own for so long she wasn't used to having someone else she could depend on. Which was a funny way to think, considering she was newly married.

"That sounds good," she said after a moment. "And don't worry about us. If things get too stressful I can always take Sophie and leave town for a little while. We haven't been away from here in the four months since we arrived."

For a moment Maggie didn't say anything. "That might be a good idea. Are you going to tell David where you're going?"

"Why wouldn't I?" She looked at Maggie. "Seriously, is there a reason why I shouldn't? You'd tell me if there was?"

"I have no reason to tell you not to tell David where you're going," Maggie said carefully.

"Maybe he could even come with us."

Maggie didn't blink. "Maybe."

"What aren't you telling me, Maggie Bannister?"

"I'm telling you everything I can tell you. If I were you I'd be very careful who I trusted in this town. People are never exactly what you think they are."

"Are you talking about David? Or Caleb?"

"I wish I knew the answer to that, Rachel. I truly do. Keep a close eye on the girls, will you?"

"At least tell me whether we're safe or not."

"As far as I can prove, you're completely safe," Maggie said, getting back in her patrol car. "Just be careful."

The house was still and quiet once Maggie picked up Kristen and Sophie. Rachel had done everything she could to talk Sophie into staying home, but Maggie was right — she and Kristen were really doing so much better together, going with the kind of cold-blooded ghoulishness that only teenagers could possess. By the time Maggie came to pick them up they'd moved on to a critical discussion of the relative hotness of the junior varsity soccer team. She watched them leave, Sophie's long blond hair tangled down her back, Kristen's dark waves beside hers, bumping into each other deliberately as they walked. They looked so innocent, so normal, so untouched.

That was why she'd come here, why she'd married David Middleton in the first place. To provide a safe, traditional, normal environment for her daughter.

And now, in this cold, rain-drenched, perfect little town nestled in the shadows of Silver Mountain, it was almost as bad as San Francisco had been. At least Sophie hadn't known the victims, and with the resiliency of youth she seemed to have forgotten that less than six months ago she'd lost her best friend in a similar manner. There were times when Rachel would have given ten years off her life for Sophie's calm nature.

She waved to Maggie, still in the patrol car, and shut the door behind them. The house was dark except for the lights left on in the family room, and she could hear the voices from the television. She started going through the house, turning on every light she could find. Most of them were those damned energy-efficient models that only cast a cool blue light. She was all for saving the planet but living in this drab darkness was enough to send her over the edge.

Once every one was lit the place looked a little less gloomy. David's Mayan death masks on the wall weren't as threatening, the twisted iron floor lamps not as tortured. She moved back to turn off the TV, then thought better of it. The noise, the motion was a companion, making the house seem marginally cheerier. She switched from *Jerry Springer* to HGTV, then headed back to the kitchen to survey the massive refrigerator David had bought her. The refrigerator that never held enough food, since David abhorred waste.

A nice rare steak and some asparagus would have been perfect, accompanied by a good cabernet. They could light the gas pilot in the fireplace, stretch out on the thick Berber carpet and have a wickedly indulgent time of it. Except that David no longer ate red meat. Or fish. Or chicken. He grew pale at the thought of blood and animal flesh made him ill. How the hell was she going to come up with a romantic dinner on a vegetarian diet?

She'd go for a quiche or pasta but now he was toying with the idea of cutting out eggs and cheese. She'd have to make do with some kind of twigs and berries. He refused to eat anything with a face on it, and while

145

she admired his ethics, there were times when her own cravings just got too strong. He was a far better person than she was.

There were Mint Milanos hidden behind the crock of whole-wheat flour, ostensibly bought for Sophie. Considering that she kept going through the packages and replacing them before she got to pass them along, she should have known better, but the latest package hadn't been opened. She ripped it apart, shoved one in her mouth, letting the richness of the chocolate slide across her tongue, and she took the first deep breath she'd taken in hours. In a world with chocolate, nothing could ever be that bad.

So, nuts and fruits and berries and twiggy grains for dinner, washed down with a nice cabernet. Or should she go white for twigs? The one thing she could do was make herself as irresistible as possible, and then maybe David wouldn't care so much about food.

She double locked the front door, then headed into her private bathroom, stripping off her clothes and climbing into the shower. Soap was a turn-on for David — in fact, he usually liked her to shower just before they had sex, and then immediately after. Which always managed to ruin the mood for her, just a bit, but he had a few hang-ups he still had to work out. She could be patient. After all, it wasn't as if she was the epitome of sexuality herself. Pleasant was good enough.

Hot sex usually led to disaster, and she hadn't had an orgasm since Jared had taken off so long ago. Then again, how could anything that brought her Sophie ever be considered a disaster?

She took a long, leisurely shower. This would be a perfect time to get past the unpleasantness of the night before. Maybe they could bring their relationship to a new level — he was oddly shy, never letting her see him without clothes. Maybe, without Sophie around, he could relax, maybe consider something new.

Tonight would improve things. Whether she was in the mood or not. She washed her hair and let it hang down her back — when it dried it would be a riot of curls but right then the weight of the dampness kept it relatively straight, another thing David liked.

Unbidden, the memory of Caleb Middleton's outrageous question came back to her. "Does he go down on you?"

He probably already knew the answer. David was sedate and pleasant. They made love in the darkness, politely, infrequently, and his performance issues were recurrent.

147

Which was fine with Rachel. David was gentle, loving, always thoughtful. It would be ridiculous to expect more — she doubted more even existed.

She pulled on a long, flowing skirt from Thailand and the sexiest top she still had — a clinging silk knit over the last Victoria's Secret bra she owned. She looked damned good in that underwear, and to top it off she put on her favorite pair of silver earrings, the ones that brushed her shoulders.

She was just finishing up her makeup when she saw the headlights in the driveway, and she rushed out of her room, a little nervous, a little edgy. She'd already opened the wine. The fruit was washed and set out, along with the grain mixture that David swore by. The message light was flashing — someone must have called while she was in the shower — but she could hear David at the door. The message could wait.

She tugged her shirt lower, so that the swell of her breasts was appetizingly visible, then bit her lips to redden them in lieu of the lipstick David hated.

She didn't even wait for him to put the key in the door. She flung it open, saying, "Hello, sexy."

And looked straight into Caleb Middleton's dark, unreadable eyes.

8

"Sorry to spoil your plans, sweetheart," Caleb said. "But all this is wasted on me. You had me at hello."

"Oh, fuck you," Rachel snapped.

"Don't let David hear you say that," he said, moving past her. The small hallway led into a wide rectangle of a living room, all angles and planes and gleaming wood floors and not a speck of dust. A fire was lit, there were candles burning and the table was set for two. He left his shoes on when he knew David insisted on their removal at the door, tossing his battered leather jacket over a chair. "Where is he, by the way?"

"That's what I'd like to know," she grumbled. To his surprise she didn't automatically sweep up his coat and hang it in the closet, the way David would have done, and she didn't give him shit about his shoes. David hadn't brainwashed her completely. Maybe there was hope for her after all.

"And what are you doing here?"

He couldn't stop looking at her mouth. It was red — he knew it wasn't left over from the kiss they'd shared hours earlier, but it was all he could think of. "My brother invited me for dinner. He thought we needed some family time. Didn't he bother to tell you?"

"I haven't seen him since I left . . . your place." Her stumble over the words was so slight that most people wouldn't have noticed. She was remembering the kiss as well. Good.

Without another word she spun around and headed for the kitchen, her skirts swirling around her long legs. Caleb took a moment to appreciate it, as well as the sway of her hips and the bounce of her tangled auburn hair, and then he followed her, just in time to hear his brother's voice on the answering machine, a pale copy of Stephen Henry's rich, Shakespearian tones. Rachel hit the delete button before he could make out the message, but the expression on her face wasn't happy.

"He's been held up," she said briskly. "Something to do with on-campus grief counseling. He's very good at that, you know."

"I expect he is."

"So maybe you'd better take a rain check. There's no telling when he'll get back." She made a move toward him, as if to shoo him out, but he wasn't in the mood.

"Oh, I wouldn't think of it, after you've gone to so much trouble."

She was just managing to control her temper. "I haven't gone to any trouble at all. David's a vegetarian — he gets twigs and berries. You strike me as a meat and potatoes kind of guy."

"I do have healthy appetites . . . What do you eat here? Hummingbird tongues?"

"He who dines only on hummingbird tongues is destined to starve to death?" she quoted back at him. "I eat meat. Just not when David's around. He's too sensitive."

Caleb said nothing, moving over to the massive refrigerator and peering inside. "You've got jackshit to eat in there. Doesn't Sophie get any junk food?"

"Sophie's none of your business," she said, trying not to look uneasy and failing completely. "In fact, she has her own refrigerator in her room, where she can have all the garbage she wants. Fortunately she's always been a wise child and she'll eat anything interesting."

He nodded, closing the barren refrigerator

151

door. Not even a beer in sight. "Where is she?"

"None of your damned business."

"It's a logical question. Clearly she's not here. You had this big seduction scene all set up so you had to have stashed her somewhere, which kind of surprises me. You strike me as an overprotective mother."

"I'm not overprotective, I'm normal," she shot back. "And Sophie's spending the night at her best friend's house, who happens to be the daughter of the chief of police."

He nodded. "Very wise. And your police chief doesn't have a hell of a lot to do now that the FBI are pushing their way around here."

"How did you know that?"

"Because they already questioned me," he said, a tossed off line, waiting to see her reaction. "Tell you what — let's go out and find something to eat."

"You're kidding."

"David isn't going to be home till late, so your Mata Hari routine is wasted, unless you want to practice on me. I'm hungry, and by the looks of your refrigerator I'm guessing you're hungry, too."

She didn't move. "You think I'd go to a restaurant with you and have dinner while half the town looks on and gossips? Fat chance."

"Good point. Though I don't know why you should let gossip bother you if you know it isn't true. Or is it the faculty-wife thing, then? Caesar's wife must be above reproach."

"I have a sense of propriety."

"Do you? You can't imagine how much that disappoints me. I thought you were a wild child with a reckless streak who simply made the mistake of marrying the wrong man. Maybe you're ordinary after all."

"It's not going to work. You can't goad me into behaving badly just because you want to injure your brother."

"I don't want to injure David."

She looked at him, startled, and he realized his tone of voice must have given something away. He smiled his most rakish smile. "And I don't care whether you behave badly or not. I just want the dinner promised me and company while I eat. You look like you could do with a few calories yourself. Where's your coat?"

"You're really asking for it," she said, and he realized she thought he was mocking her. She had the beautiful curves of a Botticelli Venus, but there was a faintly hungry air to her, one that he was more than willing to feed in any way she'd let him.

He looked at her, trying to size her up, and then he grinned. "I know your tipping point."

"I doubt it."

"Your daughter's out for the night, your husband's off counseling distraught young women, and your only responsibility is to see that your unwanted guest is fed. Get in the car."

"Go to hell."

"Not without you, babe. Get in the car and I'll fulfill your deepest, most-secret desires . . ."

"This is getting tiresome —"

"And I won't even touch you to do it."

"Ha!" She kept edging away from him, but fortunately she was heading in the direction of the front door. Maybe she thought she was leading him there. If so, she was coming, too.

"You doubt me? I won't lay a finger on you, Scout's honor. You're not my type."

That bugged her, as he'd meant it to, but she tried to hide her reaction. "Were you ever a Boy Scout?" she said doubtfully.

"Drummed out in Cub Scouts. David made it to Eagle level." Looking innocent was not a major part of his arsenal, but he did his best. "I double dog dare you."

She was wavering. "Not a finger?"

154

He resisted his flippant response. "I won't even breathe on you. Come on, Rachel. Live dangerously. This staid life doesn't suit you."

"It suits me very well," she said far too unconvincingly.

"I tell you what. If I don't bring you undeniable sensual pleasure, in absolute privacy without laying a hand on you, then I promise to leave town tomorrow and not come back." He was lying, of course. He'd left things alone for far too long, but she wasn't going to know that. As far as she knew his return was incidental and could be ended just as easily. "Now that's an offer you can't refuse."

She stared at him for a long, thoughtful moment. "Let me get my purse."

"You won't need it."

"How about shoes?"

"You won't need those either."

"And you're not —" she stopped midsentence. Poor grumpy baby — David had done a number on her. She didn't trust him, but she also didn't believe she was any kind of real temptation. Maybe the time would come when he could demonstrate just how tempting she really was, but that time wasn't tonight.

"I promise," he said, finishing her sentence.

She blew out the candles she'd set out for her seduction scene, turned off the gas fire, grabbed a brightly colored ruana and faced him, Joan of Arc at the stake. "I'm ready."

She said nothing when he opened the door of the rental Four Runner. She slid in, wrapping the shawl around her, and fastened her seat belt as he climbed into the driver's side. It was a chilly night, and he turned the heat on full blast for her bare feet, then pulled away from the house.

He knew where Maggie Bannister lived, assuming she hadn't moved in the last ten years, and people never moved in Silver Falls. He could swing by there, lure Sophie into the car, and drive the two of them, probably kicking and screaming, all the way to California or Texas or Montana, get them as far away from this town and the secrets it held before they could become snared.

But it would be hard as hell driving with two angry women beating at him, though he could probably count on Sophie to be on his side. And in fact, did he have any real reason to worry? They weren't David's type.

No, he had some breathing room. Silver Falls College had any number of students who would fit the victim profile well before either of the two women who lived with David Middleton would. To get them out of town would be a fail-safe, but probably more trouble than it was worth.

"What are you thinking about?"

He turned and looked at her. She looked a little smaller in the front seat of his car, her hair dark in the shadows, her eyes troubled and wary.

"I was thinking I might kidnap you and your daughter," he said, waiting for her reaction.

"Fat chance. I spent fourteen years traveling on my own and with Sophie — people have a very hard time getting the drop on me."

"Good to know," he said. "So why did you trade being a nomad to this kind of life?"

"It was time. Sophie needed some stability, and she needed a father."

"And you chose David?" He couldn't keep the ridicule out of his voice.

But this time she didn't rise to the bait. "I chose David. Where are we going?"

He was heading straight out of town, the streetlights getting fewer and farther between. "It's a surprise."

"I don't like surprises."

"I bet you do. You just got out of the habit of them."

She didn't deny it. That was one thing he

157

liked about her — for all that she saw him as the enemy, she didn't lie. It was a rare gift.

Now if he asked her if she liked their afternoon kiss she'd probably say no, but that was wishful thinking, not falsehood. She probably thought she was immune to him. Few women were when he put his full effort into it — it was both a curse and a gift. She'd probably prove more difficult than most. And yet he had no doubt he could do it, and would.

But he had something extra on his side, that small advantage that would sway the battle. He actually wanted her.

Sure, he wasn't going to let anything bad to happen to her and her daughter. He didn't want her the prey or even the unwitting accomplice of a madman. And he'd do anything he could to keep her safe, including scare her out of town if the need arose.

But on top of everything else, he wanted her. He glanced over at her feet — small, bare toes peeking out from under the colorful skirt. Her hands were holding the wrap around her shoulders. Good hands, long fingers, delicate but deft. He really wanted those hands on his body.

But most of all he wanted to be on top of her, skin to skin, thrusting inside her, looking into her eyes with no lies and no masks between them.

He shifted uncomfortably on the seat as he hit the interstate. Fantasies like that would only get him in trouble, distract him from his main goal. Rachel Middleton was a pawn in the middle, an admittedly delicious pawn, but a danger all the same. If David had even the faintest idea how much he wanted her then he'd have an unfair advantage over him. His undeniable attraction to Rachel was making him vulnerable, and he couldn't afford to let that happen. Not if he was going to stop David.

Except that perhaps it was already too late. David had known exactly what he was doing when he invited him over to dinner. Throw him into close contact with his wife and watch the sparks fly. He couldn't even begin to guess what was going on in his brother's tortured mind, and part of him didn't want to know. The possibilities were endless and horrifying.

At least it was highly unlikely that David was hurting anyone while he was in absentia. His needs had been very precise — like a snake who only needed to feed once a week.

But even as that iron control was coming undone, he was just as freakishly smart as he'd always been. He'd be too smart to risk making another move so soon. Unless he'd really lost it, and if that was the case, they were all fucked.

Rachel shifted in the seat as they sped down the interstate. Caleb wasn't about to tell her where he was taking her — she'd asked enough times. All she could do was sit there and realize what a total idiot she'd been to say yes.

He had just about the worst reputation in Silver Falls, as far as she could tell, and everyone in Stephen Henry's living room had tensed up when he walked in. Even her even-tempered husband had freaked out.

And suddenly women were dead. And she had willingly gotten in the car with him, without telling anyone where she was going.

She only had his word for it that David had invited him over for dinner — her husband hadn't even mentioned it in his message. If Caleb Middleton was a serial killer he could strangle her, dump her, and . . .

But he'd been too careless. Anyone could have seen him walk up to the house, seen her leave with him, which was a whole other problem. If he was really trying to get away with murder, he was doing a rotten job of it, and she suspected Caleb Middleton was as efficient as her husband at getting things done. Maybe even better. David wouldn't be able to get away with murder — he was much too transparent. She could read his feelings clearly, when he was disappointed in her, when he was feeling affectionate, his frustration over Sophie's polite distance.

Caleb struck her as much more of a liar. A manipulator, who cheated to get what he wanted, who had some score to settle with his younger brother.

It didn't make sense. In truth, Caleb was taller, better looking, more charismatic than his brother, whether she wanted to admit it or not. He was charming and manipulative — why would he envy David? David, whose very appeal was because he was safe, ordinary.

But then, nothing made sense. She remained silent when he pulled off the interstate, heading down a dark road. She'd never driven in this direction, away from Seattle rather than toward it, and she felt a little shiver slide down her backbone despite the warmth of the car.

"You know, I didn't think to leave David a message. He might come home and worry."

"I doubt it. He'll assume you've gone somewhere with me."

"I don't know that that's going to provide much peace of mind," she said, her voice wry. "Anyway, I think I'd better call and tell him where we're going. Did you bring your cell phone?"

"No service around here." They sped down the deserted road.

"How do you know? You just got home."

"I've already been down this road in the last few days."

"Why?"

A faint smile twisted his mouth. "I had my reasons."

Oh, shit, he's going to kill me. She surreptitiously squeezed closer to the door. He wasn't driving that fast, and if she moved quickly she could unfasten the seat belt and open the door at the same time, rolling out and heading into the woods at a dead run. He might not catch her, and at least it would give her a fighting chance.

He turned left, onto a dirt road, and there were no more houses anywhere around, just the road leading through the towering trees. She shifted, trying to look like she was just getting comfortable, and moved her left hand to the seat belt buckle, sliding her right hand up toward the door handle. He was looking straight ahead, paying no attention to her, and she knew she had to take her chance soon, before it was too late.

Maybe it was already too late. If she had anything left of her brain she should do something, scratching his name into her leg or something so that they could pin it on him when they found her body. There was a dip in the road up ahead, a deep pool of water lying there, and she knew he'd slow down and swerve to avoid it. That would be her chance. Her fingers played with the metal buckle, waiting, waiting.

He sped up, splashing through the puddle, moving deeper into the forest, and she knew she had to make her move, no matter how fast he was driving, no matter how slim a chance it was, and her fingers curved around the metal flange, ready to flip it up, when he slammed on the brakes, her seat belt released, and she went hurtling toward the glass windshield.

His arm shot out to catch her. Not just to catch her, but to slam her back against the seat, absolute fury in his face, and she thought faintly that this is what it's like to die.

"Tell me, just how stupid are you?" he said. "If you thought I was going to kill you then why the hell did you come with me? Why did you even open the door to me?"

She was squirming down in her seat,

momentarily intimidated by his sheer rage. "I thought you were David when I opened the door."

"Well, I'm not. And if you were afraid of me you should have told me to leave and called someone. But no, you're too fucking polite and you're going to get yourself killed because of it."

"Are you going to kill me?"

He leaned back against his seat. "No, I am not going to kill you, no matter how annoying you are. I don't kill women. I don't kill men, either. I'm trying to . . ." He stopped midsentence.

"You're trying to what?"

"Feed you," he said, putting the car in gear again.

"That's not what you were going to say."

"And *you* have such great instincts when it comes to men that you willingly came out alone with someone you thought capable of murder. I'm not impressed."

"Well, you didn't tell me where you were taking me, and this is the back end of beyond. We haven't seen another car for miles."

"Don't tempt me," he grumbled. "This is a shortcut. I grew up around here, remember? I know all the back roads. I used to come out here with my girlfriends and park."

"Girlfriends, plural? Like you brought a bunch out at the same time?" She was beginning to feel just the slightest bit foolish. He was right, she had been ridiculously naïve for blithely getting in the car with a man she didn't trust, a man who might be suspected of murder. She wasn't usually such an idiot.

"Smart-ass," he said. "One at a time. I'm a serial monogamist, not a serial killer."

"I know."

"You know?"

"Well, not about the monogamy, and I have to admit that part seems unlikely. I know you're not a serial killer."

"Then why were you ready to leap to your death to get away from me?"

"Overactive imagination," she said, pausing. "I wouldn't have gotten into the car with you if I didn't trust you."

"Now there's a mistake. There's a world of difference between thinking I'm a serial killer and actually trusting me." They'd pulled back onto a main road, with streetlamps spreading pools of light onto the wet pavement and the distant glow of neon beckoning.

His face was shadowed in the darkness, lit

only by the glow of the dashboard lights. He looked slightly brutal, slightly gorgeous, and once again the thought ran through her mind. Why him? Why now?

She straightened, peering ahead. "So you're taking me to some hole-in-the-wall bar where no one can see us and you'll be feeding me watered-down beer and playing bad country music on the jukebox?"

She managed to surprise him into a laugh. "That would probably be my first choice, though I like my beer full strength and I'm not sure if there is any bad country music. But there aren't any around here."

"No bars?"

"Nope. It's a dry county. Founded by Mormons a hundred years ago, and the laws have stayed."

"Well, I'm glad something about this god-damned state is dry," she muttered. In fact, it wasn't raining. For maybe the first time in weeks, it wasn't raining.

"So I've found the next best thing. Look over there to your right."

When she did so, she almost burst into tears and her voice filled with awe. "I don't believe it."

"Believe it. An In-N-Out Burger, straight from California. You grew up near San Diego, right? You must have had these things for breakfast, lunch and dinner. You know what you want?"

"God, yes."

He pulled up to the drive-through. "Double double, no cheese, pickles or onions, fries and a Diet Coke," he said, and turned to her.

"Shit. The same." She couldn't blow her first time at In-N-Out in seven years because of pride. She didn't care that she had the same taste as Caleb, even down to Diet Coke, though anyone less in need of a diet soft drink she had yet to meet. He'd found out she'd come from the San Diego area, something she didn't tell many people. If he'd found that out he could have guessed her particular taste in fast food as well. It wasn't as if In-N-Out had a varied menu.

Except David didn't know her taste in fast food. And he would have been horrified at the very thought. But Sophie knew — maybe she'd told Caleb.

Hell, they weren't together for that long — hardly time enough for them to get into Rachel's culinary peculiarities. It was sheer coincidence that they both liked no pickles and onions and cheese. Not a sign of something more complicated.

It was hard to stay wary with her Diet Coke and a double double In-N-Out burger.

She could feel her whole body relaxing into the soft leather of the rental car. She ought to be pissed about that — he'd made her change her clothes and then drove her down the mountain in that lousy Jeep. He liked to toy with people, and she had no desire to play the mouse to his jungle cat.

But she simply couldn't summon up any rage. Not then. Maybe later, when the fast-food bliss wore off. Tonight she was in her own little corner of cholesterol heaven.

The drive back was silent, oddly comfortable, and Rachel tipped the seat back a little, closing her eyes. Strange that she could be so relaxed with the black sheep. But after the rough day, the nerve-racking back roads drive, she could suddenly let go of everything, close her eyes and feel enormously peaceful.

Caleb had turned on the radio, and she heard the rich sound of African rhythms, the sweet tremolo of Portuguese fados, the beauty of Asian flutes. "World music station on the satellite radio," he murmured, reading her mind.

It should have bothered her. But it didn't. She was too caught up in missing the worlds she'd lived in, that now seemed a lifetime away, the color, the music, the taste and smell, the people. And for a brief moment she wanted to cry.

And then she thought of Sophie. Sophie, who made friends wherever she went, who learned to read in Brazil, who had her hair in cornrows in the Caribbean, who danced in Mozambique and sang in India. Sophie in her new, safe, ordinary world, with new friends and a better school than Rachel could have ever provided.

It was right. It was fair.

But why did it suddenly feel so wrong?

9

The house was dark when Caleb drove into the driveway, David's black BMW sitting in front of the garage like a silent reproach.

"Oh, shit," Rachel muttered beneath her breath.

"What? He's going to beat you?"

"Yeah, right. Your brother doesn't even like to swat flies — you know that. He's very Zen. No, he'll just be disappointed."

"Well, slip into bed and maybe he won't notice what time you came in."

"We don't . . . No, you're right, he probably won't notice," she said, hastily switching words.

"You don't what? You don't sleep together?"

Shit. "Of course we do."

"No, you don't. David has always slept lightly — the slightest sound would wake him up. If you shared a bed there's no way you wouldn't wake him up. He's my brother, remember?"

She could try to bluff, but the thought that she'd be tempted to do so was annoying. Her blissed-out burger buzz had vanished, and she was back in the land of tofu and lemon water. The night was dark, and it had even started to rain again. "Exactly. My thrashing keeps him awake, so we have separate rooms. And in two days I've already figured out how your mind works. Yes, we have sex. All the time. We just go to his room or mine. Or the living-room floor. Or the kitchen countertops. Or the . . ."

"With Sophie in the house?" he said mildly enough.

Double shit. She'd been getting defensive again. "She goes out often enough."

"So why were you going through your elaborate seduction routine tonight? Not that I wasn't appreciative, but if your sex life is all that good how come you have to resort to candlelit dinners and low-cut shirts?"

"I'm thoughtful," she snapped. "We're newlyweds."

Caleb's soft laugh had to be the most annoying sound in the entire world. "And it's such a love match."

"Go fuck yourself."

"I'd rather fuck you."

171

The porch light came on, the front door opened to the rainy night, with David silhouetted in the darkness.

"I'm sorry we woke you up, darling," she said as she reached the door.

David was in his pajamas, his blond hair mussed, his eyes sleepy. He looked like a little boy, and a rush of tenderness welled up in her. She stepped inside, her bare feet cold on the flagstone entry, and David leaned out and waved at his brother before he closed the door. Closing them in again.

"I'm so glad you took care of Caleb, darling," he said, brushing her cheek with his soft lips. "I meant to tell you I'd invited him for dinner but then things got out of control on campus with the news of the body they found, and I just couldn't leave."

"Of course not," she said, pulling off the colorful shawl and holding it in her arms. David never liked it — he said the bright colors assaulted his eyes and detracted from her pure beauty. Which was a ton of shit, but flattering anyway, and she did her best to accommodate him. "Sophie's over at the Bannister's."

"I know — I saw Maggie on my way back to campus. I think that was an excellent idea as well. Dear Sophie pretends to be very strong, but these things can be devastating

172

to young girls."

Sophie didn't *pretend* to be anything, but Rachel kept her mouth shut. "Do you want to come into the living room? We could turn on the fire, light a few candles, snuggle on the sofa?" And end up doing the wild thing on the ancient Persian rug in front of it, making up for the other night's failure.

David shook his head. "I'm exhausted, and I've got an early class tomorrow." He planted a soft, damp kiss on her lips. "I'll see you in the morning."

Soft and damp. So different from Caleb's kiss. Kisses. Hard and wet and . . .

"Would you like to join me tonight?" she said, wiping that erotic thought out of her mind. She needed something, she needed David to drive away the memory, the *feel* of Caleb. She needed to be held, to remember why she chose this man and this life. "I'm feeling a little shaky myself."

"Oh, Rachel, I'd love to, but it's just been too long a day," he said, sounding genuinely regretful. "You don't mind, do you? I find I have the need of solitude in order to re-group. You understand, don't you?"

"Of course," she lied. Caleb said he'd dream about her. Actually he'd said worse than that, the bastard. And without David beside her, she was going to have the same sort of dreams.

Better than dreaming about murdered young women, or thinking back to poor Tessa, only a few years older than Sophie. Gone, torn from a young life by a monster. And it was happening all over again.

But Tessa had been in San Francisco, a thousand miles away. There couldn't be any connection with a local college student, and the less she heard about the second body the better.

"Good night, dear," David said, his voice breaking through her abstraction. "You really don't mind, do you?"

She summoned a bright smile. "Of course not. I'll see you in the morning."

"I might be gone before you wake up. But I almost forgot — Stephen Henry has summoned you for lunch. I told him you could make it. One o'clock at his house."

Shit. "I had other plans. Actually I was thinking of taking Sophie and going on a little trip. Just to get some fresh air, maybe some sunshine . . ." Her voice trailed off.

He gave her a dazzling smile. "I think that's a wonderful idea. I know all this rain has been getting to you. We natives are used to it — we call it liquid sunshine — but I can understand that it might be a little hard for you two to grow accustomed to it. This

174

business up at the falls must bring up some terrible memories."

Rachel felt relief flood her. "It has. I just think it would be good for Sophie if I took her away for a few days."

"And I agree. In another week she'll have a break for Thanksgiving, and I'm sure I can get away myself. That's one good thing about Caleb's return — he can keep my father busy while you and I have some time away." A faint look of anxiety darkened his eyes. "Unless . . . you didn't specifically invite me. Maybe you wanted to go alone?"

"Of course not," she lied. He'd been so sweet, so amenable, that she couldn't possibly tell him the truth. "I was just thinking we might go a little sooner."

"There's no particular hurry, is there? You don't want to give Sophie the impression that you're running away, do you?"

"Of course not." Her smile was brittle.

"That settles it, then. I'll make arrangements for someone to cover my classes next week, and I'll even call Sophie's school for you and tell them she may be taking some extra time off. We can be gone for a week."

"I can handle it," she said.

"Of course you can." His voice was soothing. "But that's what I'm here for — to make things easier on you. In the meantime, if you wouldn't mind going to visit my father tomorrow I know he'd appreciate it. He's an old man, darling. He needs the company, and you know how he thrives on gossip. I expect he's going to grill you about Caleb, not to mention the recent murders."

"Just how I wanted to spend my afternoon," Rachel said. "I'll need to leave by two-thirty to pick Sophie up —"

"I've already made arrangements. I'll pick her up — you stay and entertain my father."

She considered pointing out that Stephen Henry was a preening old bastard, and she preferred to take care of her daughter herself, but she was learning tact, slowly but surely. Besides, David was still pushing for the adoption, and Rachel had no intention of hurrying. She could put up with Stephen Henry's nonstop monologue on his favorite subject, himself, for the sake of family harmony. At least David wasn't objecting to her leaving, even if he wanted her to wait. She could do that much.

"Thanks anyway, but I'd rather pick her up," she said. "I'll have plenty of time to visit with Stephen Henry and then make it to the school. I wouldn't want to put you to any extra trouble."

"It wouldn't be —"

"I'll take care of it." She couldn't keep the

176

slight edge out of her voice.

"Of course," he murmured, and once more she felt guilty. He'd only been trying to help. "Good night, dear," he murmured.

She resisted the impulse to slam her bedroom door behind her. The bed was neatly made, the hundred pillows she liked tossed on top of it. She was exhausted, but her feet were dirty, and a hot shower would probably help her sleep. She stripped off her clothes, leaving them lying on the spotless hardwood, simply because she knew she could, knew that David wouldn't come in and start scooping them up and hanging them in her neatly organized closet.

The hot water beat down on her skin, and the room filled with steam. She turned her face up to the showerhead, closing her eyes and breathing deeply.

And all she could think about was Caleb.

"The door's unlocked!" Stephen Henry's deep voice came from the old house, and, steeling herself, Rachel pushed it open, stepping inside. He was sitting in the living room, his books, his coffee, everything he needed at hand, a cashmere throw over his useless legs.

"Come and give an old man a kiss," he said.

She bent down and clinked cheeks with him, both sides, European style, as he demanded, and withdrew before he could prolong it. "Where's Dylan?"

"I gave him the day off. He's already made lunch for us, and I told him you could serve us."

Of course you did, Rachel thought. "Happy to," she lied, taking a seat far enough away so he couldn't grab her knee. He liked to touch women, which was one strong reason why she didn't make any effort to get Sophie to like him any better. It wasn't that she didn't trust him.

She just didn't trust him.

"What's up?" she said.

"Ah, this younger generation," Stephen Henry said, blithely ignoring the fact that he was the forefront of the baby boom. "Always in such a hurry. Why can't we be civilized, talk about art and literature for a bit?" He always pronounced it "litrachur" in particularly affected tones, which annoyed her to no end. Particularly since David had picked it up.

"S.H., I've got film to develop," she said in her sweetest possible voice. "Much as I adore spending time with you, it's sometimes difficult. Weekends are usually better, but David said this was a royal summons, so here I am, your loyal subject." She kept her voice light, giving Stephen Henry exactly what he wanted. An audience and a cue.

He chuckled. "Royal summons, eh? I certainly wish my sons were even half as obedient as you are."

That rankled enough to make her speak. "No one has ever called me obedient in my entire life."

"Ah, but you've changed. In the four months you've been a part of our small family I've seen you mature, blossom. Your wardrobe, your jewelry, your entire manner. When David first brought you back I was, frankly, appalled. You were too energetic, too wild for a sleepy little backwater like Silver Falls. But clearly I underestimated my son — he saw through the gaudy clothes and unconventional behavior to the sweet, reasonable woman beneath all that. You've curbed your impulsive nature as well. And your daughter is exquisite."

"Glad to know we pass muster," she muttered. Stephen Henry was partly deaf, and much too vain to wear a hearing aid, and she'd been docile for long enough.

"I beg your pardon, love. You were mumbling. You have to learn to enunciate. It's a sign of a bad education when people

179

mumble."

Rachel's smile grew strained. "You know me, S.H. I'm street smart. I learn from books that I choose — that way I don't have to waste my time on anything that doesn't interest me." Like self-indulgent poet snobs.

"Oh, I know you, my dear. You're too smart not to further your education. If it weren't for your unfortunate illegitimate pregnancy . . ."

Oh, she really was going to have to hit him. "But then I wouldn't have Sophie."

An indulgent smile wreathed Stephen Henry's soft pink face that never saw the sun. Then again, if he wanted sun he sure as hell wasn't going to find any in Silver Falls. "Very true. And not everyone is cut out for higher education."

"S.H., I know you didn't invite me over to talk about my educational deficiencies." Stephen Henry was oblivious to the tone creeping into her voice.

"After lunch, my dear. Dylan has made us a delicious shrimp salad and chosen an excellent wine."

Oh, yeah, that was why she hadn't made some phony excuse. Stephen Henry did eat well. And after last night's forbidden carb fest she was finding twigs and tofu even less appealing.

She had to wait through Stephen Henry's tedious monologue over heavenly shrimp salad and a crisp chardonnay, paying him only the slightest bit of attention. He was lecturing her about how sensitive David was, but right then she wasn't in the mood to be lectured, and she resisted the impulse to ask about Caleb's childhood, something that seemed to have slipped Stephen Henry's memory completely. Fortunately all she had to do was give him the right cue and he'd start off again, prattling on with his fork filled with food, hovering hopelessly near his constantly moving mouth.

Finally he was done. She cleared the dishes, dumping them in the sink for Stephen Henry's caregiver with only a trace of guilt. Anyone who had to put up with Stephen Henry full-time deserved to have the dishes done, but the sooner she got out of this airless, stuffy house the better.

Stephen Henry had moved from the dining room to the laughably labeled sunroom. The seats in there were even less comfortable, and somehow either Stephen Henry or his handsome aide had managed to find huge plants that thrived in darkness, making the room feel like an unpleasant version of a rainforest. At least she wasn't staying long. She perched on the edge of an antique wicker chair made for sylphs, propped her hands on her knees and waited.

"I wanted to talk to you about my sons. One thing about you, Rachel. You never beat around the bush — you're almost excessively direct. So I know you'll tell me the truth."

Crap. She should have known. Shrimp salad wasn't worth this. She'd hoped his monologue about David's childhood would have been enough. "Okay," she said, wary.

"My son is very attractive to women, you know."

It wouldn't do her any good to deny it. Stephen Henry, for his self-absorption, could be frighteningly acute. "I know he is," she said. "Freaking gorgeous. He's got that whole bad-boy thing going for him, and women just fall for it. Even Sophie isn't immune."

Stephen Henry looked at her in silence for a moment. "I was talking about David, my dear."

Shit. But she was nothing if not a quick thinker. "Oh, well, he has all that golden-boy charm. Both your sons are chick magnets, S.H." Not precisely true. David was charming, sweet, thoughtful and half his students had a crush on him, but he was nowhere near the draw that Caleb was. His very name sounded biblically sinful. God-dammit.

"A chick magnet?" Stephen Henry gave an exaggerated shudder which would have been seen in the third balcony if he were the Shakespearian actor he sometimes channeled. "English is such a glorious language — why must you descend to slang?"

"Because slang is a glorious part of a living language, Stephen Henry," she shot back. "The truth is, women like your sons. For different reasons, but we're agreed, they like them. That's not a bad thing, you know. But you're asking me about David. Are you trying to tell me David is having an affair?"

Odd, how the thought didn't bother her. It would explain so much — his distance, his odd disappearances, the faint unease she felt that she kept trying to ignore. Even his lack of sexual interest. It might almost be a relief — she wouldn't have to pretend anymore.

Impulsive as always, she'd jumped into this marriage, this life, without stopping to think it through. She just wanted to get Sophie away from San Francisco, and David seemed the perfect answer. She had a bad history of jumping into things without thinking, but usually the consequences weren't quite that dire.

"Having an affair? Of course not!" he said, affronted. "And you would hardly be the one I'd be talking to if he was. David has a great deal of respect for you and for the institution of marriage. Apart from that, he wouldn't think of hurting you. David's far too sensitive to ever want to bring pain to anyone."

Jesus, she was disappointed. She gave Stephen Henry the same kind of exaggerated sigh of relief that would play to the third balcony as well. "That's good to know," she said. "So what's going on?"

"I'm worried about the two of you, what with Caleb's advent on the scene. You were quite right in saying he was attractive to women. He has also tended to have a penchant for David's women. They flock to him. I don't want to see my son hurt."

"Which son?"

"Either of them." Stephen Henry looked past her, past the ominous foliage that crowded out the windows. "David lost his mother at an impressionable age, and his older brother disappeared a week later. There are times when I think none of us have healed from that hideous period in our lives. I had hopes when he brought you and Sophie back here, but now that Caleb's home and planning to stay for a while I begin to worry again."

"If you're worried that Caleb is going to steal me away from my husband I think you can relax, S.H.," she said. "It's not like I'm some irresistible cover model or femme fatale. Men don't tend to fall at my feet."

"True enough," he agreed with his lack of tact. "But that might not make a difference with Caleb. The appeal would be that you belong to David, not your desirable attributes or lack of them."

And she wondered why she always left Stephen Henry's presence feeling edgy and depressed. She gave him a wry smile. "Such a flatterer. In fact, I think you're worried about nothing. David's too busy with the crisis on campus to pay attention to whatever games Caleb might be playing, and I'm immune." She looked at him, unblinking. Willing it true.

"If you say so."

"In fact, he's told me I'm not his type."

"How interesting. And why did that come up?"

Crap. "I'm not an idiot, S.H. I could see there was a healthy case of sibling rivalry going on and I wanted to make my position clear." That was only a slight fudging of the truth, and Stephen Henry appeared to accept it.

"I lost my wife too young," he said, and for once there was real pain in his voice. "I don't want any more losses. You be careful, my dear. And keep an eye on your daughter. I don't know what's going on with these awful killings, but it never hurts to be vigilant."

She blinked, startled by the change of subject, then realized that Stephen Henry was giving her his royal dismissal. "You know me — I watch Sophie like a hawk. And as you've already mentioned, I don't fit the victims' profiles. Women like me don't get murdered."

"Anyone can be killed, Rachel," he said, his voice eerily sober. "Just keep your eyes open, and don't trust anyone."

"Not even my husband?" she said with a laugh.

But Stephen Henry didn't smile. "Not anyone."

10

Sophie wasn't waiting for her when Rachel pulled up outside the school, five minutes late thanks to Stephen Henry's manipulations and the rain-slowed traffic. She left the car on as she ran into the school, but the halls were deserted except for a few stragglers and no one had seen Sophie.

She raced back to her car, praying that they might have just missed each other, but the car was empty, and her hands were shaking so hard when she tried to dial Sophie's cell that it took her twice as long.

It went straight to voice mail. She'd either turned it off, when Rachel had told her never to do so, or she'd let the power run out.

Or someone had taken her and she couldn't get to her phone to call for help.

No answer on the phone. David was next. He was in class, the department secretary said, and no, Sophie hadn't been there. Rachel wanted to bang her head against the steering wheel in frustration. Of course she wasn't. Sophie didn't really like David.

That wasn't true. Why did that thought pop into her mind, when she'd always been nothing but sweet?

Because Sophie was sweet to everyone, and Rachel knew her daughter.

Please, God, let her be all right, she thought over and over and she drove back to the house. She hadn't specifically told her to wait to be picked up — their normal plan was to have Sophie walk or get a ride with Kristen.

So she must already be home. Rachel tore out of the school parking lot, narrowly missing a cheerleader, and raced back home at dangerous speed, half hoping that Maggie Bannister would stop her. At least she'd set her mind at ease.

She dropped her keys when she scrambled out of the car, fell when she went to pick it up, and it took forever to get through David's complex system of locks. By the time the door opened she was ready to scream, but she took a moment to calm herself. "Sophie?" she called out, trying to sound ordinary.

No fucking answer. She didn't care how it sounded, she raised her voice in a panic.

188

"Sophie, are you here? *Goddammit, answer me!*"

The house was deserted. No sign of her daughter. Rachel ran back outside, out into the street, hoping to see her coming down the sidewalk, huddled against the cold rain.

If her daughter came back, she wouldn't even yell at her. But the streets were empty, and she stood there as the rain came down, feeling sick inside, frozen in fear.

She mentally kicked herself into gear. "She's okay," she muttered beneath her breath. "She's going to be fine. Nothing's happened to her — I'd know it if it did. I just need to calm down and find her. She's okay."

The sound of her own voice helped to steady her, and she climbed back in the car, reaching for her cell phone. No answer at the Bannister's, which meant Sophie wasn't there. Maybe they'd gone with another friend, maybe they were up in Kristen's room, maybe, maybe . . .

"She's okay," she said again, and it calmed her. She set the cell phone down on the seat beside her and pulled out of the driveway. She could drive over to the Bannister's, see if anyone was home, and the next stop was the police station, just to set her mind at ease, and by that time Sophie would be home . . .

The phone made a blessed, beeping noise, signaling messages, and she grabbed it, pushing the buttons to get her voice mail. David, wanting to know why she'd called, and she deleted his message halfway through, as she realized she was crying. She disconnected, and then immediately another beep. Someone had tried to call her while she was checking messages.

"Hey, Ma, I'm up with Caleb at his house. I asked him to pick me up at school — I know you were going to the Old Goat's house, and I figured you didn't want me to walk. He'll drive me home in a —"

Rachel flung the phone across the car, not even bothering to hang up, and backed out into the street without looking, narrowly missing an oncoming car. Her tires skidded as she sped across town, hydroplaning as she reached the mountain, and she had no choice but to slow down when she started up the narrow road that led up to Caleb's half-finished house.

It took her fifteen miserable minutes to make it up there, her tires spinning, her hands cold with sweat, and when she pulled up at his place she just clipped the fender of his rented Toyota.

The stairs were slick with rain, but she

pulled herself together enough to climb them carefully, avoiding the weak one, and she forced her breathing to slow. She was going to kill someone, preferably Caleb, but she didn't need to panic Sophie.

The house had no locks, and she shoved the door open so hard it banged against the wall, shaking the entire structure. Caleb was sitting on the floor by the wood fire, his long legs stretched out, a beer in one hand, as he looked up at her.

"Where the fuck is my daughter?"

"Ma!" Sophie moved into view. She'd been sitting across the room from Caleb, a can of Diet Coke in her hand. "Chill!"

Caleb raised an eyebrow. "Yeah, Ma," he said. "Chill. I told her to call you."

"She did." Rachel came down the short flight of steps to the room. Caleb had thrown something over the bloodstain in the middle of the room, thank God, and Sophie looked both relaxed and indignant, if such a thing were possible.

Sophie had risen, a graceful fluid movement, her long hair swinging. "Are you all right?"

Don't kill them both, Rachel told herself, struggling for calm. *Even if they deserve it.* "Girls have been murdered in Silver Falls, Sophie. I was worried."

191

Sophie immediately looked stricken. "I'm sorry I scared you. You hadn't said anything about picking me up and it was raining so hard I thought I'd call Caleb and see if he wanted to. Besides, I wanted to get to know him better."

Caleb drew himself together and rose in a leisurely manner. "Can I get you a beer, Rachel? If I remember, you like my beer."

"You've been here before, Ma?" Sophie looked at her, an odd expression in her eyes.

"Caleb gave me a ride down the mountain yesterday," she said, controlling her anger. "Sweetie, would you do me a favor and go out and wait in the car? I need to talk to Caleb about something."

"Now you're in trouble. She's hardcore when she talks like that." She gave Rachel a swift kiss on the cheek. "Don't be too hard on him, Ma. He was just doing me a favor."

She waited until Sophie had left, closing the door behind her, before she turned to face Caleb. "You leave her the hell alone," she said fiercely. "Don't talk to her, don't go near her."

"Why?"

For a moment she was stopped. *"Why?"*

"Yes, why? Do you think I'm a pervert who molests little girls? Do you think I'm a murderer who strangles women and throws their bodies into the falls? Do you think I'm more dangerous than —" He stopped mid-sentence. "Exactly what *do* you think, Rachel?"

"I think that I'm barely holding things together and until they find out who killed those girls then I'm not going to let my daughter out of my sight unless she's at school."

"You're an idiot. You should get the hell out of town."

"Listen, if you're so worried about us why don't you set my mind at ease and keep your distance? Sophie might not like it but I'd appreciate it."

For a moment he said nothing, and she could see the frustration and anger practically vibrating through his body. "Do me one favor," he said finally. "Don't let Sophie wear anything in her hair."

"What do you mean?"

"No barrettes, ribbons, ponytail holders. Not even a bobby pin."

He must have flipped out completely. "I don't even know if they still have bobby pins. And she needs barrettes — otherwise her hair falls in her face."

"Let it. Even better, get her hair cut."

"Why?"

"When the women have been found

193

there's only been one thing missing from their bodies. Their hair clips. I think he collects them as souvenirs."

She stared at him, trying to ignore the sick feeling inside. "Oh, that's ridiculous."

"Ask Maggie Bannister. You'll notice she's cut her daughter's hair. Kirsten's got brown hair but Maggie wasn't taking any chances. Maybe you could dye Sophie's hair black." He moved closer, and she resisted the temptation to take a nervous step back, away from him. "Your daughter's waiting for you. Don't be too hard on her — she didn't know you think I'm a homicidal maniac."

"I don't."

He made an impatient noise. "Then what's your problem?"

"There's a difference between what I think and what I know. And I can't risk my daughter's safety based on my instincts."

For a moment he looked distracted, staring down at her. "Your instincts tell you to trust me. Why won't you listen? If you won't leave, then you need to be very, very careful. Don't leave Sophie alone with anyone unless you've given your permission. And don't give your permission. I don't want to have her body turn up at the bottom of the falls, with her barrettes missing and her hair floating in the stream like Ophelia, caught in the branches."

"Stop it!" Rachel cried, horrified. "That's a hideous image."

"I was the one who called in the first murder. I saw her like that. I don't think I could stand it if it was Sophie." Before she realized what he was doing he reached out and pushed a tangle of her red hair away from her face. "I don't think I could stand it if it was you."

For a moment she didn't move, wanting to rise into the touch of his hand. But an instant later sanity came back, and she stepped away from him. "Nobody else is going to die. It was a transient serial killer and he's gone. I've read enough about sociopath killers — they don't murder in their own backyards. It's all about keeping their little hobby a secret. Whoever did these things is long gone. But you're right, I'm not going to take any chances. And that includes letting you anywhere near Sophie. Understand?"

"I understand," he said. "Doesn't mean I'll do it."

She turned on her heel and stomped out of the house, slamming the poor, abused door behind her, narrowly missing the damaged step. Sophie was sitting in the passenger seat, looking subdued.

"I didn't mean to scare you," Sophie said softly when Rachel got in the car. "I just happen to like him. And no, he's not some creep who's into little girls — you've taught me to spot them a mile away. I have perfect perv-radar. I figured he's my uncle, and he's funny, and I ought to get to know him."

"How can he be your uncle when you can't look at David as a father or Stephen Henry as your grandfather?"

"Number one, Stephen Henry is as big a perv as you can find. Oh, I think he's pretty well behaved, and stuck in a wheelchair there's not a lot he can do. I could always outrun him, and besides, I think his aide is his boy toy. He just gives me the creeps."

Rachel had never lied to Sophie in her entire life, and she wasn't about to start now. "Yeah, he does me, too. But David adores you, and you and I have talked about him adopting you."

Sophie's face didn't change. "I know he adores me, Ma. And he makes you happy, so I like him. But let's hold off on the adoption stuff, okay?"

"We'll take as long as you need. And if you never want it then that's cool, too." She'd never told Sophie that she was doing all this for her, and she never would. Sophie didn't need that kind of pressure. Sooner or later she'd settle in, start to see Silver Falls as her home, David as her family. David and Stephen Henry.

And Caleb?

He'd be gone. Stephen Henry said always he came back to cause trouble for his brother and then left again, usually without warning. She just had to be patient, and wait. Once he was gone she wouldn't be looking at David's placid good looks and finding them boring. Once he was gone the safety and normalcy of this shadowed town would wrap around her like a soft blanket.

Except what the hell was so safe about murdered students and a serial killer?

Maybe Caleb was right. Maybe she should leave.

She turned to Sophie as she slowly drove the car down the mountain. "Do you feel like taking a little break from here? Maybe a minivacation, just you and me? We could go somewhere sunny, eat food that's terrible for us, maybe go find some street fairs and markets. We wouldn't have to come back for weeks."

There was no missing the hope and delight that sprang into her daughter's bright blue eyes, but a second later they were shuttered, blank. "What about David?"

For a moment Rachel was at a loss for words. "He says he can get some time off if we wanted him to come with us. We do, don't we?"

Sophie said nothing.

"What with all the things that have been going on, he doesn't really feel he can leave right away. Or that we should leave. But maybe in another week or so."

"Sure, Ma," Sophie said, sounding singularly unenthusiastic. "That would be great. But you know I'm really busy right now anyway. I'm just about ready to be bumped up a class, and if I go away now I'll have more catching up to do."

"Honey, you're already working on college level math."

"That's because you taught me to go for it, Ma. I just have to fill in the gaps with English and chemistry and I'll be just fine. Give me three weeks and we can take off."

"If we left then we'd be gone over Christmas."

"I don't think David is terribly invested in Christmas, do you? He doesn't seem the type," Sophie said.

"I think he's been looking forward to a real Christmas with his first family." She tried to keep the disappointment out of her voice. Christmas was her favorite thing in the world, and she loved going to strange, new places and celebrating it with local customs. The local custom here was probably The Festival of Coal.

"We'll see," she continued. "In the meantime I need you to stay close to home. Don't leave the school with anyone but me or Maggie Bannister. Don't walk home, don't accept rides, and don't let anyone but me get you from Maggie's house."

Sophie looked at her. "Not even David?" she asked.

Rachel thought back to Stephen Henry's words. *Don't trust anyone.* "Even David," she said finally, the words tasting like acid in her mouth.

Too many people, people she distrusted, told her not to trust anyone. If the liars and tricksters warned her then the situation had to be pretty bad.

But they'd make it through. Sophie was too young, and as long as Rachel was vigilant she would be perfectly safe. Absolutely no one would want to harm her.

No, if they just kept their heads together and didn't panic then everything would be resolved. And in fact, Sophie would like Christmas here as well. A traditional American Christmas was just as foreign as celebrating it in the Sudan or South America.

And maybe the three of them would finally start feeling like a family.

In the meantime she simply had to stop thinking about Caleb Middleton, his dark warnings, and Stephen Henry's odd behavior. She needed to get home, immerse herself in her darkroom, secure in the knowledge that Sophie was planted in front of the wide-screen television, and not think about anything but exposure and negatives and the safe, dark world of photography.

He was going to have to do something, Caleb thought, watching them head down the mountain. The stubborn redhead wouldn't listen, and if he told her the truth she'd be even more resistant. She would believe it was some demented sibling rivalry or childhood vengeance.

There were a number of ways to get rid of her, short of kidnapping and dumping them five states away. If he could only think of something. Right now he'd tried every way of telling her and none of them had made a difference. Nothing would, short of the brutal truth, and the fact is, he had no proof. Nothing but circumstantial evidence that could lead to him as easily as it could to his brother.

Maybe he could sabotage her car. If she

banged herself up a little bit then it was too damned bad. He'd like to bang her head against the wall to make her listen to him, and that was far from the only thing he'd like to bang, but she was too busy protecting David and fighting her attraction to him. His first plan had been to use that interest, enough to scare her into leaving, but that wasn't getting him anywhere and besides, he was finding it all a little too tempting. Things were bad enough — he wasn't going to take his brother's wife, no matter how much he found himself wanting her. That would just convince the old biddies in town that he was exactly as David had painted. A jealous, treacherous lecher, who took everything David had ever wanted and more.

Nobody noticed that it was David who'd bought the architect's house, three years after Caleb had picked up the man's half-built disaster. He hadn't stolen Libba away from David — they'd been secretly going together for a long time before David decided to put moves on her.

The problem was, he'd had such a hellish reputation that Libba hadn't wanted to tell her mother, and they'd kept the affair, the first and best of his life, a secret. But David had known. There was no way he could have missed it. And when he started publicly courting her, public opinion swung directly against Caleb, as it had so many times before.

He wondered where Libba was now. He hoped to Christ she was happily married, with children. He hoped the scars had healed. Even with them crisscrossing the left side of her face she was still beautiful.

He'd been blamed for that as well. He'd been driving David's car and David had followed. By the time he woke up in the hospital David had explained it all to everyone else . . . how his jealous older brother had chased after them, ramming their car with his trashy beater.

David had the story right. He just had the roles reversed. And Libba's concussion had taken care of the rest of the truth.

He should never have taken the rap for the cat so many years ago. It still made him sick to think of it, no matter how many atrocities he'd witnessed overseas, but he couldn't stand to see his apple-cheeked baby brother painted as such a horrific creature. So he'd made excuses — a spilled can of gasoline, a careless cigarette — and they'd bought it, sort of, looking at him funny and knowing he was lying. They just didn't know who the lie was protecting.

It was too late to save David. He could no

longer ignore the fact that he'd graduated to killing women, and by saying nothing, doing nothing, despite his suspicions, he was guilty as well.

But he wasn't covering up anymore. Wasn't walking away. This was going to stop, stop now, before anyone else got hurt.

But first he had to get Sophie and her mother out of the line of fire. Or they might be the next to go.

Stephen Henry Middleton waited until his personal assistant drove out of the driveway. Dylan was a charming boy — the generous salary Stephen Henry paid him was going a long way toward covering his college expenses, and he was smart enough not to notice anomalies. Or if he did, not to mention them.

The curtains at the front of the house were drawn, the lights were on, the doors were locked. No one would stop by unannounced, not his argumentative sons, certainly not his snooty daughter-in-law who liked to think he didn't realize that she considered him a dirty old man. It amused him to play into it. In fact, he much preferred his sexual partners to be experienced, mature and male, though he kept that as one of his many secrets.

He set the brakes on his top-of-the-line wheelchair, kicked up the foot plates and rose. It was a good thing his house had wall-to-wall carpeting — there'd be no telltale scuffs on his shoes. He walked over to the small drinks table Dylan had set up, pouring himself a generous glass of his favorite Scotch, the one he never shared. Most palates were too unsophisticated to appreciate it. And besides, he wanted it all to himself. At his age he deserved to indulge himself.

He was going to have to do something about the current situation, though he wasn't quite sure what. In his worst nightmares he could envision total disaster, but he firmly believed that things couldn't be as hideous as they seemed. He simply wouldn't let them be.

He was a selfish old man, lazy to a fault, greedy for attention and not particularly interested in other people's needs, even those of his sons. He had no illusions about himself, not at his advanced age.

But he also didn't want the extremely comfortable life he'd arranged for himself be shot all to hell by a nutcase for a son.

He moved into the sunroom, staring out through the dark, leafy houseplants, to the backyard and the rainy evening. He didn't deserve that kind of lousy luck, and he preferred to think positively. A psychopath for a son would put a real damper on his golden years.

Therefore he simply wasn't going to consider the possibility. Life was too good for him right now — he was waited on hand and foot, the attention was constant and flattering, and even if it looked like his sons had made some unfortunate choices, they couldn't be as bad as he suspected. Plus there was no way the college could kick a cripple out of his plush faculty housing.

Positive thinking, that was the ticket.

And he raised his glass to his reflection in the window, a silent toast, before he headed back to his chair.

11

Rachel had always liked working in the darkroom. It was a safe place, an isolated haven where magic happened, and when she was in there she could pretend that outside was sunny and warm.

She picked up the contact sheet and put it in the development bath, watching as the tiny pictures came into focus. People always wondered why she didn't just use a digital camera, why she chose to immure herself in darkness when she loved the sun. She never bothered to explain. In this tiny section of the world she was in complete control. The rest of the world was crazy, but in here it was black and white.

She took the contact sheet out and hung it on the line she'd strung. Pictures of Silver Mountain, of Sophie and Kristen, their heads together, pictures of her new family.

Stephen Henry, right before his reading and the return of the prodigal son. He looked surprisingly tense, and she realized that he had stage fright. The man who craved the spotlight paid for his addiction with sick nerves.

There was one she'd taken of David when he wasn't paying attention. It fascinated her. He was looking at something, Rachel couldn't tell what, and the expression on his face was something she'd never seen. Almost sly. Avid. Needy.

What the hell was he looking at? The photo was taken in the kitchen, and as far as she knew there'd been no one in the house besides the three of them. And Caleb, of course.

So what had put that odd expression on his face, captured when he was unaware, a look she'd never seen again?

She went back to her most recent roll of film. She usually loved times like these, but for some reason she couldn't get into her Zen-like calm. Not today. Today she didn't want to shut out the world — she had to keep one part of her attention focused on Sophie in the next room. She needed to hear if someone came into the house and started talking to her. If the phone rang with bad news, if David returned home. She needed to hear if Caleb followed them down the mountain, if he came into the house, and she'd pull him into the darkroom and tell him never to come near them again. . . .

No, she wouldn't. She wouldn't get in any dark, enclosed place with him, because the crazy mixed-up feelings inside her were stupid and wrong and dangerous. It didn't do any good to deny it, to berate herself. The only way to get past it was to accept it for what it was, and then say no.

She wanted Caleb Middleton. It was that simple, that stupid and self-destructive. She'd spent most of her life blissfully free of emotional or sexual involvements, since they usually ended up being not worth the trouble. With just her and Sophie, traveling the world, she couldn't afford to take chances, and relationships had been few and far between, and eventually she'd stopped even thinking about it. The first year after Jared had dumped her she'd been too mad to be interested. After that, too caught up in her miraculous daughter. Love and sex were for other people. She'd always thought when Sophie went off to college she'd consider looking around and seeing if she was interested again.

But that was before Tessa had been murdered and David Middleton had come into their lives like a white knight. Safe, sweet, so apple-pie normal and removed from their nomadic, communal-living ways that she grabbed on to him when he first made advances. He was everything their lives weren't. He was safety. He was salvation.

He was boring.

And she was a shallow, evil bitch to even notice. And even worse, secretly she was responding to his rotten brother's advances, no matter how much she was "no, no, no" like Amy Winehouse and rehab. Then again, Amy Winehouse really needed to go to rehab, and Caleb was the very last thing Rachel needed in her life.

Smarten up, she told herself, pulling the sheet out of the developer. There was no way she was going to risk the best thing that ever happened in her life for some irrational attraction.

Except David wasn't the best thing that had happened, Sophie was. And if it hadn't been for Tessa's murder, maybe she wouldn't have jumped into marriage with someone who was practically a stranger at such short notice. It was that damned impulsive streak, the one that made her run off with her teenaged boyfriend, flaunt her asshole father and wander the world. Ironic to think that same impulsive streak had pushed her into settling down sooner than she should have.

Enough. Maybe Caleb was right. Maybe she should just pack Sophie up and head out of town, no matter how much she protested. Just long enough to get her head on straight, long enough for —

The bright light of the opening door momentarily blinded her, and she let out a shriek as a day's worth of work was instantly destroyed.

"What the f— ?" She stopped midword. David was standing there, looking both sheepish and stern, an odd combination. She took a deep, calming breath. "David, the red light was on."

"This couldn't wait."

Oh, shit. He had that professor who doesn't believe the dog ate my homework voice going, and Rachel inwardly cringed. He couldn't have known that Caleb kissed her. Or worse, that she'd kissed Caleb.

"I went to the lawyer, since you kept finding excuses. He said you never had him draw up the adoption papers."

"Can we discuss this somewhere else?" she said, stalling for time. "Let's have a glass of wine and talk about it."

He looked at her, his baby-blue eyes flinty with anger. Funny, she couldn't remember seeing him that angry before. "I take this very seriously, Rachel. You lied to me."

210

"No, I didn't," she said, lying. Funny, when she'd spent most of her adult life trying to be scrupulously honest, avoiding everything but the gentlest of white lies. "I talked to Blanchard, and I simply told him to hold off for a little while. Until Sophie got more settled."

"That wasn't the impression he got."

"I can't be responsible for his impressions, David. I can only tell you what I said. This has all been a tremendous upheaval for Sophie, and I didn't feel she was quite ready for one more huge change. I'm sorry I didn't discuss it with you but I thought there was no big hurry. Unless you're planning to murder me in my sleep so you can get your hands on my daughter."

"Given the current happenings, I find that joke in very poor taste," he said stiffly.

"Sometimes you can either laugh or cry."

"I'd prefer if you'd do neither, particularly in public. Sophie told you she didn't want me as a father?"

And lie number two. "Of course not! You know she thinks you're wonderful. This was my decision. I thought things were happening too fast for her. We rushed into this marriage without a whole lot of thought —"

"And you're regretting it," he filled in. "Suddenly, when Caleb comes to town,

211

you're having second thoughts about marrying me."

"Don't be ridiculous," she snapped. "We
rushed into this marriage because we loved
each other and I wanted to get Sophie out
of San Francisco and you had to come back
to Silver Falls, and we didn't think living
together was appropriate given your position at the college and Sophie." She softened
her tone. "We would have gotten married
anyway — we just got married sooner. And
it wasn't a bad thing that we did, but there's
reasonable fallout and I want to make
Sophie as secure as possible before making
any more changes."

He didn't look appeased. "One more
change isn't going to make that much difference. Don't you think knowing she has a
father to count on in case anything happened to you would simply increase her
sense of security?"

For a moment a stray chill ran across her
backbone, distracting her. "Why would
anything happen to me?"

"Accidents happen all the time, Rachel,"
he said, patiently explaining to an idiot
child. "You could get hit by a car while
crossing the road, you could choke to death
on a piece of pizza. You could even be the
random victim of a serial killer. There are

no guarantees that anyone is safe from the evil in this world. Everyone, everything dies."

He was sounding so pompous that her alarm faded. "I'm the wrong physical type for the Northwest Strangler. He likes young, thin blondes, not strapping redheads."

He looked startled. "The Northwest Strangler?"

"That's what they're calling him. Apparently Sophie picked that up in school."

"That's ridiculous! Who came up with such a completely unimaginative name? For that matter, why do they think he only works in the Pacific Northwest? I don't think he should have a pseudonym at all, like Ted Bundy, who you have to admit was the greatest of the serial killers."

" 'Greatest?' " Rachel echoed, startled.

"At what he did," he said impatiently. "Don't play semantics with me, Rachel, you know you'd only lose. When you think of serial killers, what name comes to mind?"

"Jack the Ripper," she said promptly.

She'd managed to surprise him. "You're right," he said, thoughtful. "And of course he was never caught. Maybe having an extra name isn't such a bad idea. Too bad it's such a boring one."

"They don't know enough about him to

give a better description." Despite the macabre oddness of the conversation at least they weren't talking about the adoption anymore. "Maybe they could call him the Blonde Murderer. But that might suggest that he's blonde, not his victims. Have they been able to link any other murders to the same man?"

David shrugged, some of his earlier irritation vanishing. "I gather there might be a connection between the murders of several young women, mostly college students, in Oregon and Western Washington, but as far I know they haven't figured out anything definitive. Who knows, the killer might have traveled even farther afield."

"I'd just as soon he would," Rachel said, her stomach knotting. "Until he's gone for sure it makes me nervous. Could we stop talking about this? I need to see what we're going to have for dinner and I don't want Sophie to see that I'm upset."

"Certainly. And I've taken care of the adoption papers."

She raised an eyebrow. "You have?"

"Blanchard drew up some generic papers for you to look over. You may want to change some provisions — for instance, you may want her to spend time with her biological father, or have your parents have visitation rights if anything happens to you."

"Jesus, you're gloomy."

"Language, Rachel," he chided gently. "You know how much I hate it when you curse. And I'm just being responsible."

"And I'm not?"

"I didn't say that." He was very patient. "I'm just saying that this is a simple matter that needs attending to, and since you've been avoiding it I've gone ahead and taken care of it. Just tell me what changes you want Blanchard to make and I'll tell him. I already assume you want to ensure that Sophie has no contact with my brother. What about your family?"

"You know that my parents have nothing to do with me and prefer their safe little fundamentalist world in Oklahoma where they can concentrate on two obedient children. As for Jared, he died in a plane crash three years ago, still never having even met Sophie."

"So you see, it's even more important that Sophie be taken care of," David said. "I promised Blanchard you'd take a look at it and sign off. Otherwise he's going to charge us double, and you know how obscenely expensive lawyers are. Unless, for some reason you've changed your mind?"

"I haven't changed my mind, David." She

215

was getting a headache. "I promise I'll look at it after dinner. For now could we just stop talking about the papers, about serial killers, about your brother, about anything depressing? And that leaves out the weather as well."

David smiled his charming smile, the one that had first attracted her, touching her cheek. Caleb had touched her cheek earlier, pushing her hair out of her eyes, and it had been electrifying. David's touch was soft, affectionate. Safe. And that's what she wanted. Safe.

"Of course. It's been a miserably long day for me as well, and I think we both need to relax. We'll have that glass of wine, and you can tell me what my father had to say when you had lunch with him."

Shitsticks. "You get the wine," she said in her sweetest voice. "I'll start dinner and then come join you."

He took his dismissal with relatively good grace, putting the papers into her unwilling hands. She wanted to go back into the darkroom and see if there was anything she could salvage. She wanted to rip the adoption papers in half and stomp on them. She wanted to grab Sophie and run like hell, not from the danger Caleb kept warning her about, but from temptation and frustra-

216

tion and sheer boredom.

She headed into the kitchen, grabbing the vegetarian casserole she'd taken from the freezer and putting it in the oven. The details of David's diet were so complex that she could only face cooking once a week, and she usually spent a whole day concocting all sorts of unsavory things with soy and grains, all thanks to the cookbook David had given her as a wedding present. The one time she'd tried something new he'd protested, even though she'd adhered strictly to his dietary demands. "Too spicy," he'd said, and she'd ended up tossing it.

Back in San Francisco, when they were dating, she found his regimen charming, and there were enough inventive restaurants in the city that she never noticed how limited her choices were. If she took Sophie and ran away for a few weeks she could eat anything she wanted, without having to worry if the smell of cooking chicken was going to turn a quiet evening into a major event.

But Sophie was right. David had already insisted on coming with her. It would be no escape at all.

Sophie was sitting at her usual spot, in the family room, cross-legged in front of the wide-screen TV, working on her homework while mournful girl singers crooned in the background. Sophie had the ability to study anywhere, and in fact, found dead silence distracting. She had her golden head buried in a book, but a moment later she looked up, sensing her mother's eyes on her. "Hey," she said, grinning.

"Hey, baby girl," she replied, and the knot in her stomach loosened. No matter what mistakes she made, no matter what anyone else did, as long as she had Sophie then things couldn't be that bad. "Lentils for dinner tonight."

"Barf. Do I get a frozen dinner?"

"Even better, sweetheart. You get sushi. I had Sakura deliver it before I went into the darkroom. David gets so bothered by the smell of meat cooking that I thought this would be a good compromise."

"David can . . ." Sophie stopped herself. "David can eat his lentils, while I get sashimi. Did you get Ahi tuna?"

"Would I neglect your favorite? You're the only thirteen-year-old I know who loves sushi. Save a piece for me, would you? There is only a certain amount of lentils that a normal person can eat in a week. I can't imagine how David can survive on them."

"Well, if he ever flips out and starts hacking people up with an ax he can use the lentil defense. Not as good as the Twinkie defense but it will do. The grains made him do it."

Rachel laughed. Not even for a moment did she stop and wonder how Sophie knew about the infamous "Twinkie defense murder" in San Francisco so long ago. The depth and breadth of Sophie's knowledge sometimes astounded her. "I'll mention it to him if he starts to crack at the seams."

She expected Sophie to reply with another wisecrack, but her daughter's grin had faded. "You'll notice long before that, won't you, Ma? If anyone starts to get twitchy you'll see it, right?"

"Don't let this doom and gloom atmosphere get to you, sweetie. I'm sure the crazy man is halfway to San Diego by now. Or up in Canada. He's long gone."

"That's not what Sheriff Bannister says. Or Caleb. They say there's bad stuff going on, and to be very, very careful."

Funny, that was essentially what Stephen Henry had told her, in between his endless self-praise and egocentric reminiscences. And that's what her instincts told her, those treacherous, irrational instincts that were pushing her in Caleb's direction.

Her brain knew better. Caleb's bantering and flirtation were a way to get at his brother, nothing more. It would almost be worth taking him up on his sexual offers just to see the look on his face.

Almost. She pulled the chilled bottle of chardonnay out of the wine cooler. David was waiting for her in his study, looking at something in his drawer when she walked in, and he closed it carefully, locking it.

"Something interesting in there?" she asked, taking the sofa and setting the tray down on the walnut-inlaid table.

"Nothing but confidential student material," he said easily. "Ridiculous to lock it up in my own house but you know how touchy the lawyers can be about confidentiality. They wouldn't let me take the records home unless I swore on the grave of my mother that I'd keep them locked at all time."

"Then you should." She leaned over to struggle with the wine opener.

"Here, let me do that," David said, rising from his desk and moving around to the sofa. "It seems as if we've had no time together recently. We need to get out more. We could take a weekend, go up north. I know my father would be more than happy to have Sophie stay with him."

For some reason the idea, which would have seemed like a gift from heaven a week ago, no longer sounded so appealing. "But what about my idea of taking Sophie away? Maybe I could do that first, leaving you some time to visit with your brother." She ignored his doubtful expression. "Besides, it sounds as if the campus is in turmoil after the murder, and I'm sure you're needed. What if he strikes again and you're not here? I think I should just take Sophie away for a bit. You and I could go later."

David smiled tenderly. "If you go then I'm going, too. I hate to admit it but I've really gotten dependent on your presence — it would feel so empty here without you. But there's no need for you to go anywhere. I don't think there's going to be any more problem with the killer. He's long gone — I sense it in my bones."

She kept the disbelief from showing in her face. Maybe the killer was gone. She just couldn't bring herself to believe it. "And just how reliable are your bones?"

He poured her a glass of wine, a little more generous than the one he did for himself. "Sometimes very reliable. They told me you were the woman I'd been waiting for. And they were right about that, weren't they?"

She wanted to say something flippant, some light, sexual innuendo, but she knew

David wouldn't like it. "Absolutely," she said, taking a sip of the icy chardonnay. She'd missed having wine with her meals.

And she had to stop mocking David's diet. Indeed, she respected his refusal to eat or wear things that came from animals — no leather shoes for him, and Caleb's leather jacket must have been an appalling affront to his sensitive soul. But then, it was quite clear that Caleb's very existence was an affront to David, no matter how he tried to hide it.

"You'll sign those papers, won't you, Rachel?" he said, taking a cautious sip of his wine. He took her hand in his, running his thumb over the back. He had soft, delicate hands — someone who used his intellect for a living, not his body. He had a fair amount of strength in his hands despite his scholarly life, though he never used his strength when they made love. She might have even liked a little more forcefulness. . . .

"We should sleep together tonight," he said softly, almost reading her mind. "It's been too long."

In fact, it was just four days ago that he'd come to her room, but apparently he was going with selective memory, and the least she could do was match it. "I'd like that."

And then realized, with absolute horror, that that was the third lie she'd told him today.

12

Rachel was curled up in the oversized armchair in the family room, watching television while Sophie worked on calculus. *CSI* was on, but she wasn't in the mood for graphic crime scenes, particularly when they had one not five miles away, still cordoned off by the police and now the FBI. They'd TiVo'd *Lost* — castaways on a mystical island worked well enough to distract her — right now reality was highly overrated.

David was in his study, working. He'd barely touched his wine and the tomato-and-cheese casserole, but his lingering glance when he excused himself made it clear he hadn't forgotten his plan for that night.

She could easily count the number of times they'd made love. She'd simply assumed that David hadn't much of a sex drive, and that was a good match for her. She had no particular interest in grand passion or long, energetic nights of sex, particularly when it seemed more like exercise than anything else.

It had been different with Jared, but then, she'd been so damned young. Sixteen, and in love, and even his glance could send erotic shivers down her spine. She'd gotten over that quickly enough when her parents kicked her out of the house and they'd lived together. She'd enjoyed the sex, even if Jared was too fast and totally uninterested in cuddling afterward. But in truth, she hadn't missed it once he abandoned her and his baby.

So why did David suddenly decide he wanted to make love when he'd barely touched her the last two months? Was it to make up for the debacle four nights ago, the one they were going to pretend hadn't happened? Was it to prove something to her or himself? Or did it have something to do with the greatest threat to his sense of manhood, Caleb, coming back to town?

It didn't matter. She just knew it had nothing to do with actual affection or desire, and she had no idea how she was going to derail him without hurting his feelings. She could always make up some excuse with Sophie, and he'd go along with it, asking no questions, but it was bad enough she was lying like a felon. She didn't want to drag her daughter into it as well. Especially when it had to do with avoiding sex.

She heard the commotion at the front door, and for a moment she didn't move. Sophie lifted her head. "You want me to go see who's here, Ma?"

"David can answer it. I'm sure it's for him." There would be nobody to visit her. In the few months she'd been in town she'd been singularly unable to make friends. Everyone was either old or younger, and uniformly conventional. Even though Rachel tried her best, the young women of Silver Falls could see through it. Maggie Bannister was the closest thing she had to a friend, and she wasn't the type to just drop in for a cup of coffee. Not at this hour.

A deep voice carried to the family room at the back of the house, and Sophie made a comical face of despair. "It's Stephen Henry." And then she perked up, as another voice followed. "And Caleb." She jumped up from her seat on the floor, shoving her hair behind her ears, the silver barrettes from India beginning to slip.

Rachel wisely kept her mouth shut, just in case David heard the words she really felt like using. She didn't want to move — with luck they'd just go into the living room with

David and she could pretend the television was too loud to hear anyone arrive.

No such luck. "My father and brother are here, darling," David said, putting his head in the door. "Why don't you two come join us?"

Sophie used every excuse under the sun to keep away from the Old Goat, as she called Stephen Henry, so Rachel readied her excuse. "Sophie's got a lot of homework."

"That's all right, Ma," her daughter said with surprisingly good cheer. "I was just finishing up anyway." She'd already moved past David, heading toward the living room.

"That's nice," David said, waiting for her slower, more reluctant approach. "I knew she'd like the old man if she took the time to get to know him."

She still wasn't taking the time. She was over to one side, talking to Caleb a mile a minute, while Stephen Henry sat in state by the gas fire, a glass of whiskey in his hand.

The room looked welcoming for a change, with the artificial fire burning. Every light was turned on, filling the space with a cool glow. Even the Mayan death masks on the wall, which usually creeped her out, seemed suddenly benevolent. She never could figure out why David even had them, though admittedly they went well with the austere interior and the geometric lines of the room and the furniture.

Stephen Henry was already holding forth. "I hope you don't mind, my boy, but I asked Caleb to help himself. You wouldn't begrudge your da a drop of the finest, now would you?"

He was doing his Irish poet thing now, Rachel thought, dismayed. And then his eyes caught Rachel's, and she could see the same, inexplicable warning that had been there earlier in the day.

She must have imagined it, because a moment later it was gone. "Come sit beside me, Rachel," Stephen Henry commanded. "I had Caleb bring me over since it had been so long since I'd seen dear Sophie, but like most women she's already smitten with the black sheep of the family. I don't know how he does it."

"Sophie." Rachel raised her voice. "Come here and talk to Stephen Henry. You haven't seen him in ages."

Sophie rose immediately, good manners a second nature to her. Stephen Henry would never guess that her daughter found him infinitely creepy, but Caleb clearly had a pretty good idea.

"You go entertain Caleb, Rachel," Stephen Henry said grandly as Sophie sat near him, just out of reach. "You two are practically strangers, and now that he's decided to rejoin the family you should get to know each other. I promise you he's not nearly as wicked as he pretends to be."

"Isn't he?" Rachel said in a neutral voice. David had taken a seat beside Sophie, and for a moment she thought she saw her daughter stiffen. But a moment later she laughed at something Stephen Henry said, totally at ease.

She could make an excuse, go in search of coffee or dessert or anything to make this unexpected visit go as planned. But Caleb was watching her, and she could still hear the challenge in his voice. David was watching her as well — if she refused everyone would make a big deal out of it, when it was nothing more than a slight aversion to the man.

Who was she kidding? She had an aversion to how she reacted to Caleb, and that wasn't precisely his fault. Though he seemed to be doing his best to manipulate her.

"Can I get anyone coffee?" she asked brightly. "Something to drink?"

"We're fine, Rachel," David said, as if talking to a stubborn child. "Go talk with Caleb while my father and I catch up on

Sophie's last few days."

It shouldn't have bothered her so much, leaving her in the company of the two men. She'd be five feet away, watching them all the time. This was the man she loved and trusted, the man she married, the man she intended to eventually be the legal father to her daughter. Just not right now.

As for Stephen Henry, he was nothing more than a self-important pain in the ass, and even if he had wandering hands Rachel would be watching, and she wouldn't hesitate to clobber him with the nearby fire poker if he did anything inappropriate.

"Sit down, Rachel." Caleb's voice was full of amusement. "I promise you, I'll kill the old man myself if he touches her." She looked at him for a long moment before taking a seat just out of reach, shielded from her husband by the back of the chair. "And I'm wondering just why you'd think he would?"

"Why would *you* think he would?" she said.

"Because you're watching him like a chicken hawk. Or are you just looking for excuses not to talk to me?"

She turned back to him. He was wearing the worn leather jacket that would be an affront to David's nothing-with-a-face policy, and he was the one looking at her like he was a hawk and she was a darting field mouse.

The hell she was. When it came to her daughter she was a panther, and she'd rip his throat out before anyone hurt her.

"I don't think I like that smile," he said. "It looks far too evil to me. What were you thinking?"

"What I'd do to you if you did anything to hurt my daughter."

To her surprise he grinned. "Good to know. You're not going to believe this, but comparatively speaking, I'm quite harmless."

"Compared to whom?"

"Compared to the Northwest Strangler." There was no more levity in his deep voice. "Having second thoughts about going on a little trip?"

Not with David hovering, she thought. "No."

"You're pretty fucking stupid for such a smart woman," he said in a low voice.

"Caleb, your language!" David had somehow managed to pick up on the forbidden word. "There are children present."

Rachel glanced over at Sophie, at the mischief in her eyes, and she knew it was a testament to Sophie's self-restraint that she

231

didn't tell David to leave Caleb the fuck alone. She simply grinned.

"Christ, David, are you still living in Victorian times?" Caleb drawled. "I think Sophie's heard that word before. Probably used it a time or two."

"Not my darling Sophie," Rachel protested, in mock horror. "She's had a rarified upbringing."

"She will from now on," David said firmly.

Sophie made a comical face of dismay, so swift that neither David nor Stephen Henry noticed. "Absolutely," she said staunchly.

"I'm thinking maybe we should have coffee," David said. "Decaf for me, darling. The Sumatran roast, I think. Caleb, why don't you go help her?"

For a moment Rachel froze, about to protest, when Caleb kicked her in the leg. "We'd be happy to. Just give a shout if you need anything," he said as he rose, and the back of the chair shielded the sight of him hauling her up, too. "Won't take more than a minute."

She glanced back at Sophie as Caleb was shooing her away, but her daughter simply nodded, and she followed her obnoxious brother-in-law into the kitchen.

He waited until they were out of hearing range. "What the hell do you think you're doing?" he said. "Are you really going to tell them you don't trust them to be alone with Sophie?"

"I do," she protested unconvincingly. "I just wanted to keep an eye on her. She's had a lot of things going on in her life in the last few months, and I don't like to leave her . . ."

"Sometimes you have to. I can understand why you don't want her around me, but you don't really have an excuse not to leave her alone with David and my father. Or do you?"

"The situations are different."

"I know they are. But do you have any reason not to trust my father or David? Any concrete reason? If you do you need to tell me," he said.

"Of course not," she protested. "You're making a fuss over nothing. I'm just a little rattled, which is perfectly normal given what's just happened in this town."

"Given what happened in San Francisco."

"Sophie trusts you too much," she said in a cranky voice.

"And you don't trust me enough. Let's stop fighting and get this coffee made. Otherwise David's paranoid enough to think we're having passionate sex on that kitchen table."

She couldn't help it — her eyes immediately went to the sturdy table. She knew her body well enough to recognize her reaction, but she ignored it. "He's the one who sent you out here with me. Why would he do that if he doesn't trust you?"

"Now that's a very interesting question."

She reached for the coffee beans, then turned. "Would you do me a favor?"

"You're asking me for a favor?" He was startled. "I thought you considered me the spawn of Satan."

"You're the spawn of Stephen Henry, so you're not even close."

"Actually I think spawn are biological offspring, so I'm not sure . . ."

"I'm not going to argue semantics with you," she said. "Will you do me a favor or won't you?"

"Yes."

"That simple? No questions asked?"

"No questions asked. Unless you're going to ask me to leave town."

She sighed. "I figure that's a lost cause. No, I want you to go back out and stay with Sophie. Don't ask me why — I know I'm not being reasonable. But I'm perfectly capable of making coffee by myself, and if David's throwing us together as some kind of test I don't want to play that game. But

234

most of all, I just want someone to be with Sophie. And I don't trust you with David's million-dollar coffeemaker."

"You're serious?" he said, not bothering to hide his astonishment.

"You'd probably break it —"

"I'm not talking about the coffeemaker. I'm talking about the fact that you apparently trust me more than David and Stephen Henry when it comes to your daughter."

"There's safety in numbers," she said in a neutral voice. "Besides, she likes you. A great lapse of judgment on her part, but there it is."

"If you think it's such a lapse of judgment why are you sending me back there? Why don't you tell me why you don't trust David and Stephen Henry?"

"I don't know," she snapped, goaded.

"Then why do you trust me?"

"Because I'm crazy!"

Silence. He looked at her, long and hard. "But you do trust me, don't you?" he said in a low voice. "Don't bother denying it. Maybe there's hope for you yet." He pushed open the door before she could refute it. "I take my coffee black and strong, full of caffeine."

"I don't think I'm going to be in the habit

235

of getting you coffee."

He grinned, and for a brief moment the darkness that had settled around her heart lifted. "You just might be surprised," he said.

Caleb strolled into the living room. David looked up, a frown on his face, but a moment later it was gone.

Stephen Henry was the center of attention, as always, regaling his captive audience with stories of his youthful follies that somehow always seemed to reflect well on his taste, wisdom and talent. Sophie was curled up in a chair, her legs tucked underneath her, looking like the picture of rapt attention. Rachel had done a damned good job of raising her alone. She was smart, she was sweet, and she knew how to hide it when she was ready to scream with boredom.

He deliberately moved between David and Sophie, pulling a chair up beside her. "Rachel kicked me out. She said I was more trouble than I was worth."

"That's what I used to tell your mother," Stephen Henry said fondly. "But she wouldn't hear a word of it. There were times when I think she loved you even more than the fruit of her loins."

David didn't blink.

"Gross," Sophie muttered.

"Heavens, no, Sophie dear," Stephen Henry intoned. "The phrase comes from —" Before he could go off on a philosophical rant Rachel reappeared, bearing a tray with four miniscule cups of coffee. She set it down on the table and brought each cup over — Stephen Henry first, David second, and Caleb's extremely milky brew last.

"Just the way you like it," she purred.

"Nonsense, child," Stephen Henry said. "Caleb is lactose-intolerant."

She laughed heartlessly. "How can the big bad wolf be lactose-intolerant? That really doesn't fit the image."

"Don't tease him, Rachel," David said, putting a fond, possessive hand on her arm. "He went through misery with it when he was young. And even though Mother did her best, he'd get the most awful stomach attacks."

Caleb leaned back, still holding the tiny cup in his hand. "It was strange how milk products managed to get into things."

"That's why you didn't order a milkshake," Rachel said.

Everyone turned to look at her. "When would he have had a milkshake?" Stephen Henry demanded.

She was flushed. She had pale, Irish skin to go with that red hair of hers, and she'd probably have freckles as well if she ever lived someplace with sun. He'd always been a sucker for freckles.

He watched her, wondering if she was going to lie. David had a faint half smile on his face, enjoying her discomfiture, thinking no one had noticed. Caleb noticed everything about his baby brother. Had she told him they'd gone out — she must have. If she didn't, lying would play directly into his hands.

"David invited me over for dinner last night and then forgot to show up or tell Rachel. I ended up kidnapping her and taking her to the In-N-Out Burger over in Monasburg," he said easily.

"There's an In-N-Out Burger nearby?" Sophie demanded in tones of awe. "And nobody told me?"

"That food is disgusting," David said with a frown. "You shouldn't be eating it."

"And who are you to be telling the girl what she can eat?" Stephen Henry said with his usual malice. "She's not your daughter, after all. Unless the adoption papers went through and you neglected to tell me."

Only Stephen Henry could make David squirm like that. Normally Caleb had taken

238

a certain amusement in it. Now it seemed much too dangerous.

"It's just a question of time," David said in an even voice. Sophie's face was expressionless, as was Rachel's. The very lack of reaction was more damning than anything else.

"I'll get Caleb another cup of coffee." Rachel broke the sudden silence, turning.

He was about to go after her when he saw the headlights. With David's tastefully orchestrated landscaping he could only see the lights on the top of the vehicle outside. A visit from Sheriff Bannister was going to make everybody squirm, and he wasn't going to be immune. That woman was a hell of a lot smarter than she let on, but he couldn't count on her seeing her way through the smoke screen his family had set up.

Caleb was up a moment before the doorbell rang. "I'll get it."

He ran into Rachel in the hallway, carrying a cup of black coffee. "Better get another cup. We've got visitors." He took the coffee from her hand. "Rat poison?"

"Tempting, but no. Just strong black coffee." She headed for the door, but he moved in front of her, opening it.

"Good evening, Sheriff Bannister," he said politely.

Maggie wasn't impressed. "Professor Middleton's housekeeper told me I'd find you all here. Mind if I come in?"

"Who is it?" Stephen Henry's loud voice wafted from the living room on liquid tones.

"Sheriff Bannister, S.H.," he said. "Looks like the jig is up."

"Very funny," Maggie said sourly. "Hey, Rachel."

"Hey, Maggie. What's up?"

For a moment she didn't answer. "Good news, bad news."

"Come in here, oh, minion of the law," Stephen Henry bellowed, and Rachel rolled her eyes, then realized Caleb had caught her. For a moment she didn't know what to do, and then she simply shrugged.

"Sorry," she said. "I have a hard time taking your father as seriously as he takes himself."

"Don't underestimate him," Maggie said, handing Rachel her coat. She was still in uniform, and he wasn't sure whether that was good or not. She moved past them, sure of her way, and he glanced over at Rachel.

For the first time he could see the signs of strain around her eyes, and he knew that he'd put some of them there. He couldn't

240

regret it. He did what had to be done, and if she got hurt in the meantime then at least she'd be alive.

"Still in uniform, Maggie?" Stephen Henry was saying. "Am I to assume this is a professional visit?"

"Hardly," David said with his easy charm. "Unless someone's been speeding." Everyone immediately turned to look at Rachel.

"Hey," she protested.

"Speeding's the least of my worries," Maggie said, looking around at each of them in turn. "There's been another murder."

And Stephen Henry promptly dropped his coffee, letting it smash on the hardwood floor.

13

Rachel moved swiftly, pulling the brightly colored scarf from the back of the chair and dumping it on the broken cup, scooping up shards of china and spilled coffee. David had always hated that shawl, the one piece of color in the austere living room, so she figured he wouldn't object. There was no way she was going to leave the room without hearing what Maggie had to say.

She dumped the shawl and its contents into a wastebasket before turning back. Everyone had composed themselves — they were all looking solemn and unsurprised.

"What happened?" David said, sounding distraught. "Not another student?"

"Not another student. They found a young woman's body over by the Idaho state line. The good news is that apparently the Northwest Strangler has moved on, and so has the FBI."

"Thank the good lord," Stephen Henry,

the atheist, said with devout piety.

"Yes, thank heavens," David said. "The entire campus has been in a state of panic. Now that the danger has passed maybe we can get back to our normal lives."

Caleb wasn't saying anything at all.

"Not necessarily," Maggie drawled. "The FBI is sure they've got a good lead on the man, and they've handed local authority back to me."

"But you're not convinced," Rachel said, a statement, not a question.

"No, I'm not. Maybe the FBI's right, and we have nothing more to worry about. We were just a pit stop for a monster making his way across the Pacific Northwest. But I don't like unanswered questions. This doesn't smell right to me."

"Don't you think you should let it rest, Maggie?" Stephen Henry said in his most dictatorial voice. "If the FBI is satisfied then you should be, too."

"Professor Middleton, I've never been the kind of gal who takes someone else's word for things. I make up my own mind, and right now Rachel's absolutely right. It doesn't feel right to me. I'm not letting go of it until I'm convinced the murderer is hundreds of miles away from here. In the meantime, I'd like to talk to each of you, alone."

"At this hour?" Stephen Henry exploded. "Don't be ridiculous. This is hardly the time for social calls."

"Didn't I just tell you that this is far from a social call?" Maggie drawled. "Now you can meet with me, one by one, in the dining room, or you can come with me down to the station. Makes no difference to me — I'll get the job done either way."

"It can't wait until tomorrow?" David said, his forehead furrowed.

"I'm afraid not. I do think the killings have stopped for the time being, whether or not the murderer has moved on. Maybe he's thinking he's managed to fool everyone, and he's too smart to jeopardize his position right now. For the time being people are safe. Unless he's gotten totally out of control and can't help himself." She looked over at Caleb, who met her gaze with a calm, steady expression.

"Sophie, I think you should go to bed," David said. "Maggie won't be needing to talk to you and I know how upsetting this must be."

Rachel didn't miss Sophie's instinctive pout.

"I'm afraid I meant it when I said I need

to talk to all of you," Sheriff Bannister said. "I can take Sophie first so she can get to bed sooner."

"Don't be ridiculous!" Stephen Henry said, his voice raised to almost bellowing levels. "You can't tell me you suspect my granddaughter of being a serial killer!"

"Sheriff Bannister just wants to talk with me, Stephen Henry," Sophie said calmly. "She probably wants to know if I've seen anything, noticed anything out of place or peculiar. It's no problem — I don't mind." She rose. At age thirteen, she was already nearing five feet seven — in another year she might be taller than David. "I was getting pretty tired anyway."

"You mind if we use the dining room, Rachel?" Maggie said.

She could sense David's irritation that he wasn't being consulted. "It's fine with us," she said deliberately, giving David his ounce of power. And annoyed with herself for doing so.

"Don't any of you go anywhere. You stay and keep the boys from killing each other, Rachel." With anyone else that would be a joke. Coming from Maggie's flat, affectless voice it sounded far too real.

"This is ridiculous," Stephen Henry fumed once Maggie and Sophie disappeared. "I don't know what's gotten into that woman — she should know better than to harass members of one of Silver Falls's most important families."

"Oh, come on, Father," Caleb drawled, still sitting a little way off. "Don't be modest. What's this 'one of' bullshit? You know that no one else in the area comes near our exalted level."

Stephen Henry didn't deny it. "I was being tactful," he said, drawing up his dignity around him, ignoring Caleb's mockery. "Which is something you could work on, my boy."

Caleb's dark, wicked eyes met hers for a brief moment before he turned back to his father. "Tact is for pussies."

"Caleb!" David said, shocked.

"Oh, come on, David!" Caleb said. "You're just too damned easy to rile. Loosen up. There are all sorts of perfectly good, Anglo-Saxon words with effectively crude meanings. I bet Stephen Henry approves of them."

"I do, indeed," the old man said. "I don't know how you became such a little prig, David. I would have thought marriage and the love of a good woman would have loosened you up, but you've still got that revolting little minister deep inside you.

Sometimes it's much more fun to raise the devil."

"You'd know," David said with far less than his usual grace. He glanced toward the hallway. "How long do you think this imposition is going to last? Why couldn't she wait until tomorrow to talk to us?"

"Now that's the interesting question," Caleb said. "Why does she come after us the moment she gets control of the case back? Kind of makes you wonder?" He leaned back, perfectly at ease.

A moment later Maggie appeared in the door. "Rachel, you want to come next?"

Stephen Henry rolled his wheelchair forward, bumping into the coffee table. "I'm an old man and I want to go home to my own bed," he said peevishly. "If you want to talk to me you're going to do it now. In front of my children."

If Maggie was impressed by his bluster she didn't show it. "All right. I'd like to know your schedule for the last four days. Where have you been?"

"At home, of course. You think I miraculously climbed out of my wheelchair, strangled and raped some poor girl, carried her up the mountain and dumped her into Silver Falls before climbing back down and getting back into my wheelchair? Don't be absurd."

Maggie didn't even blink. "Why did you put it in that order?"

"What do you mean?"

"You said strangled and raped, not raped and strangled. I don't think that bit of information was made public. That she was raped post-mortem."

Stephen Henry looked at her blankly. "This is a small college town, Mrs. Bannister. If you think there are any secrets here you're sadly mistaken."

"It's Sheriff Bannister, Professor. Or Maggie." Her voice was even. "And you'd be surprised at the secrets some people can keep." She looked over at Caleb, who was lounging off to one side, seemingly at ease. He gave her a faint smile.

"Answer her question, Father," David said in a weary voice. "She's not going to leave us alone until she gets what she wants."

Stephen Henry looked sulky. "Most days I wake up, my aide dresses me and puts me in my chair and rolls me into the bathroom. I take care of my bodily functions. I come out and Dylan rolls me into my study, where I set to work on a new collection of poetry. Dylan leaves for the day, returning in time to assist me in getting ready for bed, and one day is pretty much the same as the next.

Do you need any other details?"

"What about yesterday? Any phone calls? Did you check your computer, answer e-mails?"

"E-mails are an invention of the devil, the single greatest contribution to the wretched illiteracy of the masses. I won't have a computer in the house."

"Luddite," Caleb said sweetly, and Rachel resisted the impulse to grin. David was almost as bad — he used a computer only when he had to, and if Rachel hadn't insisted he would have continued to survive on dial-up in the house.

"So you have no witnesses to your whereabouts between the time your aide left and the time he returned."

"You're talking about yesterday? David," he said promptly. "He came over in the middle of the day. We needed to have a family powwow, and he cancelled classes and came to talk to me."

For a moment David started, and he glanced at his father so swiftly Maggie probably didn't notice. But Rachel did.

"And I presume Caleb was there as well."

"Not me, Sheriff," Caleb said. "I think I was the family problem they were discussing."

"Is this true, David?"

David hesitated. "Yes, it is. That we met, not that we talked about Caleb."

"Then why didn't he join you?"

"I assume he was busy elsewhere," David said, glancing at him. "Maybe you should ask my wife where he was."

Rachel froze. "I beg your pardon?" she said in her iciest voice.

David turned to look at her. "You've been up at his place. It only seemed logical."

"*Sheriff* Bannister isn't interested in your brother's tomcatting ways, David," Stephen Henry said.

Rachel looked over at Caleb, who simply looked back at her, unperturbed. "Caleb's tomcatting ways have absolutely nothing to do with me," she said, not certain who was pissing her off the most.

"There's no need for anyone to get edgy," David said with his usual easy charm. "I'm sure we're just one of many families she'll be talking to. That's how police work is done, isn't it? Patient footwork, talking to dozens and dozens of innocent people until you find the clue that puts it all together."

"That's the way it usually works," Maggie said evenly.

"So tell me, Sheriff," Caleb said suddenly. "Why don't you think the murder over in Idaho was committed by the Northwest

Strangler?"

"I didn't say that."

"Then why don't you think our two little murders were committed by the same man?" David asked.

"We haven't established that the second body found was actually a murder victim. And I wouldn't exactly call our crimes little. No death is ever small."

Rachel noticed she didn't answer that question, but went on as if it had never been asked. "It's turning out that our Northwest Strangler might not be that localized. There have been similar cases as far away as Portugal and West Africa."

"Then that leaves our family out," Stephen Henry said triumphantly. "Except, for perhaps . . ." His glance strayed toward Caleb, who was listening to all this with no more interest than if he were watching a trial on television.

"Except for me, Maggie," he said. "I've been in Portugal, West Africa, Kuwait, Saudi Arabia, Russia . . . you name it, I've been there in the last fifteen years or so. Now all you have to do is find similar murders in each country, check my whereabouts at the time and you've got your man."

"That's not funny," Rachel snapped.

His smile was oddly sweet. "I don't know,

I can find a certain black humor in it. What is it, Maggie? You want to take me in? I won't put up a fight."

"Well, I certainly will," his father said. "Neither of my sons have a violent bone in their bodies, and —"

"Now that's definitely not true, S.H.," Caleb said. "I can hold my own in a bar fight, and I've got the scars to prove it. I fight dirty, I'm ruthless, and I can do what I have to to get the job done. Seems to me I'm the perfect candidate for murder."

"And then there were the dead animals," Maggie said, her voice even. "I'm not sure that torturing animals is something you just outgrow."

It hit her so fast she was shocked. Rachel had been sitting there, an unwilling witness to all this, when her stomach suddenly lurched. "Excuse me," she said, bolting from the room, barely making the bathroom before she was sick.

It seemed to last forever, which, considering how little she'd been eating, didn't make sense. When she'd finally gotten rid of everything in her stomach she leaned back against the wall, closing her eyes as her breathing slowly returned to normal. No one had ever said a word about tortured animals — the very thought almost had her hurling again. She took calm, shallow breaths as a cold sweat covered her. What the . . . fuck . . . had she gotten herself into?

She heard the sound of voices in the hallway outside the powder-room door — Stephen Henry's sculptured tones, David's measured ones. She pushed herself up, splashed water on her face and rinsed her mouth out before opening the door.

Her bright smile must have been a little wavery. "You okay?" Maggie asked, and Rachel realized with shock that she was the only one in the room who actually cared. There was too much going on in the tangled mess of the Middleton clan to pay much notice of a married-in stranger.

"Just a touch of the stomach flu," she said, forcing her voice to sound stronger.

"Yeah, that's been going around," Maggie said, covering for her. "Caleb's taking Stephen Henry home and then coming down to the station. I'm finished with David. He's been real helpful."

She couldn't look at him. Not without thinking about it, not without having to turn around and head straight back into the bathroom. No wonder David had been so adamant about not having animals. She didn't even want to think what he went through as a child, having a sociopath for a

253

brother.

She'd spent far too much time reading about serial killers — before Tessa was murdered. Once that happened, she'd found the very thought of it so revolting that she'd had to avoid certain sections of the bookstore. Some of the other parents had wanted to read everything they could, trying to understand the how and the why of Tessa's death. Rachel didn't want to understand anything. She'd simply wanted to take her daughter and run to a safe place as fast as she could and David had appeared, deus ex machina, to protect her, when she'd never thought she'd needed protection before. And now here they were, in a place that was anything but safe.

She wouldn't, couldn't look at Caleb. He'd told her to leave town, and she should have gone at the first warning. She should have listened. If Maggie was right, and you didn't outgrow torturing helpless creatures, then chances were he'd moved on to bigger and better victims. And sending her out of town would have been the perfect setup. David would insist on coming with her and there would have been no one left to stop him.

Or maybe Caleb had some sick, strange compulsion and he was trying to stop himself. Maybe that was why he wanted to send her away, to somehow keep her safe from his own monstrous hands.

"Give an old man a kiss, Rachel," Stephen Henry said, still with that annoying tone that had become part of his everyday speech.

She leaned down dutifully, trying not to look at the man standing behind his chair, the hand that rested on the handles, strong and long-fingered and tanned by the sun. Hands that had done things too horrific to even think of. Even if he'd been a perfect Boy Scout from there on out, there was a darkness of the soul that would never leave you.

She brushed Stephen Henry's cheek with hers, but before she realized it, Caleb had caught her chin in his hand, tilting her face up to his, forcing her to look into his dark, endless eyes for a long, silent moment.

He had to see the disgust and condemnation there, even while she tried to hide it, and then she pulled herself away, stepping back. "Good night, Rachel. If Maggie hauls me off to prison without giving me a chance to see you again I hope you'll be very happy with my brother." There was that malice again, hidden beneath the polite words, malice that only Rachel seemed to hear.

"That's not going to happen, Caleb," Stephen Henry said. "As soon as I get home I'll call our lawyer."

"Not necessary, Father. I'm sure Sheriff Bannister and I can come to some kind of understanding. If not, I think I can manage to escape before she calls out the bloodhounds."

Maggie didn't blink, didn't respond. "You take care of yourself, Rachel," she said, turning her back on the men. "You and Sophie mean a lot to us Bannisters, and I need to make sure you two are safe. Nothing's going to happen to either of you, not on my watch. But it doesn't hurt to pay attention."

Attention to what? Rachel wanted to ask. But they were already heading out the door, leaving her behind.

At the last minute Caleb turned back to look at them, an unreadable expression in his eyes. David put an arm around her. For some strange reason she wanted to throw it off, but she remained still, motionless, the perfect image of a devoted couple.

And then they were gone, the door closing behind them. David took a step away from her, almost as if she were an infection. "I'm going in my study for a while, dear," he said smoothly. "I'll see you in the morning."

At least his earlier amatory mood had vanished. The thought of fending off one of David's rare romantic moves was enough to make her want to head for the powder room again.

But she composed her face in a Madonna-like smile, and kissed the air beside his cheek. "Sleep well, then."

His smile was benevolent. "I will, my love. I will."

14

It was a good thing he didn't have to make conversation with Stephen Henry in the car. His adopted father kept up a monologue that wouldn't have allowed the most determined chatterbox get a word in. Because if he had, Caleb would have probably slammed him up against the side of the car, shook him till his teeth rattled, and demanded to know what the fuck he thought he was doing.

Since Stephen Henry wouldn't have told him, and since putting hands on the old man was probably not a good idea, it suited him just fine to chauffeur the old bastard back to his pilfered house and his highly paid houseboy.

It wasn't until Dylan, a graduate student with the patience of a saint, was extricating Stephen Henry from the car that his father finally decided to address him directly, smugly assured that Caleb wouldn't say anything in front of the help.

"You've been very quiet, my boy," he said as Dylan settled him back into the chair. The old man was heavier than he looked. "Are you troubled about something?"

Caleb looked down at him. "I was just wondering about something. When you told Maggie Bannister that lie about David being over here, was it to give *him* an alibi or *you*?"

For once he'd managed to shock the old man into silence. "When you figure out what your answer is you can let me know," he added, climbing back into the car and pulling out into the road without looking. Good thing no one was driving by to smash into, ruining his melodramatic exit, he thought sourly as he drove down the road. Though maybe it wouldn't be so bad after all. He had no particular death wish, but things had just gotten a hell of a lot more complicated.

She must be pregnant. He'd been a fool not to realize what was going on, but the thought of his brother actually breeding had been too far-fetched to even consider in his darkest nightmares. No wonder she refused to listen to him and take her daughter the hell away from there. If she was carrying David's child she wouldn't very well bail on him, any more than she would harbor any unacceptable suspicions.

Of course, suspecting the black-sheep brother was just fine. She'd looked at him like he was Jeffrey Dahmer after Maggie dropped that bomb about animal torture. He'd have to thank the sheriff for that little extra. As if things weren't complicated enough, now his sister-in-law was going to consider him the man most likely to become a serial killer.

Shit. He didn't mind that part as much as he minded the fact that she was pregnant. It explained a lot about her. The gorgeous, female curves of her body, her pale, almost luminous skin. The fact that she was both attracted to and repelled by him. Hormones run amuck. He couldn't thank his own reliable magnetism. She was simply knocked up.

Which made everything a lot more difficult. Maggie didn't believe the serial killer had moved on, and neither did he. He'd love it if he was wrong, if life was just a series of ugly coincidences, if he could just head back to Africa or wherever the bureau decided to send him next and not have to think about what was happening in Silver Falls. Maybe he'd been wrong all this time.

Yeah, and maybe pigs could fly. Maggie

might be right, and there'd be no more murders in Silver Falls, at least not for a good long time, long enough for people to forget.

But there had always been long waits in between victims, a studied methodology designed to outwit even the most trained of criminologists. And now there'd been at least three in the last few months. Maybe more.

Maybe David could bring it back under control, maybe he couldn't. And maybe Caleb should just tell Maggie Bannister what was going on. The trouble was, he didn't have an ounce of proof. Everything was pointing to him just as easily as it pointed to David, and he had to start thinking there was a reason for it. The crimes that were turning up, the murders around the world. He was willing to bet his life that they happened during David's infrequent visits to his older brother.

That could point to him just as much as it could point to David. And if Maggie decided not to believe him, which was more than likely given his experience in this rotten little town that had always been ready to accept that the adopted kid was the monster, then he'd be locked up and there'd be no one to stop David.

He couldn't let that happen. He could stonewall Maggie. She'd believe what she'd want to believe, but she wouldn't come up with any evidence unless his helpful father decided to go one step further in protecting David. It was the way it had always been, with even their mother keeping a close eye on her damaged birth son. In the end it had killed her, and if he'd had any proof at the time he would have killed David himself.

But he hadn't, everything had pointed to him, once again, and he'd gotten the hell out of there. He'd gotten out and kept on going, running until he could run no more. Until he'd heard his twisted baby brother had married.

One mistake he'd made was to be too careful. David wasn't going to screw up without more help — he was cunning, deliberate, totally in control. He had no emotions, no weaknesses as far as Caleb could see. If he was waiting for David to screw up he was going to be stuck in this hellhole for a long time.

In the meantime he had to get Rachel and her daughter out of town. She wouldn't listen to his warnings, she wouldn't listen to her own instincts. So he had no choice but to take it one step further.

Maggie Bannister was waiting for him,

and he'd have to undergo what he'd been through so many times in his life. Denying his guilt without implicating David, at least overtly. He'd been doing it since David was ten and Stephen Henry had beaten him for supposedly lying about his brother, though he suspected the old man had known perfectly well who the guilty culprit really was. Not that Maggie could believe him if he tried.

If he was going to stop David he'd have to do it on his own — there'd be no help from their father. Sooner or later David's little tricks could come back to bite him in the butt, and he could let go of the guilt.

Once that happened he'd be long gone, continents away, and he wouldn't even need to think about it. Think about his niece or nephew growing up with a monster for a father. Soon enough it would all be over.

But first he had to get rid of Rachel.

Sophie woke up early, just after dawn. She took a quick shower and threw on the school uniform that she hated, the dull greens and grays of the ordinariness that her mother had only recently seemed to prize. She grabbed a soda from her fridge, a Butterfingers from her stash, well out of Rachel's sight or they'd be long gone. She brushed her hair, working her fingers through the snarls, and reached for her barrettes.

Her fingers skimmed the intricately chased silver ones David had given her. He always asked her why she didn't wear them, and she always told him she was saving them for something special.

Like when her mother came to her senses and left the creep.

That wasn't going to happen anytime soon. The murders had just brought back all the fear and horror of Tessa's death, and if Sophie knew her mother, and she did, she'd dig in even harder.

Maybe she wasn't madly in love with David after all. There was no missing the tension that was simmering beneath the surface. So far Sophie had tolerated him for Rachel's sake, but if her mother wasn't as blinded as she had been in the beginning then maybe there was a chance for them to get out of there.

She'd certainly picked the wrong brother. Caleb was everything David wasn't — funny, relaxed, treated her like an adult instead of some creepy, precious doll. Her mother had always had excellent taste in friends and the occasional boyfriend. It was only with David that her instincts had gone haywire.

Sophie crept silently to the door, her Asics in her hand, moving the chair out of the way and unlocking it without making a sound. Her mother had no idea she locked her door, had locked it within a week of getting there. She herself didn't quite know why — it just made her feel safer. Which was kind of weird, because she left her windows open on the warmer nights. Whatever threatened her was inside the house, not out.

But she wasn't going to think about that. The house was still and silent — David and Rachel were asleep, and she hoped to God they weren't asleep together. That was just too weird and gross to consider. She scribbled a note, put her shoes on and walked all over David's spotless floor, and a moment later slipped out into the cool Northwest morning.

For the first time in weeks it wasn't raining, though the clouds threatened. She pulled up her hoodie anyway and started walking, past the bungalows and Victorians, toward the center of town. By the time she got to Ray and Lucy's Diner the fitful light of day was at its strongest, and she went inside, hopeful.

Caleb was sitting at a booth, nursing a

cup of coffee, and he gave her a brief smile when she slipped in across from him. "I thought you might be in jail," she said.

"I think Maggie was doing that more for show." He rubbed a hand across his brow. "She's too smart to spend her time chasing ghosts."

"Is the Northwest Strangler a ghost?"

"I hope so," he said, but he didn't sound optimistic. "Why don't you and your mother get out of town?"

"We have to wait until David can get some time off."

"Go without him."

"Easier said than done," Sophie muttered. "I don't think she'd go if he couldn't. She's madly in love with him."

"You sure about that? I haven't seen any signs of it."

"Why else would she marry him and drag me up here, when we could be somewhere, anywhere? We were doing just fine before she met David. She could make enough money for us to live well enough, especially overseas, as long as we weren't too fussy, and we both liked living with the locals. But suddenly she just threw everything away, our plans to go to New Zealand, and married David. What other reason could there be besides true love?" She sounded disgruntled and jealous and she knew it, but she couldn't help it.

"You'd be surprised, kid," he said. "I talked with Maggie. She wants you to stay with her family for the next week or so. I think that's probably a pretty good idea."

"Why?"

Caleb would have been pretty cute if he weren't so old. If her mother had any sense she would have seen it herself — he made his younger brother seem about as interesting as oatmeal. "Just trust me on this."

"I need to look after my mother. She tends to jump into things without thinking them through."

"Leave your mother to me. I promise you I'll make sure no one hurts her. Can you trust me on this?"

She considered it for a moment. In her life she'd been used to trusting her mother first, and then the people her mother trusted.

But her mother trusted David, which was a big mistake in judgment as far as Sophie was concerned. And Rachel didn't trust Caleb, who was the only adult around who was honest with her. Not even Kristen's mom told her the truth.

She nodded. "I can trust you. What am I going to tell my mother?"

"I told you. Leave your mother to me."

Sophie repressed a romantic sigh. If only her mother had better taste, she could do just that.

As it was, her mother had taught her early on that you played with the cards you were dealt, and life had dealt them David. At least for the time being.

"I'll give you a ride to school," he said, tossing some money down on the table.

"I can walk."

"I'm giving you a ride. And from now on you only ride with the sheriff, your mother or me. You got that?"

She grinned at him. "Bossy, aren't you?"

"You bet your ass. Are you going to do what I say?"

"Don't I look like an obedient child?"

"You look like your mother's daughter, a pain in the ass," he said. "You're also smart enough to do what's best."

"Okay, pops. You can drive me to school."

" 'Pops'?" he echoed, startled.

"You come on all parentlike, that's what you get," she said cheerfully. "Okay?"

"Christ," he grumbled. "Teenagers." And he followed her out of the diner, a reluctant grin on his face.

It had taken Rachel forever to get to sleep,

and when she finally did, her dreams were horrific. No secretly shameful erotic dreams about the bad boy — in these someone was chasing her, and she kept stumbling over dead women. Every time she turned to look at her pursuer his face changed. From David to Stephen Henry to Caleb. From her judgmental, fundamentalist father to Jared, who'd abandoned her, to all the faceless men she'd avoided over the years, only to make a mistake . . .

She woke up in a cold sweat, the dream still haunting her. She took deep, calming breaths, trying to shove away the sick, awful feeling that still lingered. Marrying David hadn't been a mistake — it had been the smart thing. For once in her life she'd done what her head had told her, not her heart.

She managed to push herself out of bed, moving across the polished hardwood floors to open the heavy linen curtains. The dull, gray day was like every other day, and she wanted to beat her head against the thick glass. And then she noticed that despite the darkness of the weather, it was later than she realized.

She looked back at the clock, and let out a shriek of panic. It was after ten — Sophie was due at school by eight. Grabbing her ancient silk kimono she slammed out of the room, calling Sophie's name.

The house was empty, all the lights off, making the place thick with gloom on such a dismal day, and she ran into the kitchen, ready to call everyone, including the National Guard, the FBI, the CIA, and the president himself until she was sure Sophie was safe.

There was a note by the phone. *Got a ride with Kristen's mom — going there this afternoon. Get some rest.*

She almost burst into tears of relief. She'd been an idiot, panicking over nothing. Despite Maggie's suspicions, Rachel knew that the killer was long gone, and her daughter was out of danger. In the cold, gloom of a northwest day her worries seemed ridiculous.

David had left for the day as well. She moved through the house, turning on the lights. Today she wasn't going to go anywhere. If by any strange miracle the sun actually came out then she could change her mind, but the chances of that happening seemed astronomically small, and she really couldn't stand the thought of going out into the rain one more time. After she showered and dressed, she'd go see what she could salvage of the disaster in the darkroom.

The adoption papers were lying on her worktable, prominently displayed with a pen right beside them. She picked them up, planning to scan them, then set them down again. Right now she didn't want to think about anything. She wanted to immerse herself in her work. There'd be time enough to deal with legalities later.

She only emerged from her studio once, to find something to eat. The message light was blinking, but before she pushed the button she picked up the phone to check caller ID. Two calls from David, one from the lawyer. They could wait.

It was late afternoon by the time she closed the door on her makeshift studio. The house glowed in the artificial light, but beyond the windows the darkness loomed. More messages. They could wait.

She was free for the next few hours. With luck, free for the rest of the night. David had said he'd be home late and he meant it — he usually didn't come in until long after she was asleep. She might be able to get through the entire day without seeing him.

And why did that suddenly seem so desirable? She could blame Caleb for putting those doubts in her mind. Caleb, who tortured animals and taunted his brother, who was driven out of town and whose occasional return was barely tolerated. Caleb the monster.

Except that he didn't seem like a monster. In truth, he seemed like someone who didn't bother to hide who he was, daring people to accept him or not. He clearly didn't give a damn. Unlike David, who went out of his way to charm people, who'd twice been voted the most beloved professor on campus, a fact that had rankled Stephen Henry no end until he decided they weren't considering professors emeriti, he'd informed her.

Suddenly the yogurt lunch began to feel meager indeed, and she wanted, no, she needed another In-N-Out burger, a double order of fries, a Diet Coke, with a chocolate milkshake on the side, a total pig-out in the confines of her Volvo. Why hadn't she paid more attention to Caleb's route?

Well, because she'd been a little preoccupied with panic at the time. But once she'd driven it herself she'd have it memorized, and an In-N-Out burger could get her through a lot of long, dismal days.

She headed for her computer, but the site wasn't up-to-date, and there was no listing anywhere in the state of Washington. Now that she'd decided she had to have one there was no way she could just let it go. She had a fairly good sense of direction, and despite the fact that it had been dark and she'd been an idiot, she could probably find her way back if she just trusted her instincts.

Of course, if she had Caleb's cell-phone number she could simply call him and ask him. Though it would be a cold day in hell before that happened. Besides, Maggie probably had him behind bars.

She dashed out into the rain, locking the door behind her, and got into her car. She turned the key, listening to the motor turn over as the sound of freedom. Putting it into Reverse, she started to back out into the street.

Someone was coming, and she put her foot on the brake. The pedal went straight to the floor, and she went careening backward, straight into the middle of the road, directly in the path of an oncoming SUV.

She slammed the car into Drive and gunned the motor, praying that the transmission still worked. The Volvo shot forward, jumping the curb and tearing up the manicured front lawn until it came to a stop at the trunk of an aging apple tree, snapping it in two.

She reached out with shaking hands and turned off the motor, then tried to pull the key out. It was stuck, until she realized she was still in gear. She shoved it into Park, yanked the key out and sat there, trembling, as the rain poured down around her.

She didn't know how long she stayed there. Someone rapped at the window, and she turned, dazed, to see a dark, hooded figure looming over her.

Panicked, she fumbled for the locks, but it was already too late, the door was opening and hands reached for her, pulling her out, out into the darkness.

"What happened?" Caleb demanded, shoving the rain hood away from his face.

It's all right, she told herself. *People are nearby, it's not that late, he's not going to hurt me.*

"My brakes failed," she said.

"That shouldn't have happened. This is a new car, isn't it?" His face was unreadable in the darkness.

"Yes."

"You need to have it looked at. I've already called a tow truck."

The panic was finally receding. "Well, yeah, I kind of think so, considering my new car is now sitting in the middle of my yard," she said. "I can't very well drive it like that."

"I'm not talking about just fixing it. You need to find out what went wrong. If someone cut the brake lines."

"Why the hell would someone do *that?*"

"You tell me," he said, his voice dark. "All I know is that brakes don't suddenly fail, not in a town where a serial killer has been active."

"The killer is gone."

"You sure of that?" he said.

"You know I can't be sure of anything. But there's no earthly reason why anyone would want to hurt me."

He looked at her like she was an idiot. "Maybe not that you can think of. Sometimes people don't need reasons. I told you . . ."

"Yes, I know what you told me. But the fact is, the only person I'm afraid of around here is you." The moment the words were out of her mouth she wished she could have called them back. Not that it wasn't the simple truth. Not that she was worried about hurting his feelings. Simply because she didn't want him to know how deeply she distrusted him.

He said nothing, looking down at her. "Where were you going? And where's Sophie?"

"A. None of your business. B. None of your business."

"A. She's my niece and I'm worried about her. I want to make sure she's safe. B. I'm a

275

nosy bastard. So why don't you answer my questions since I saved your life."

"What do you mean, you saved my life?"

"If you hadn't been trying to dodge me you might have found out your brakes were gone once you were on the highway. If that was where you were heading."

"How convenient that you just happened to show up at the right time."

"What's that supposed to mean?"

"Never mind," she said stiffly. "I'm not making any sense. If you'd been out to hurt me you wouldn't have waited around and then rescued me, if this can be called a rescue. Unless you had second thoughts."

"I don't waste my time with second thoughts. I do what needs to be done. Are you going to answer my questions?"

"Right. Sophie is spending the night at Kristen's house — I asked Maggie to keep her there. It's the only place I think is safe nowadays, thanks to you."

"What do you mean by that?"

"You've got me suspecting murder everywhere I turn. I don't even trust my husband completely anymore. So you've won. You've taken what David wanted."

His eyes narrowed. "I don't give a shit about David, as long as you and Sophie are safe," he said, and she almost believed him.

"So if you weren't on your way to get her, where were you going?"

She didn't want to tell him. Wasn't going to, except her reluctance annoyed her. "I was headed out to find the In-N-Out Burger place."

He stared at her. "That's way over in Monasburg."

"I had a craving."

For a moment she was actually able to shut him up. "Not the best actual diet," he said after a moment.

"I get plenty of healthy food when I eat with David. Every now and then one needs a little variety. Things don't always have to be good for you."

"I've been trying to tell you the very same thing," he said in a low, seductive voice. "Since your daughter's out and presumably David's not around, why don't you come back to my place with me? I can't feed you burgers but I can distract you with other things that aren't good for you."

"Give it a rest, Caleb. I'm going back inside and locking the doors and calling a tow truck. I'll be just fine without fast food or . . . or you. I don't like you. I wish you'd go away — you make everything worse."

"And just how do I do that? My father's delighted to see me, David professes to feel the same, your daughter adores me. How do I manage to alienate you so thoroughly when I'm just doing my best to be a good brother-in-law?"

"You're about as good a brother-in-law as Jack the Ripper."

"Ah, but we don't know if Jack ever married or had siblings. It would be very interesting if he had a brother. How do you think the brother would feel, knowing he'd grown up with a monster? Do you think he tried to stop him? Or did he follow in his footsteps?"

She turned, reached in her car for her purse and then slammed the door, giving herself time to recuperate. "You know how you keep telling me to go away? Why don't you take your own advice? Why don't you get back in your car and drive the hell away from here? You're nothing but trouble."

"I've been told that all my life, and it hasn't stopped me yet. I tell you what. You agree to take Sophie and leave and I'll get out of here myself. Leave town and your husband and my father will get by on their own. Wouldn't that make life a lot simpler?"

"I'm not going anywhere."

He stared down at her, and she could sense the anger simmering beneath his dark expression. And then something seemed to snap. "Yes, you are," he said, and before she realized what he was doing he'd scooped her up, slapping a hand over her mouth, and started dragging her toward his waiting car.

She tried to scream, but his hand muffled the sound. She bit his hand, but he didn't even flinch as her teeth clamped down hard enough to draw blood. He managed to yank open the door of his Toyota long enough to throw her inside, then shoved in after her. "Put your seat belt on," he growled.

She was already fumbling with the door handle. He grabbed her wrists in one hand, holding them so tightly it hurt, as he put the car in gear. "You fight me and you just might end up killing us both. I'm trying to save your fucking life."

"Right. You do that by kidnapping people and torturing animals."

"I never tortured any animals," he said in a tightly controlled voice.

"Then what was Maggie talking about? She doesn't make things like that up." His fingers were like iron around her wrists, and she tried to bend over to bite him again, but he simply yanked her upright.

"She didn't make it up, she just didn't have the right person. I didn't torture birds, set fire to cats, hang my dog . . ."

"Stop!" she said, gagging.

"Oh, Christ. You're not going to puke again, are you?"

She managed to swallow the bile that rose in her throat. "If you didn't, then who did?"

"Who do you think, Rachel? Your sweet, angelic husband who's so sensitive he won't even eat meat that someone else has butchered. If you're wondering who the budding sociopath in the family was, you're looking in the wrong direction. Just as everyone else in this fucking town did. Now settle down and stop fighting me, or I swear to God I'll clock you one."

She glared at him. He was crazy, he was a bully and a liar. His hatred for his younger brother had clearly put him over the edge.

He was also much stronger than she was, and he already had her at a disadvantage. "Okay," she said with deceptive calm. "If you'll tell me where you're taking me."

"Somewhere that my brother can't get to you. Long enough to talk some sense into you. Are you going to stop fighting me?"

He was focusing on the dark, rain-slick road, and in the reflection of the streetlights his face looked almost frightening.

He was going too fast for her to jump out of the car. She forced herself to breathe slowly, trying to look at him objectively, and

280

as she did, she calmed. He might be batshit insane, but he wasn't going to hurt her. Totally deluded, but he wasn't the Northwest Strangler. Of that, at least, she was sure.

"I'll stop fighting you," she said. Wondering if she'd just made the worst mistake of her life.

15

David came back late. Rachel's car was gone, and he smiled smugly, until he noticed the tire tracks in the lawn. He let out a moan of pain, parking his car and stumbling over to the damaged apple tree. The trunk was split in half — in a matter of months, maybe sooner, it would be dead. He knelt down on the muddy lawn, tears in his eyes as he touched the dying tree. The loss of its perfection seared his soul.

It was her fault. He'd brought her into his life, with her exquisite daughter, sure that she would adapt, become a graceful complement while he watched Sophie blossom and mature. He'd been so sure it would fill that dark, empty hole inside him.

It hadn't. She was too bright, too brash, her colors clashing with his muted palate, her music ripping through the calm of his house. She stood between him and Sophie, thwarting him, when she'd promised to love and obey him. They hadn't used those words in the judge's office in San Francisco, but she knew they were implied.

Instead she'd taken over his house, turning his breakfast room into a studio for her silly photography, she'd put bright scarves over the furniture in her bedroom, and she used crude language in front of her angelic daughter. He thought she'd be reasonable. Instead she was a disaster.

But he was a man who knew how to deal with disaster, he reminded himself, brushing away his tears as he rose from his muddy spot on the ground, keeping his eyes averted from the ruin of the lawn. She refused to even look at the adoption papers, she kept coming between him and Sophie, when clearly Sophie adored him. The answer had been beautiful in its simplicity.

His brother had returned. His brother, who had always taken everything David had ever wanted. When Caleb was around, no one would look twice at David. Even the stray mutt he'd picked up would whine and cringe when David came near it. He'd taken care of that, of course.

The girls as well. Caleb had an unerring instinct for picking the girls that David would have fallen in love with. It was cosmically unfair — he never realized he loved them until Caleb would bring them around. And he'd made them pay. But Caleb had haunted him all his life. Even his mother had preferred the stranger to her own flesh-and-blood son.

He'd dealt with that as well. It had been Caleb's fault, of course. If it weren't for him he never would have had to do the terrible things he did.

And in truth, only the ignorant ones would think his actions were terrible. He understood his choices, understood his needs and his calling, and he needed no approval from anyone. True visionaries always had to go it alone, and he preferred it that way.

She didn't double lock the door when she left. Every light in the house was on. He stripped off his muddy clothes and shoes, double locked the door and moved through the house, methodically turning off lights. He could see very well in the dark — he'd trained himself, since so much of his most important work took place in the dark. The bright electric lights hurt his eyes. He went to the kitchen last, and as he flicked off the lights the bright red glare of the blinking light on the answering machine assaulted him.

She'd never checked the messages. He

pushed the button and deleted each one, pausing long enough to admire the smoothness of his tone. He frowned at the lawyer's voice. Blanchard was being far too conscientious — he didn't need to talk to her. He'd made her wishes clear himself — enough that it should hold up in court.

The final message from Maggie Bannister was the best. The car had been towed to the local impound, and it was clear the brakes had been tampered with. But he hadn't touched them.

It was typical of Caleb, always trying to outdo his younger brother. He must have thought that David loved her, as he'd loved those girls Caleb had brought home. It served his purpose beautifully, whatever his brother's reasons were.

But really, it was all falling into place so beautifully that he knew it was meant to be. There was no proof, not even enough to suspect David of the things he'd done. He'd been far too careful. He was invulnerable.

But Caleb wasn't nearly as smart. He would have left some trace behind, and that would be enough to convict him. Particularly once Rachel was dead.

He went outside to mourn his apple tree.

Caleb kept a close eye on her as he drove.

As long as he kept his speed up she wouldn't try anything — she wouldn't want to hurt the baby. She seemed to have given up fighting for the time being — maybe she was finally beginning to realize just how big a mess she was in.

He couldn't count on it. Sophie was safely out of the way, staying at the sheriff's house. That couldn't have worked out better if he'd planned it, and it must infuriate David. Maggie Bannister was a levelheaded woman — she might not trust him further than she could throw him, but she didn't trust David, either. She was smart enough to look beneath the surface of everything, including Stephen Henry Middleton, Professor Emeritus.

He'd taken a chance last night when Maggie had questioned him. He'd half expected her to push him into a chair at the police station and shine a bright light in his face.

"Have a seat, Caleb. Can I get you some coffee?" She'd been businesslike, pleasant, but he didn't make the mistake of relaxing.

"I'm fine," he said, taking the seat at the table. There were U-shaped iron hooks there, presumably to lock onto handcuffs. Normally he'd think that was overkill in a sleepy little town like Silver Falls. But not now.

Maggie took the seat opposite him, her gray eyes seeing everything he didn't want her to see. "So why don't you tell me why you came back home this week? You've only stayed here one or two nights at the most in the last twenty years, according to David. Suddenly you've moved back in, ready to take your place in Silver Falls society at the same time a serial killer shows up, and I'm wondering if that's a coincidence. Because I have to tell you, Caleb, I don't believe in coincidences."

"Maybe after twenty years I was getting homesick. Time to revisit my roots."

"Maybe," she said. "Or maybe you had another reason. When did you hear David got married?"

Why the hell was she asking that question? He couldn't very well lie — it would be too easy for her to find out. In fact, his best bet would be to tell the truth as much as possible. Easier that way. "Last week. Stephen Henry sent me the announcement from the paper. I've been trying to forget about this town, so I'd purposely steered clear of any word of it online or off."

"So you decided to come home. Wasn't that short notice for the press service you work for?"

He wasn't surprised she knew about his

job — Maggie Bannister was a thorough woman. She probably knew his boss's name, the names of the last three women he'd slept with, how much he weighed and what his favorite brand of beer was. "I've worked for them for a long time and I'm a valued asset. They want to keep me happy and I wanted to come home. To meet my new sister-in-law, of course," he added.

"Did you know she had a young daughter?"

"No."

"Were you worried about something?"

He stared at her, stone-faced. He had to be very careful what he said. If he tipped his hand everything could blow up and there'd be no way to stop the nightmare that had been haunting him for so many years.

"What would I have to be worried about, Maggie?" he said, stretching his legs out in front of him. "Are you worried about something?"

"I've had one senseless murder and another corpse show up in my town, and the FBI is calling them serial killings. What do you think?"

"What do you want from me?"

"The truth," she said, her voice flat.

He was almost tempted. He needed to stop David, by any means possible. The best of all possible outcomes would be to get him locked away, where he couldn't hurt anyone.

But that wasn't going to happen until they found more proof. David was smart and cunning. He'd have to screw up big-time to let that happen.

The good news was that he had started making mistakes. But people were still dying, and Caleb couldn't let that happen. He'd turned a blind eye to the unthinkable for too long.

His mother had wanted him to look out for David. She'd known David was damaged goods, and Stephen Henry did, too. The difference was that her husband was happy to throw his older son to the wolves, just to protect David.

Caleb couldn't let that happen any longer, not with the stakes so high. If Maggie couldn't find proof in the next couple of days then Caleb would have no choice but to do the unthinkable.

Stop David himself. By any means possible.

He looked across the desk at the sheriff. Underestimating Maggie Bannister was a mistake a lot of people made, but he wasn't a lot of people. In the end, he had to put a stop to David.

He leaned forward. "I'll tell you one thing, Maggie. You should keep Sophie at your house until this is over. Don't let her go home, don't let her go out without you and your daughter. I don't care what kind of excuse you have to make, just don't let her go home."

She didn't blink. "And that's all you're going to say? I'll listen, you know."

He leaned back. "That's pretty much it."

She looked at him for a long time, her eyes searching his face. "What about Rachel?" she asked suddenly. "Don't you think she's going to put up a fuss if I keep Sophie?"

"I think you're smart enough to figure out a way to convince her."

"But you *don't* think I'm smart enough to have a pretty good guess what's really going on?"

For the first time in his life someone in the claustrophobic little town of Silver Falls looked ready to believe him. "You tell me," he said.

She shook her head. "When you decide to be honest with me I might return the favor. In the meantime I'll look after Sophie. You keep an eye on Rachel. I don't want to lose anyone else."

It was as close to a declaration of trust as he could have hoped for. "I won't let anything happen to her."

And Maggie had nodded, satisfied.

Of course she hadn't expected him to sabotage Rachel's brakes and then haul her out into the wilderness by force. Chances were a law enforcement officer like the sheriff wouldn't approve, but then, he'd never been one to do what was expected of him.

He shifted the Toyota into low as the road grew muddier. Rachel had her arms across her chest, her face averted, and she was radiating anger. Maybe he should be glad that she was such a fighter — it had probably kept her alive so far and would continue to do so. But for now it was annoying the hell out of him.

She was the one to break the charged silence. "I don't suppose you let your brother know you carted me off like a sack of potatoes?"

"How much do you want to bet he already knows?"

She didn't respond to that one. "Sophie," she said, her voice thick with tension. "I need to make sure Sophie is okay."

"Sophie's with Sheriff Bannister, and she'll stay with her until this is over."

She turned to look at him. "Why?" she demanded.

"You know why," he said in an even voice. "You just don't want to admit it. Sophie's not going back to that house and neither are you."

She exploded. "Don't be ridiculous! If you're trying to tell me that David is some kind of serial killer, then you're wasting your breath. You've barely seen him during the last twenty years — I've been living with him for the last four months. David wouldn't hurt a fly."

"Maybe not. But he'd hurt you." They'd reached a deserted stretch of road, and he slowed, looking for the turn.

"What kind of proof do you have? I'd trust him a hell of a lot more than I'd trust you!"

"I know. Which is why I kidnapped you." He took a sharp right, heading down the rutted road. "He's not going to have time to find you — he's going to be too busy try-ing to frame me."

"Oh, I forgot, you're the poor innocent and David's the sociopath," she said, her voice rich with scorn. "Where the fuck are you taking me?"

He almost wanted to smile at her use of David's forbidden word. "As far away as I can drive in one night. I'll dump you some-where that David can't find you and then come back here and finish this."

"Dump me or my body?"

"You're pissing me off."

"Why? Because I don't like being dragged off in the middle of the night? Because I don't trust you? Because I sure as hell don't like you!" Her voice was getting stronger as her fear was fading.

Good. Because he didn't want her frightened of him, not when he was the only thing that stood between her and death.

"Now that's a lie," he drawled. "Your problem is you like me too much and you're feeling guilty about it."

"Oh, please!"

"David knows. He's always been able to figure people out. He would have known the moment he found us outside my father's kitchen door that you were attracted to me. And he's done everything he can to foster it." He glanced at her. "Haven't you figured that out yet?"

"The only thing I've figured out is that you're batshit insane."

"You've got the wrong brother."

"I'm *with* the wrong brother," she said. "And if you think I'm going anywhere without my daughter you're even more deluded than you appear to be."

"You're here, aren't you?" He pulled the car to a stop and killed the lights.

"And exactly where is here?"

"Bates Motel," he said.

"What?"

He turned off the motor and slid from the car. "That's just what we call it. This was supposed to be the route the state road took, and years ago someone built a motel here. Then someone paid someone off, the highway got rerouted, and the motel closed."

"Great. And now Norman Bates wanders around dressed like his mother . . ." She looked at him. "That reminds me. Where is your mother buried?"

"Damn, woman," he said, opening her door. She sat there, furious and unmoving. "You're really trying to get on my nerves. Good thing you didn't try it with David — you'd be dead already."

"Your brother is not a rapist and murderer," she said in the flat voice of absolute certainty.

He reached over and unfastened her seat belt. She hit at him, trying to stop him, but he simply hauled her out of the car, ignoring her struggles. "And you know that . . . how?"

"I just know. And if you think I'm going with you into the creepy place you're out of your mind."

"Haven't you figured out that you don't have any choice?" he countered. He clamped a hand on her wrist. He didn't want to risk hurting her or the baby, but keeping her alive came first.

The sign for the Sleeping Bear Motel had long ago faded, the neon tubes burst by kids throwing rocks. The place really did look like something out of *Psycho,* but the Silver Falls police used it as a safe place to stash people. Material witnesses, abused wives and girlfriends, runaway kids whose parents might be worse than the streets — the motel had seen them all. If it weren't for his connections he wouldn't have known about it. People steered clear of the place, and David didn't know it existed.

"I'm not going in there," Rachel said, pulling back.

She was far from a lightweight, and scooping her up was no easy task, but years of rough living had made him strong enough to deal with one hundred and thirty pounds or so of squirming female. Hard to unlock the door at the unit on the end, but he managed, turning the knob and kicking it open.

The musty smell spilled out — the place hadn't been used for a long time. He crossed the room, dumped her on the double bed and then shut the door behind them, bolting and locking it before turning on the lights.

It looked both better and worse than he'd expected. The place was clean enough — just a thin layer of dust on the rabbit-ears television which was probably black and white, and the bedspread looked like something out of the 1950s. The angry woman sitting in the middle of it was the anomaly, and for a moment he didn't move, looking at her.

Thank God she was pregnant. Because otherwise he'd be hard put to keep his hands off her. Though she'd probably clobber him if he tried. He had to be as crazy as his brother to even notice how attracted he was . . .

Hell, that wasn't it. It wasn't lust pure and simple. Or not so pure, and definitely not so simple. Because he didn't just want to fuck her absolutely ripe, luscious body. He wanted her quick mind and quicker tongue. He was drawn to her as he'd never been drawn to anyone before, and all he could think was maybe Stephen Henry was right after all and he'd just been deluded. Maybe he was obsessed with her because she was David's.

Except that he'd had no interest in the meek college librarian David had been dating the last time he came to town. Or the physics teacher several years before.

But Rachel was a different thing altogether, and even looking at her was making him hard.

"You got a problem?" she snarled. "Did I grow another head or something?"

He turned away, pulling the threadbare curtains and the blackout shade. "Just thinking about something else," he said. Which was true enough. He was thinking about how he could justify touching her, kissing her after he'd kidnapped her, and he was coming up empty.

"So you think I'm just going to do what you say and stay here?" she said when he turned back.

"Well, I could always tie you to the bed. I'd certainly enjoy it, but I don't know how happy that would make you. If you leave you'll have a long walk in a deserted part of the country, and there are bears."

"Don't try to scare me," she snapped. "In case you haven't figured it out yet, I don't scare easy."

"You ever hear the term 'foolhardy'?" he said.

"You ever hear the term 'fuck you'?"

"Do you ever stop fighting?"

"Never," she said, and dove for the door.

He caught her before she could unfasten the chain, spinning her around and pinning her against the solid pine. "I told you not to do that," he said. He was too close to her, his body pressed up against hers, and he knew he was in deep trouble. He had to fight it, to get the hell away from her before he made a big mistake.

"Haven't you figured out I don't listen?" she said, looking at him out of steady eyes.

He didn't move. Neither did she. They stayed the way they were, pressed up against the door, and he could feel her heart pounding against his through the layers of clothing, and what he saw in her eyes was nothing but wishful thinking on his part, he was crazy, but he was going to kiss her anyway, just kiss her, because he wanted to and what the hell difference would it make?

So he lowered his head and put his mouth against hers.

16

He had her pinned against the door of this shit motel, Rachel thought. And if she had any sense she'd bring her knee up hard enough to send him screaming to the floor, and she'd get enough of a head start. She could even hot-wire his car if he didn't leave the keys in there, and if she couldn't she could disappear into the woods and to hell with the bears, and then he lowered his head and she thought, *if he doesn't kiss me I'm going to die.*

And he did. His mouth covered hers, rough, demanding, and she broke her arms free enough to put them around his waist, pulling him closer, while she kissed him back.

It was heaven. It was hell. It was slipping into a darkness so deep and rich that she never wanted to emerge. She closed her eyes, to shut out the cold motel room, the glaring light, the reality of what she was doing, she just let herself feel the sensations of his lips, his tongue in her mouth, and she shivered, needing more, wanting more, her hands moving between them, sliding up to his shirt, pulling at the buttons.

He pulled away, so abruptly his shirt tore, buttons flying. He moved out of reach, a dark, unreadable look in his eyes.

She could reach behind her and unfasten the lock and it would take him too long to catch her. Or maybe he'd move fast enough and then he'd kiss her again and this time he wouldn't stop.

But she was smarter than that. She'd gotten caught up in the moment. Momentary insanity, that was it. "What in hell was that all about?" she demanded after a moment, trying to look affronted. "You really have to hit on all your brother's women?"

He ran a hand through his tangled hair. "That was mutual."

"The hell it was," she shot back, ignoring the simple truth of his statement.

"Are you in denial about everything? You're married to a monster, you're attracted to his brother, you're living a life you hate, trying to be someone you're not and never wanted to be. Does that pretty much sum it up?"

"And you're such an expert on me," she

said sweetly. "Why do you think you know anything at all about me?"

"Because I do. Because we're alike, you and I. We're wanderers, adventurers. Neither of us belong in a dead town with no sunshine, trapped into playing a role that has nothing to do with who we are. Where are your parents? Why didn't they help raise Sophie?"

"None of your damned business!"

"They kicked you out, didn't they? You were the bad girl, just like I'm the black sheep. You've been wandering, looking for a home, and you found the wrong one."

"What if I told you my parents were dead, but they'd never been nothing but loving and supportive of me and Sophie?"

He looked at her for a moment, considering. "I'd tell you you were lying," he said.

And she didn't lie, not if she could help it. Not to him. "At least my brother isn't a sociopath," she snapped. And then she realized what she'd just said, and the simple, inescapable truth of it was horrifying. "Oh, holy Christ," she moaned, sagging a little.

He was across the room in a flash, catching her, and there was concern, not lust in his eyes as he picked her up and put her on the bed. She wasn't used to being picked up. The sensation was oddly threatening and yet comforting at the same time. Almost erotic in the protective feel his body gave hers.

"It's not true," she said, turning away from him, burying her face in one of the limp pillows, breathing in the smell of dust and mothballs. It couldn't be true. But the moment the words had left her mouth she'd known.

She felt the sagging mattress give beneath his weight. He'd sat down beside her, all sexual threat vanished. "I know," he said. "I've spent most of my life telling myself that. I just couldn't keep lying to myself, knowing people might have died because I never said something, never pushed it to the edge to find out the truth."

She turned to look at him over her shoulder. "How long have you known?"

"Known for sure? A couple of days. Suspected? Since I was a child. I may have been the one blamed for torturing the animals, but I knew who'd really done it."

She shuddered. "It still doesn't make sense. Are you absolutely sure? Maybe I'm just reacting to your manipulations."

"You haven't signed the adoption papers. You must have a reason for that. I do know that it's made David very angry, and it's dangerous to make my baby brother angry."

She shook her head, still trying to take it all in. "You don't understand, he doesn't . . ." She couldn't bring herself to say it, so she simply wrapped her arms around herself, hugging tight. "Sophie's safe?"

"Sophie's more than safe. No one will get anywhere near her," he said. "I think Maggie Bannister suspects. Or at least she doesn't take everything at face value the way people have in the past. And for what it's worth, I don't really think David will hurt you. You're too precious to him."

"Precious? Hardly." Her ironic voice couldn't hide her pain. "I'm an assault to his nerves and the peaceful beigeness of his life. I still can't figure out why he married me."

"Can't you?"

Rachel closed her eyes. "Sophie," she said finally. "But he's never made advances, done anything icky. I just don't get the weird child-sexual vibe from him. He doesn't feel like a pervert."

"He's a serial killer who rapes his victims after he kills them. Just because he's not out to have sex with your thirteen-year-old daughter doesn't mean he's not a pervert. He's just waiting for her to get a little older."

"Please, stop," she said weakly. "I really

303

don't want to think about it. Besides, it doesn't make sense."

"Why would you think a sociopath would make sense?"

She rolled over on her back to look at him. "That's not what doesn't make sense. The killer rapes his victims. Your brother . . . has problems in that area."

"What kind of problems?"

God, did she have to spell it out for him? "He has a hard time with sex. He's not that interested in it. We've only managed to do it a few times. We only had sex once before we got married, and he was nervous then, so I didn't realize he had performance problems. I've been patient, waiting to work it out. So why would he rape dead women when he can barely manage with me?"

"Rape has nothing to do with sex," he said slowly, staring at her. "It's an act of anger and aggression."

"Against a dead woman? He's already killed her — what more does he need to prove?" This conversation was taking on a nightmare tinge — maybe she'd wake up in her own bed and find out she'd been having some hideous dream. Which would serve her right, for being inexplicably attracted to the one man she couldn't have.

"Total domination and destruction," he

304

said, almost absently. "But . . . if he can't get it up, then who's the father of your baby?"

"I didn't even know your brother fourteen years ago. Sophie's father is dead."

"I mean the one you're carrying."

She looked at him, simmering. "Are you telling me I'm fat?"

"What? No. But you're pregnant, aren't you?"

"No," she said.

He sat on the bed, staring at her, motionless. And then he dropped back beside her, almost touching her, and she edged away carefully. "Thank God," he said. "The thought of my brother reproducing is enough to give me chills."

"Why in the world did you think I'm pregnant?"

"You threw up. You had cravings. You . . . you . . . glow."

"Animal abuse makes me ill, In-N-Out burgers are worth craving, and I'm not radioactive. What do you mean, I glow?"

He turned his head to look at her. It was strange lying side by side on the bed, like two lovers on the sagging mattress. "Hell, I don't know — you just have this luminous quality about you. I thought it was hormones."

For some extremely bizarre reason she was feeling almost lighthearted. "You're probably right about that, but it's your hormones, not mine. You already told me I'm not your type, but clearly the stress of the situation is making you deluded."

"When did I say that?" He seemed astonished.

"The night we went to In-N-Out Burger."

"Well, I lied."

"No, you didn't. I'm definitely not the type of woman you get involved with."

"What do you mean by that? How do you even know what my type is?" He frowned at her.

"Just by looking at you. You like leggy blondes, right? Model-thin with muscles."

"No."

"All right, then you like petite brunettes, who are fragile and delicate."

"No," he said. "I like big, curvy redheads, who aren't afraid to fight back."

She stared at him, looking for lies, looking for trickery, looking for a hidden agenda. Either he was as much of a sociopath as his brother, or for some insane and unbelievable reason he really wanted her.

"Those are hard to come by," she said slowly.

"That's why you can't afford to let them

get away, just because the time isn't right or she's married to the wrong person. Whether it makes sense or not, whether the timing's right or screwed all to hell, you have to grab what feels right when you can, or the chance might not come around again."

"You're a liar."

"I am," he said. "About a whole lot of things. But not about this."

She didn't move. If she had half a brain she'd get off the bed, fast, before he could stop her. She'd try for the door, and if he didn't let her out she could always sit in the one straight-back chair the room boasted. Or she could sit cross-legged in a corner, as far away from him as possible.

If she had half a brain. "I'm your brother's wife," she said.

"You're married to a man who kills women for pleasure. Do you think you owe him anything?"

"I don't have any proof."

"You don't need proof," he said, sitting up and swinging his legs over the side of the bed. "You know it, deep inside. He's a sick fuck and you know it — you've just been afraid to look at things clearly."

"So I'm ready now. Take me home, I'll get Sophie and I'll get out of town."

"It's too late for that. He'll follow you.

You're safer here, where I can look out for you." He got off the bed, moving over toward the door. He'd hooked it with the chain when they'd first come in, but now he unfastened it. "There you go. If you want to risk it, want to go back to him, then I won't argue. Just keep Sophie away from him. You don't have the right to risk your daughter's life because you're being stubborn."

"All right." She got off the bed and headed for the door. He didn't move out of the way.

"I'm going back home," she said. Because she had to. If she stayed she was going to do something really stupid, something she hadn't done in years. She was going to sleep with the wrong man simply because she couldn't help herself.

Hell, maybe she'd never given in to this kind of overwhelming temptation. She couldn't even remember feeling this way. She had an iron will, and she wasn't easily swayed. Keeping Sophie safe had precluded romantic entanglements — she didn't want her daughter to have a series of "uncles," never knowing who she could trust, which one was a constant.

And now, suddenly, as the worst possible time in the world, she was ready to throw everything to the wind just to have him touch her again.

She was crazy, but not that crazy. "Open the door," she said.

He didn't move. "You can't go back to him. He's too dangerous."

"I haven't done anything wrong. He has no reason to want to hurt me — I'm not in any particular danger. I'll keep Sophie away until I find out the truth of what's going on. You're right — I can't risk her. But he's not going to hurt me."

He didn't move, looking at her out of narrowed eyes. "He knows you're attracted to me. Don't you think he'll see that as the ultimate betrayal?"

"No. Because I haven't done anything about it."

He moved then, turning his back to her, and she expected him to unlock the door. Instead he slid the chain back in place. "Then I guess we're going to have to do something about it."

She felt a fluttery little leap inside. "What do you mean by that?"

He leaned back against the door, reaching out and threading his long fingers through her curly hair, cradling her skull, pulling her closer. "I mean you won't go back to him if you've cheated on him. Which means you're going to cheat on him. Right now."

"I'm not —" His mouth silenced her. It

was a full kiss, hot and hungry. When he'd kissed her before he'd been holding back — not this time. Her body slid up tight against his, and there was no chance of her not kissing him back.

He could kiss like a devil, or maybe a saint. No one had ever kissed her like that, with such single-minded dedication and intensity, and she wanted to dissolve into the kiss, just drift away on a tide of sensuality. Her eyes closed, and she felt his hands on her shirt, unfastening the buttons.

Her eyes shot open. "No."

"Yes," he said, pulling her shirt free from her jeans, moving his mouth down the side of her neck, sinking his teeth into her earlobe, a move that sent sparks directly between her legs, and she moaned because she couldn't help it.

"No means no," she whispered, as he pushed the shirt from her shoulders.

"That's right," he said, reaching for the snap of her jeans. "No means no, except when the mother's life is in danger. Then all bets are off."

She needed to get it together, push him away, but it was too delicious. "You're getting your issues confused," she murmured. "We're talking rape, not abortion," she said as he moved his mouth down and kissed the swell of her breast above the lace. She heard the sound of her zipper, and it should have been enough to galvanize her into action. Instead it made her knees weak with longing.

"This is a very bad idea. It's wrong," she said, as he put his mouth against her navel, licking her skin so that she shivered.

"It's for your own good," he said, shoving her jeans down her hips, taking her panties with them. "Just close your eyes and think of England."

She opened her eyes at that. "Fuck you."

"Now you're getting the idea." He scooped her up and deposited her on the bed, pulling her jeans off her as she landed. "You can get under the covers if you're feeling shy, but we're doing this."

"We are not." She'd already pulled all the buttons off his shirt earlier, and he shrugged out of it, then reached for his belt buckle. She let out a little shriek and yanked the chenille bedspread around her. "Don't take your pants off!"

"It's a little tricky to manage if I leave them on," he said. "Not that I couldn't do it, but you'd really be more comfortable without my zipper rubbing against your thighs."

"I don't want any part of you rubbing

against my thighs," she said in a tight voice, trying to control the treacherous way her body was reacting. Even the enveloping chenille bedspread felt luscious, sensual.

"Sure you do," he said, kicking out of his jeans and getting on the bed with her. "You just won't admit it." He slid up next to her, pulling her cocooned body into his arms, and he let his lips feather across her stubborn mouth, his tongue touching the corners, teasing her.

She was having a hard time keeping her body rigid in protest. She'd told him no and he hadn't listened, she reminded herself, trying to drum up outrage. But his body felt too good up against hers.

He caught the edge of the bedspread with his hand, slipping his fingers beneath it, cool against her heated skin. "I tell you what. You can hate me. You can have me arrested. But you'll be alive, and that's all I care about." And before she realized what he was doing he'd pulled the bedspread away from her, wrapping his body in it as well, and he was kissing his way down her body, his mouth latching on to her breast, sucking it into his mouth so hard she arched up off the bed. The pleasure was so fierce she couldn't deny it anymore. She wanted, needed more, and when he moved to her other breast she almost came from the power of her response. Her deep, guttural groan filled the room, and she gave up, leaning back to give him better access to her shrouded body.

He put his wicked mouth between her legs, and she remembered that he'd said he would, and a tiny orgasm shook her body. He slid his long fingers inside her, and a more powerful one hit her, hard. He made it last, so long that she was sobbing, her fingers digging into his shoulders, clutching at him, as wave after wave shook her body, and before she could even begin to come down he pushed her legs apart, slid up and over her, and she could feel him, hard and heavy against her.

She slid her hand down his belly, wanting to touch him, wanting to wrap her fingers around his silken length, and he made a muffled sound of barely controlled need. It made no sense to fight this — she needed it too much, wanted it too much. It felt too damned good to stop, and she guided him to her, leaning back and lifting her hips for his deep, hard thrust.

She put her arms around his body, her face against his neck, lost in the feel and the scent, the sounds and the sensations, and she was trying to hold off, to keep from

313

coming. If she was going to be bad then she wanted to be really bad — she wanted it all, an orgasm so powerful her rational mind would disappear and there would be nothing but feeling, rich and powerful and wicked.

He'd wrapped the bedspread tight around them both, trapping her against his body, his cock inside her, the sensation was frustrating and delicious. She wanted to break free. She wanted to stay trapped forever. And her orgasm was coming closer, dancing along her nerve endings, making her tremble, and she didn't want to let go, didn't want this to end, but he was moving faster, deeper, harder, and she clutched the sheets beneath her, trying to hold on.

He put his mouth against her ear, his breath hot and moist. "Stop fighting, Rachel. Give it to me. Come for me. Come now." As his words filled her head his hand reached down between their bodies to touch her, hard, and she was lost. She screamed, for the first time in her life, as her body felt blown away into a million pieces. She felt him go rigid in her arms, and she knew he was there, too, and she thought about condoms, and she didn't care and all she wanted was him, inside her, around her, making up her entire world, so that she

314

could lose herself in him, in the feelings, in the desire that went hand in hand with love. . . .

That was enough to bring her back to earth with a thud. Stray tremors danced across her body, and he pulled away, turning his back to her for a moment.

"You used a condom," she said in a rough whisper.

He looked back at her. "Of course I did. What kind of man do you think I am?"

She pulled the bedspread around her, shivering slightly in the cool room. "The kind of man who forces his sister-in-law to have the best sex of her life even when she says no."

There was a faint grin on his brooding face. "Best of your life, eh?"

"I said no," she repeated, clinging to it.

"Yes, you did. And now you're ruined, you can never go back to your husband. Mission accomplished."

The faint chill grew worse. "Very noble sacrifice on your part," she said, trying to keep her teeth from chattering, trying to keep her emotions at bay.

He turned and smiled at her with such devastating sweetness that her defenses almost came crashing down. "I'm a helluva guy," he said. "Now this time let's do it

315

simply because we want to."

She started at him. "This time?"

"The night is young, and you've been haunting my dreams since I first saw you skulking around Stephen Henry's kitchen door. I want to fuck you any way you'll let me, and then I want to do it again. I want us to make love until we're too weak to move, sleep for a little bit, and then start all over."

"I don't think your brother's going to need further convincing."

"I don't give a shit about my brother. This one's for us." And he pulled the bedspread from around her, spreading it out so he could look at her in the shadowy light of the motel room. "Okay?"

"I think it's too late," she said gloomily. "I'm lost."

"I know you are," he said with a faint smile. "I am, too. Maybe we can find our way back together."

He was close, not moving, and she realized it was up to her. He wouldn't push it again.

So she rose on her knees with one fluid movement, slid her arms around his neck, pressed her naked breasts against his hard, smooth chest, and brushed her lips against his mouth, slowly, tantalizingly, until he grabbed her with a hungry growl and they fell back among the covers, rolling and tumbling with delight.

17

Taking a shower in the Bates Motel was probably not the smartest thing she ever did, but lying in bed with Caleb Middleton wasn't an option. Because if she had a choice she could have stayed there forever, and her life hadn't turned out that way. The rain-soaked light of day brought reality crushing back. She had responsibilities. She had Sophie. She had managed to drag her daughter into a mess so deadly and so complicated that they might not survive, and there was no way she could keep hiding away.

She should never have gone to bed with him. The awful truth was, he was right. One look into his dark, cynical eyes outside Stephen Henry's kitchen door and she'd fallen into some kind of crazy infatuation, and her marriage vows, her determination for a safe, ordered life, suddenly hadn't meant shit. If she had the choice, she'd grab Sophie and take off with Caleb and never look back.

But he hadn't asked. He'd been manipulating her since the moment he'd met her. He'd slept with her because it suited his agenda of keeping her away from David. She'd feel too guilty to go back to him, and Caleb had known it. Even if it turned out that David had nothing to do with the murders there was no way she could ever live with him again. Not after betraying him. Not after realizing what a stupid mistake she'd made in thinking she could make her life over in somebody else's mold.

Maybe it would be better if a crazy person came in and stabbed her in the shower. At least then she wouldn't have to think about it, wouldn't have to blame herself anymore.

The door to the bathroom opened, and through the cheap shower curtain she could see him. He pushed it out of the way and simply climbed into the tub with her. And then pulled her into his arms.

She hadn't even realized she needed it. One moment she was calmly dissecting the utter destruction of her safe new life, in the next she was sobbing in his arms, her body shaking, as he held her.

He said nothing, simply stroked her hair, her face, letting her cry. The kiss was comfort, nothing more. The second kiss was deeper, and she stopped crying. By the third kiss he had her pushed up against the cheap tile on the wall, as hungry as she was for more.

They moved without words, hands and mouths and bodies intertwining, stroking. She sank down on her knees in the narrow tub and took him in her mouth and he put his hands in her hair, holding her there for moments that she found unbearably arousing. He stopped her before she finished, pulling her up so that she straddled him, wrapping her legs around his waist, taking him deep inside, and it was slow and sweet and gentle, and when she came she cried.

He set her down carefully, and her knees were weak. She leaned back against the cheap wallboard and looked at him. And she saw the regret in his face, and she turned her own away, unable to look at him again.

Stephen Henry woke early, just past dawn, with a bad feeling about the day. David had come by late last night, his eyes glistening with pleasure, too excited to sit still, and there was no way Stephen Henry could ignore the foreboding. Things were going very well for David apparently. Which was seldom a good thing.

According to David, Rachel had run off somewhere with Caleb. Not that Stephen Henry could blame her. Caleb had that bad-boy charm that most women found irresistible. They found presumably safe men like David much too boring. Unfortunately they never knew just how unsafe David was capable of being.

It wasn't like Rachel to run off without letting anyone know. He'd watched her try to cram her larger-than-life personality into her role as faculty wife. She'd tried to tame her hair, her clothes, her voice, her behavior, but no one was fooled. She was too exotic for the likes of Silver Falls, Washington. She just didn't want to admit it.

She married the wrong brother. She belonged with someone like Caleb, always on the move, exploring new places, new things. And David had probably known it — that was why he'd chosen her. One more stab at his older brother.

But it appeared that David had pushed Caleb one step too far. Rachel's car had been sabotaged, and David said everything pointed to Caleb. He'd find that hard to believe if he didn't know that David was absolutely useless when it came to cars, and Caleb had loved them since he was sixteen and started rebuilding an old Corvette. The

Corvette had been destroyed in the garage fire, just as Caleb was finishing it. David had said all the comforting things. And hid the matches he'd used.

There was no peace with the two of them around. Caleb incited David to do horrible, horrible things. If he just stayed away then David could keep his impulses under control. Even if Rachel wasn't a perfect match for him, she gave him stability, a family. There might still be hope. He couldn't let his son be destroyed in front of his eyes, no matter how many hideous things he might have done. There was a chance he could still be saved.

But right now the forces of darkness were closing down on his family, and he couldn't see any way to get free from them.

One of his sons was going to die. And he had no idea how to stop it.

"I need to go home," Rachel said flatly. She wasn't sure where to look — not into his eyes, not anywhere near his face or his body. She felt vulnerable, ashamed, and the sooner she got away from him the better.

"That's not a good idea."

"I want to go home, pick up my daughter and get the hell away from this place and everyone here."

"Everyone?"

At that point she did look him at him, calmly, squarely. "Everyone," she said. "I want to forget this place ever existed. I never signed the adoption papers. I'll get an annulment or a divorce and move on with my life and forget about all of you."

"Are you sure you didn't sign those papers? David's a talented man. He had my handwriting down pat by the time he was twelve."

She fought against fear. "He'd need witnesses. A legal hearing of some sort."

"Don't underestimate my brother's charm. He knows how to get what he wants. Even if the adoption papers weren't signed it might turn out that you left a will."

She couldn't hide her stricken expression. "He wouldn't —"

"There's nothing he wouldn't do. And if I were you I wouldn't be in any hurry about the paperwork," he said, unmoved by her reaction. "You'd have to be in touch with David to do it, and the only way to be truly safe is for him not to know where you are. At least until things change."

He was right, and it pissed her off. "Well, hell, maybe I'll stay married to him until you can manage to get him convicted of murder. That way when they execute him I can get his pension from the college."

"I think they might put a stop to his pension considering he killed at least one student and two teachers."

"What?" She was too horrified to be annoyed.

"You don't need the details. Neither of them were ever seen again, and I'm not naïve enough to think that's a coincidence."

"That doesn't make sense. If he murdered other women he dated then why wouldn't he kill me?"

"Because they were tall and thin with long blond hair," he said simply.

"I don't even know if I believe you. I was stupid last night, scared and angry and upset, and you took advantage of me."

"Yes, I did. I took advantage of you this morning, too. I enjoyed it."

"I want you to take me home. Now!"

"I don't think that'll be necessary." He shoved a hand through his long dark hair.

"And just why not?"

"Because your husband and a police car just pulled up outside the motel, and I imagine they're going to crash into here, guns blazing, and rescue you."

She didn't move. "Do I need rescuing?"

"Not from me. You'd probably disagree. We don't have much time," he said, moving toward her, his previous laziness vanishing. "You need to listen to me. Don't believe what anyone tells you, even Maggie Bannister. There's more going on, and I had my reasons. Whatever you do, don't trust . . ."

The banging at the door drowned out whatever he was saying, and a moment later it slammed open. Not just Maggie and David, but two uniformed policemen with their guns drawn. As was Maggie's.

"Get away from him, Rachel," David said, with real fear in his voice. *"Don't let him touch you."*

Caleb took a step back, raising his hands in a mock gesture of helplessness. "What do you think I'm going to do to her?"

Maggie paid no attention. "Caleb Middleton, you're under arrest for the attempted murder of Rachel Middleton. Read him his rights, deputy."

Caleb held still as one of the beefy deputies came forward and put him into handcuffs. "Why aren't you charging me with the other murders, Maggie?"

"Because I don't have any proof yet," she said, her voice flat and emotionless. "I'm not charging you with anything that might not stick — I don't want a murderer walking free because I made a mistake."

"Is that what you think I am, Maggie?" he

said softly, ignoring the deputy's rote reading of the Miranda rules.

"I don't know what I think. I've got proof you sabotaged Rachel's car — fingerprints and a witness, and that should be enough to keep you for a while. You can deny it all you want."

"Oh, I don't deny it," he said, not looking at Rachel. "I cut her brake line."

It was like a blow to the stomach. She heard her own swift intake of breath, and then David was beside her, putting his arm around her, drawing her close. "Let me take you out of here," he said in his gentle, comforting voice. "I know what a shock this is. But he's managed to fool smarter women than you."

For a moment everything became cloudy, and all Rachel could think was, *fuck you, I'm as smart as any woman you ever met.* She caught Caleb's eye, by accident, and everything came back into focus. He was trying to tell her something, still manipulating her, and she turned her face into David's shoulder. "Take me out of here," she whispered.

She half expected Caleb to call out after her as they left the dingy hotel room. But there was nothing but the sound of Maggie's voice giving orders.

David settled her into the front seat,

solicitously, even bringing a cashmere blanket to wrap around her in the early morning chill. The foul smell that had plagued the BMW had finally vanished, replaced with the somewhat overbearing scent of laboratory-created roses, and she leaned back against the leather seat, closing her eyes, as David pulled away from the motel, back down the narrow, twisted road.

"How did you find me?" she asked in a low voice, not looking at him.

"Maggie called me to tell me about the accident. Fortunately one of the neighbors saw him hustle you into the car, so we knew he'd taken you, and there were only a couple of places he might have gone. Oh, Rachel, I was so frightened!" His voice was soft, earnest. "I was afraid we wouldn't get to you in time. I always thought this might happen, that sooner or later his control would snap. I'm just so sorry that I couldn't protect you."

Her eyes flew open, as his words sank in. "You think he's the serial killer? But he hasn't even been living here."

David reached his hand over to pat hers in a reassuring gesture, never taking his eyes off the narrow road. She let her hand lie still beneath his. "Maggie told me on the way over," he said. "The deaths in this country coincided with the times he was visiting, and there have been identical murders in the cities where he's lived over the past twenty years. I hate to tell you this, Rachel, but he was even in San Francisco six months ago."

Her stomach turned inside her. "You think he killed Tessa? Isn't that just too big a coincidence? That he chose a random victim who ended up connected to his sister-in-law?"

"It was no coincidence," David said. "I've been suspecting Caleb for years, too afraid to find out the truth. When I heard about Tessa I deliberately sought you out, to see if I could find any way to tie Caleb to the newest horror. But then I fell in love with you and Sophie, and it became even more important that I keep you safe."

Her head was spinning. None of this was making any sense, and David's soft, calm voice was making it worse. She wanted to scream at him to shut up, but she bit her lip. She just needed silence to work this out. She'd not only broken her marriage vows, she'd had sex with a serial killer. Several times. The very thought was revolting.

She forced herself to speak. "David, I have to tell you —" she began, her voice thick with horror and shame. "He wouldn't let me leave the room, and I —"

"Hush, love. You don't have to say it. Rape has always been part of his bag of tricks."

It would be an easy out, but she despised herself too much to take the easy way. "It wasn't rape. It was —"

"I don't need to hear it," he said calmly, drowning her out. "My brother can be very charming — that's how sociopaths get their way. Even if he didn't tie you down and force you, it was still rape."

She wanted to believe him. She wanted to be absolved, cleansed, forget it ever happened. But she could still feel Caleb's hands on her body, his mouth against hers, the rough tenderness of his touch. How could she have had the best sex of her life with a serial killer? Was she as twisted as he was?

"We'll get you back home where you can take it easy," he said in that same, soothing monotone. "Maggie will want you to make a statement at some point, but for now I think you can just rest. It's been a harrowing few days for you. I think you need Sophie with you as well. I'll go pick her up after I get you settled."

"No!" The objection was instant, irrational, irrefutable. She managed a weak smile. "I don't want her to see me like this. I'd feel much better if she stayed at Maggie's."

"But there's no need," he murmured, shooting a glance her way. "They've caught the killer — you and she aren't in any danger."

It didn't feel that way. Everything seemed upside down, twisted, and the buzzing in her head, David's soft drone, made it impossible to put it all in order.

"I want her with Maggie," she said stubbornly.

She expected anger, or at least that deep disappointment he sent her way far too often. Instead he nodded. "Of course, my love. Whatever gives you peace of mind. She can come back on the weekend. I don't know how the justice system works, but I don't think they'll be holding Caleb in town. There must be some kind of maximum-security prison where they keep the dangerous ones. As soon as they find enough evidence to charge him with the murders everything should be fine."

A shiver danced across her backbone, one she couldn't define. "But what if they don't? If he's gotten away with it for this long, why do you think he'd incriminate himself now?" she said, trying to stay calm when she wanted nothing more than to bury her face in her hands and cry.

It was starting to rain, and David turned

on the windshield wipers before he spoke. "He's been losing control, Rachel. He always used to kill sparingly — years would pass between his crimes. He had perfect timing. He'd wait until I came to visit before acting. He was passing through San Francisco on his way to the far east when we met for dinner. That was the night Tessa died."

"Oh, God."

"I blame myself," he said, his voice solemn as he pulled out onto the main road. "There's some deep kind of anger that runs inside him, and I bring it out, no matter how hard I try to show him I love him. There's something wrong with him, something deeply twisted, and there was nothing any of us could do to fix it, to help him."

"What if they can't find any more proof? What if he gets out on bail? And comes back here, where Sophie is, and —"

"That's not going to happen. Maggie will find the box of souvenirs hidden somewhere up at his house, and that will tie him to every murder. And then, no matter what he says, he'll be convicted of thirty-seven counts of murder, and they'll execute him. Do you know they still hang people in the state of Washington? I'd have to go, of course, just so he knows that someone who still loves him is there, but the idea horrifies me." There was an undercurrent in his voice, one she couldn't identify.

"Thirty-seven? He's killed *thirty-seven* people?" Rachel cried.

For a moment David looked confused. "I don't have any real idea how many he's killed. That was simply a guess. When they find the souvenirs they'll find the number."

"What souvenirs?" She was no longer slumping in her seat. Her critical mind was beginning to take over, and this was feeling just too wrong. "How do you know about souvenirs?"

"It's been in the papers, Rachel," he said gently, as if explaining to a small child. "His victims all have long, blond hair, and they wear barrettes. Apparently they're always missing when a body is discovered, and it's been surmised that he's been keeping them. That's what serial killers do, you know. They like remembrances of the horrific crimes they commit."

"I'm afraid I'm not particularly well-versed in what serial killers do," she said, her voice getting stronger.

"I know you haven't been reading the papers, my love." He voice was solicitous. "I don't blame you. I can tell you anything you need to know. They simply have to find the barrettes and they'll have an open and shut case. Means and opportunity. As for motive — a serial killer doesn't need a motive. Though Caleb had one, illogical as it was. He was trying to frame me. He's always been jealous of me, and childhood with him was a living hell. My parents tried to protect me, but they didn't want to throw poor Caleb to the wolves. My mother paid with her life for that."

They were finally back at the house. He pulled into the driveway and turned off the car. Rachel looked around her. She could see the deep grooves her tires had made in David's perfect lawn, the split apple tree where her car had ended. All proof that this wasn't a hideous dream.

He hadn't denied it. He'd been right there, waiting for her after he'd tried to kill her. If Maggie and the police hadn't shown up who knows what might have happened? She might be one more murder victim at the Bates Motel.

No, that wasn't right. The strangler raped his victims post-mortem. And what had happened in that hotel was a far cry from rape, no matter what David said.

She got out of the car before David could come around to open the door for her. She thought she'd be unsteady on her feet, but the ground was firm beneath her, and the rain had stopped again. At least for the moment. The clouds were thick overhead, and it was only a matter of time before the darkness descended again.

"You go in and rest, Rachel. I'll bring you a cup of tea before I go tell my father what's happened. Do you want any lunch?"

She shook her head, every muscle in her body tight with her last effort at self-control. "Don't worry about me. I can get my own tea if I want any. You're right, you'd better go talk to Stephen Henry."

"He'll be devastated," David said solemnly. "We've both been expecting this, both hoping we were wrong."

From somewhere in the depths of her fast-draining reserves she managed to drag forth a smile. "You go see him. Give him my love. I think I'll just go to bed."

He came around the car and kissed her on the cheek, soft lips, so different from Caleb's hard ones. "We'll get through this," he murmured. "Just sleep." He brushed the hair away from her face, and unaccountably, she shuddered.

A moment later he was gone, and suddenly she could breathe again.

She went into the house, kicking off her muddy shoes, double locking the door behind her, moving through the muted darkness to her bedroom, leaving the lights off. She should call Sophie, just to make sure she was all right. Though in Maggie Bannister's house, how could she not be?

She could also be reasonably sure that Sophie never knew she'd been missing. Maggie would have seen to that.

Besides, she was probably on her way to school right about now. There was no need to alarm her. She'd take a nap — she was bone tired and not up to facing anything. This afternoon would have time enough.

She almost took another shower, just to wash his touch off her skin, but the idea reminded her of what had gone on under the stream of water, and she couldn't stand to think about it. It was going to be baths for a while, until she could stop thinking of him. Of what he'd done. Of what she'd done.

But right now it was bed. She stripped off her clothes and dumped everything in the trash, even her underwear.

She grabbed another pair of panties and a tank top, and all she could think of was Sigourney Weaver in *Alien,* blasting the bad guys. She climbed under the covers, pulling them up around her ears, and closed her eyes. She still wanted to talk to Sophie, to make sure she was all right, but just then she couldn't bring herself to do it. Sophie would be heartbroken — she'd been charmed by David's psychopath brother, as he'd meant her to be. The thought that she might have been his next victim was so horrifying that she almost bolted from the bed.

Empty your mind, she told herself.
Sophie's safe, everyone's safe.
Nothing bad will happen. It's all right.
Everything's all right.

And she closed her eyes and slept.

Sophie heard the rumors in fifth period. They weren't talking loud enough for her to hear, but the odd looks cast her way, the sudden silences when she got close to classmates tipped her off that something was really wrong.

There were strict rules about using your cell phone in school. You were supposed to turn them off, but Sophie simply put hers on vibrate. Her mother had taught her early on that following rules and doing what was expected of you could lead to disaster, and the moment she could she slipped into the handicapped bathroom, the only private place in the entire building, and dialed her mom.

No answer, and her mother's cheerful

voicemail prompt should have reassured her. It didn't. She tried David's house, but the phone kept ringing, the answering machine never picked up. Then she did what she should have done in the first place — called Caleb's phone. But that was turned off. Something bad had happened, something very bad, and she wasn't going to calculus and pretend everything was cool.

She waited until she heard the bell ring and she knew the halls would be empty, and then she opened the door. To find Kristen waiting for her.

"I saw you go in there," she said, her voice as flat and no-nonsense as her mother's. "What did you hear?"

"Nothing. But I know something's going on. No one's answering their phone, and everyone's giving me funny looks."

"They arrested your uncle for murder. They think he's the Northwest Strangler."

"My . . . what? You mean Caleb? That's crazy!"

"Not according to my mother. Actually he got busted for trying to kill your mother — he cut the brake line on her car. They haven't been able to tie him to the other killings yet, but that's just a matter of time."

"That's impossible," Sophie said flatly. "I don't believe it."

"For what it's worth, neither does my mother, but she says there's nothing she can do. He came right out and admitted he'd tampered with your mother's car. He hasn't confessed to the killings yet but that comes next." Kristen hiked up her heavy backpack. "At least it means we're safe."

"No, it doesn't," Sophie said. "Caleb didn't kill those women. I don't care what he said about the car, I know he's not a killer. The M.O. is completely different."

"Then who is?"

"You wouldn't believe me," she muttered.

"Try me."

"It's —"

"*What* are you two young ladies doing, standing in the hall and gossiping when you should be in class?" Mrs. Wenberg, the scourge of eleventh grade, loomed up. And then her eyes narrowed as she recognized Sophie.

"Oh, it's you, dear," she said. "I'm so sorry about your troubles. Perhaps you might like to go to the guidance counselor. Miss Bannister, you may accompany her." She pulled out her omnipresent pad of pink paper and scribbled on it, tearing a page off with a well-practiced flourish and handing it to Kristen. "This should keep the hall monitors from bothering you. You take care of her, Miss Bannister. Stay with her until someone can come pick her up."

"But no one's supposed to . . ." Kristen began, but Miss Wenberg had already strode off, in search of other miscreants.

"Come on," Sophie said, plucking the pink slip from Kristen's hand. She headed straight for the side door, the one that led through the parking lot. It was at the back of the old brick building with few windows overlooking it — no one would see her leave.

"Where do you think you're going?"

"I'm going to see what the hell is going on. I know perfectly well that Caleb didn't kill anyone, and if he sabotaged my mother's car he would have had a damned good reason for doing it."

"Let me go back and get our jackets," Kristen said.

Sophie shook her head. "You're not coming with me. You know your mother would kill you, and she wouldn't be too pleased with me if she caught us skipping out. Which she would — your mother can find out anything."

"Let her," Kristen said. "You need someone with you."

"No, I don't. I need to find my mother. If you want to help, cover for me if anyone asks."

"Don't I always?" Kristen said, offended.

Sophie grinned. "I'll see you back at your house. No one will ever know we separated. Just tell them I'm in the bathroom if they ask."

"Are you sure you should be doing this?" But Sophie was already gone.

18

When Rachel woke up the house was dark, like a suffocating tomb. She rolled over in the big bed, restless, achy, and pulled the pillow over her head, then pushed it away. There was no light in the house, no noise. She didn't have to bury her head.

She reached over and turned on the lamp. It made a meager blue pool of light by the side of the bed, and she squinted at the tiny numbers on the clock. It was only a little bit past noon on another miserable day and yet it felt as if she had slept for twenty-four hours.

The rain had returned with a vengeance, and she allowed herself the luxury of a muffled curse. She dragged herself out of bed, shoving her hair away from her face. David was always after her to get it cut, get it straightened, get it dyed a more subdued color. He had no idea that she surreptitiously had the red brightened from the

341

naturally sedate auburn — he would have been horrified. But she'd changed enough for him and her new life. New clothes, new shoes, new attitude, even if the old one kept popping up every now and then. And she had even more reason to be grateful. She'd betrayed him, distrusted him, broken their marriage vows and he'd forgiven her.

She went into her bathroom and splashed her face with cold water, then looked up at her reflection. She had that haunted look in her eyes, the one that had been there when they'd first found Tessa. Right now she didn't think it would ever go away.

She needed Sophie. To hell with David's wise advice. If the killer was caught . . . Why was she still thinking in terms of *if?*

Because it didn't feel right.

She opened her closet, looking at the rows of gray and beige clothing. Classics, David had told her when he took her shopping. They made her look younger, slimmer, prettier. And how could she argue with that?

She shoved them aside, grabbing her old jeans and tie-dyed T-shirt. Her raggedy, hand-painted sneakers were still there as well. Her oldest, most comfortable clothes had started disappearing a month after they'd arrived in Silver Falls, and she'd actually been fool enough to hide these to keep them away from him.

Why hadn't she realized how slowly, insidiously he was controlling her? This whole life had been so foreign to her that she'd taken her cues from him. And she'd been an idiot.

Now that the danger was over she was going to do the thing she should have done in the first place. She was going to take Sophie and get the hell out of this town, find a place with no memories. Maybe she'd call David when she got someplace where she felt safe, maybe not. She didn't want to be around for Caleb's trial, she didn't want to hear the gossip. Didn't want the horrific details. She'd avoided the newspapers for good reason when Tessa died — she didn't want to read them now.

The only way she could miss all of it was to take Sophie overseas. It would be spring in New Zealand this time of year. The sun would shine, and it would be exquisitely beautiful, and she could finally get her head clear, without David's disapproving influence, without the constant rain rotting her brain and growing mold on her soul. And for the first time in the last twenty-four hours her heart lifted.

Finding suitcases was her first task, and she finally discovered them in the back of the garage, in the neat shed where David kept the few tools he used. She could still smell the dead-animal scent back there, and she pried open the window, letting in the damp air and probably more rain. He'd have a fit if his tools were damaged.

So what. There were two huge suitcases underneath the smaller ones, and she dragged them through the house, closing the noxious odor away from her. In the end she hadn't needed that big a suitcase. She wasn't going to take any of the beige and gray, the black and brown and navy blue. She wrapped her cameras in her bright shawls, tossed in the jeans and T-shirts and colorful wraps, and at the last minute she pulled out her hiking shoes. They still had dried mud on them, an anathema in this shoeless house. She pulled them on and laced them up, then headed into Sophie's room.

David hadn't gotten very far in subduing her daughter's natural liveliness, Rachel thought. Thank God. Her clothes were still intact and there'd be no need for school uniforms. Never again.

She scooped up the toiletries, the teen magazines, the Nintendo DS and the handful of games, then headed for the bureau. The brushes, ponytail holders, the barrettes that David had given her . . .

No, she'd leave them behind. They were solid silver, and valuable, but Sophie didn't like to wear them. In fact, Rachel would be happy if Sophie never wore barrettes again. Too many memories.

She'd been a fool not to listen to Caleb's warnings. He really had been trying to save her. It just turned out that he was trying to save her from himself. So now, when all danger was past, she decided to listen. The depths of her idiocy knew no bounds.

When she finished the second suitcase was filled to the brim, while her own was half empty. It didn't matter. As soon as they got to a major city she'd buy more things for herself, bright, comfortable clothes, clothes that made her feel like herself. She'd eat like a pig, gain back the ten pounds David had talked her into losing, and she wouldn't give a flying fuck.

There was no phone book near the phone in the kitchen. David didn't like telephones — the only other one in the house was in his study. He didn't realize the extent that Rachel and Sophie depended on their cell phones, and he probably never would. He was almost as much of a Luddite as his father.

And she could hear Caleb's low, sexy

voice, using that word with affectionate mockery. A murderer's voice, beguiling, charming, seductive. And she didn't want to be thinking about that.

She was going to have to rent a car. Not that that should be a problem — she had money and credit on her own. She didn't touch the allowance David gave her to run his perfect household.

She wouldn't have to think about that anymore. She wouldn't have to think about allowances, and lightbulbs, and vegetarian meals and washing three times before David would have sex with her and then pretending she liked it. She and Sophie were going to be free. And she threw back her head and laughed out loud at the very idea.

The phone book had to be in his office. The door to his office was locked, which was odd in itself, but she knew where he kept his keys, tucked behind the King James version of the Bible. As an English professor, David said only the King James would do, and he assumed his boneheaded wife wouldn't touch it.

That was his mistake. His wife was neither boneheaded nor incurious. Her father had been a proponent of some new translation, which always seemed to be full of dire warnings, and one day she'd pulled out the King

346

James to see if it was as bad. She'd fallen in love with the music of the words, reading it for an afternoon, and when she went to put it back she noticed the keys.

She'd meant to say something to David about them, but she'd forgotten all about it. Until she'd come up against an unexpectedly locked door.

For some reason she felt nervous, edgy, like Bluebeard's wife, as she fumbled with the keys. Would she find seven dead wives inside? No, that was ridiculous. It was David's brother who killed women.

She opened the door and breathed a sigh of relief. It looked as it always did, neat and orderly.

She moved over to the desk, pulling the leather chair back and sitting in it. The phone book lay on its side beneath the utilitarian telephone, and she took it out, pushing the neat pile of papers out of the way.

And then froze. They were newspaper clippings, all referring to one thing. A string of murders.

Tessa's was the fourth from the top, and she looked into her sweet, cheerful face and wanted to weep. Her hair was pulled back with the tortoise-shell barrettes Sophie had given her for her fifteenth birthday, the barrettes that were missing from her body when they pulled it out of the Bay. No one had thought anything of it — her body had been in the water long enough that even identifying her had been difficult.

But now those missing barrettes seemed far more sinister, according to David. Were they really up at Caleb's dilapidated half-built house, locked away so he could gloat over them, stroke them, remembering choking the life from poor Tessa?

"No." She jumped, then realized she'd said the word out loud. The house was still and empty. She shook her head, as if to clear it, and shoved the newspaper clippings away from her, unable to bear looking at them. She could understand David's morbid fascination. After all, he was trying to do the unthinkable, to catch his beloved older brother in a series of crimes so unthinkable that Rachel hadn't even been able to read about them.

She started thumbing through the Yellow Pages. Silver Falls wasn't large enough to have a car-rental agency, but if she could find one within fifty miles then she could talk Maggie into driving her there. She'd have to pick a time when David wasn't around, so he wouldn't try to stop them, or, even worse, go with them.

Maybe she was overestimating her importance. But something told her he wasn't going to let her go easily — his sweet demeanor only went so deep.

He'd left the BMW behind and gone out in his beloved Range Rover. It wouldn't be that awful if she took the BMW and drove to the car-rental place three towns over and left it there. People wouldn't think very highly of her, abandoning her poor husband during such a difficult time, and abandoning his car, but she was tired of caring what the small-minded people of Silver Falls thought of her. They were the same ones who'd condemned Caleb without proof.

But they had been right about him after all, hadn't they? So why was she fighting it?

She closed the phone book without calling anyone. She had a sick, restless feeling in the pit of her stomach, and she couldn't figure out why. She picked up the clippings again, looking into the sweet face of Jessica Barrowman, moving past to the articles about the missing librarian with the mane of blond hair, the young girl in Portland, almost a clone of Sophie, the dead girl from eighteen years ago, another student from the college, her glittery butterfly barrettes giving her an oddly frivolous look.

She went through the papers, looking at

each face, trying to somehow honor them as an act of penance, when she froze. Elizabeth Pennington, from Santa Fe, New Mexico, found raped and strangled in 2003. Her blond hair was pushed back from her sweet face, held in place by a pair of silver barrettes. The same barrettes Rachel had left on Sophie's dresser.

She didn't think, she moved. The drawer beside her was locked, and none of the keys worked. She picked up David's letter opener, one in the shape of Excalibur, and forced it open, breaking the blade, scarring the walnut of the desk. She yanked it open, to see the pile of confidential student papers, just as David had told her.

She looked at them for a moment, a feeling of dread washing over her. David would never forgive her, he'd kill her —

She yanked the folders out and threw them on the floor. There, at the back of the drawer, was a tiny velvet pouch, like the kind used to hold jewelry. She drew it out, her hands shaking, and emptied it out on the desk.

Thirty-six barrettes. Counting Sophie's, that made thirty-seven, the number David had given her. The supposedly random number. She reached out a hand to pick them up, then pulled it back. She didn't want to touch them.

She pushed away from the desk. Caleb had been right all the time. He wasn't the serial killer or a sociopath. He was Jack the Ripper's brother, trying to put an end to murder. She picked up the telephone, her hands shaking, planning to call Maggie.

There was no dial tone. Somewhere in the distance she could hear a door close, and she froze in place. She wasn't alone in the house after all, and the man she'd been stupid enough to trust, the man she'd been stupid enough to marry, was coming for her.

The window behind her was locked. She looked around her for a weapon, but there was nothing, and at the last minute she grabbed David's chair. It was heavy, but she managed to lift it, using all her strength, and fling it through the window. The glass shattered, the mullions smashed, and the chair ending up on the flagstone patio. And she followed after it, feeling the shards of glass rip at her arms, disappearing into the wet afternoon just as a shadow appeared in the ruined window, calling after her. Her name was lost in the wind as she ran.

Sophie knew how to get around Silver Falls. The light rain gave her the excuse to pull the hood over her hair, and she walked with her head down. She dumped her backpack in the playground on her way — too bad if someone took it. She was bored to tears with the schoolwork anyway — even the college-level courses were too easy.

She was heading straight for the one place she had any chance of getting an honest answer. Straight for the Old Goat.

He was sitting in his wheelchair in the study, reading a techno-thriller, one he immediately put down when he saw her standing in his door. "How'd you get in?" he said, sounding less than welcoming.

"The door was unlocked. I want to know about your sons."

The Old Goat had recovered himself. "Why don't you come over here and sit beside me and we'll talk . . ."

"I can hear perfectly well right here," she said in a stony voice, no longer bothering to do her Miss Charm thing. "I don't trust you."

The Old Goat looked affronted. "What are you accusing me of? You think I'm a child molester?"

"No. You're just a dirty old man who thinks he's a lot more interesting than he is, and I don't want to get any closer. Where's David?"

"Your father is —"

"*Not* my father," she snapped. "And you're not my grandfather. Where is he?"

Stephen Henry managed a dignified pout. "I have no idea. He said he had some arrangements to make. This has all been extremely difficult, and I know what a sensitive child you are. Let me call your mother . . ."

"I'm not sensitive, I'm pissed off. Why is Caleb in jail? You know he didn't kill anyone."

"Do I?" he replied, refusing to meet her accusing stare. "I'm not sure what I know. I've never been certain."

"Certain about what?"

He leaned back in his chair, and it was clear he wasn't going to give her any answers. "I don't think they'll hold Caleb for very long," he said instead. "They can't have any proof."

"Why are you so sure of that?" Sophie persisted.

Stephen Henry looked at her with clear dislike, something she much preferred to his fawning. "Did anyone ever tell you you were too inquisitive for your own good?"

"Next you'll be saying curiosity killed the cat. My mother has always encouraged me to have an inquiring mind."

"Your mother needs to learn not to be so

impulsive," Stephen Henry said in a grumble. "Things were doing fine until she came here."

"I beg your pardon?" Sophie said, still trying to be polite. "What's my mother done?"

"Set him off," Stephen Henry said in a low, empty voice.

"I don't believe you. Caleb wouldn't do these things and you know it. Besides, he likes my mother, I can tell."

"Of course Caleb likes your mother. He likes anything that belongs to David," the Old Goat said in a cranky voice.

Now Sophie was getting pissed. "My mother doesn't belong to anyone. And I don't know what you think is my mother's fault, or why, but she has nothing to do with Caleb being arrested for something he hasn't done."

"She has everything to do with it, and you're an idiot," Stephen Henry said, any trace of charm long gone. "Go away and leave me alone. I don't have time for inquisitive little girls right now."

"Not until you tell me what's going on. If you know Caleb didn't kill anyone then why aren't you doing something about it?"

"Caleb can take care of himself. He always has." Stephen Henry put his hands on the wheels and tried to turn himself away.

354

Sophie crossed the room and yanked him back. "If your son didn't kill these women then who did?"

The Old Goat looked anything but lecherous and smarmy. He looked broken, sad and empty. "I never said my *son* didn't kill these women."

She froze, as everything clicked into place. "You knew?" she said, her voice filled with horror. "All this time, you knew that David was . . ."

"I never knew for certain. He's my son," Stephen Henry said with the merest trace of dignity.

"He's a monster. And you're one, too, for covering for him, for letting him get away with it, for letting Caleb take the blame and doing nothing."

"Go away," he mumbled. "You're too young to understand."

"God, I hope I never get as old as you then," she said bitterly. "I have to go warn my mother."

"Sophie!" His voice followed her, still with those rich tones that made her want to hurl, but she was already out the door.

She started running, taking the shortcuts through backyards, ignoring the barking dogs, the pelting rain. She reached for her cell phone — even if she couldn't reach her mother she could call Kristen's, but her battery power died just as she began to dial, and with a sob she threw it, running again, desperate to get to her mother, to warn her . . .

Her mother's car wasn't in the driveway, and for a moment she panicked, until she remembered about the car accident. She didn't for one moment believe that Caleb would have tried to hurt her. Like most stupid-ass adults, he wasn't going to admit such a thing, but he had a wicked case of the hots for her mother, and if her mother weren't so blinded by her idiotic adoration for her creepazoid husband she would have felt the same way. Caleb was old, but then so was her mother, in their thirties at least. Old enough to know better.

There was no sign of anyone — the lights were off in the house, a sure sign that either her mother wasn't there or that David was. When her mother was alone in the house she turned on every single light. She said the darkness was eating her soul.

She moved closer, keeping to the edge of the overhanging trees, trying to look in the windows. She'd get a better view from the back, but she'd have to go through the garage to do so. The Range Rover was gone, only the BMW was still there, and she knew

David would never have let her mother drive the Rover. Even the kind, sane David wouldn't let her near it. The crazy monster beneath the surface would . . .

She couldn't think about that. The door to the garage was open, and she slipped inside, skirting the big black car that still smelled faintly of dead animal, moving around the front to the back door. She could just sneak out there, peer in the windows and if she saw her mother she could warn her.

The backyard was dark and shadowy. There was a light from David's study, and she froze, peering through the shadows. There was something on the terrace, something large and bulky, too big to be a person. She took a few steps closer, leaving the safety of the hedge, and recognized a chair lying sideways, with the smashed window behind it.

She had to get help. Run to the nearest house, use their telephone and call the police. She turned, and froze.

"Hello, Sophie dear," David said. "I've been looking for you."

19

Caleb was stretched out on the bunk in Silver Falls's one jail cell. It wasn't the first cell he'd been in. Hell, it wasn't the first time he'd been in this particular jail.

Sometimes he'd deserved it. Joyriding in old Professor Morton's beloved sports car, underage drinking, fighting. There was no doubt he'd been a hellion. But there were other times, bad times, when David's shit had been laid at his door. Malicious stuff, meant to hurt.

He could hear a commotion outside the small cell area, and a moment later Maggie Bannister showed up, keys in her hand.

"You're being released on your own recognizance," she said.

"Oh, yeah? I don't have the best reputation in this town. Why did the judge decide to trust me?"

"I vouched for you," Maggie said in her flat voice.

"I'm charmed by your faith in me," he said, not bothering to hide his sarcasm. "So what are the terms? I'm guessing I'm supposed to stay away from Rachel."

"I imagine she'll take care of that by herself."

Caleb wanted to hit something. "You're keeping an eye on her, aren't you?"

"We are. Right now she's at home, asleep."

"And where's my brother?"

Maggie looked guilty. "I don't know. On the record we have no reason to follow him."

"And off the record?"

"We both know what's going on. But I can't move unless I have probable cause, and right now I have shit," Maggie said. "Your brother doesn't know I see through his games. I've always seen through his games. He'll think he's won, and he won't be wanting to make any mistakes."

"Maybe," Caleb said, doubtful. "He's closer to the edge than you think. He fucked up, and he knows it. I need a car."

"I don't want you going anywhere near him."

"I'm not. I'm going up to my house to pack."

"So you're just going to leave? Just like that?"

"Go to hell," Caleb snarled. "You know I

can't do that."

"You can take Rachel's car. It's drivable, they fixed the brake line, and maybe it'll make you think twice about half-assed schemes to scare people that can backfire."

"It worked. I had her where I wanted her."

"You had her where you wanted her an hour before we got to the hotel, asshole. If you'd kept it in your pants we wouldn't have had this problem. He wouldn't have flipped out."

"Yes, he would have. I just made it happen sooner."

"And what about Rachel? How do you think she'll feel, married to a monster, used by his brother?"

"She'll be glad she's alive," he said, his voice flat and cold. "Where's her car parked?"

"Out back. The desk sergeant will give you the keys. And don't go thinking you'll find her and 'explain.' I don't think she's going to listen, and I don't want to tip David over the edge. Sophie's safe at my house, Rachel thinks you're a crazed killer, and David thinks he's gotten away with it. Let's leave it like that for now. Understood?"

Caleb said nothing.

"I can throw your ass back in jail," Maggie warned. "I'm sick of the whole lot of you. Rachel's my friend and you've fucked her over, and I don't take kindly to that."

"I'll leave her alone," Caleb said. And he'd try. Because Maggie was right — for the moment David thought he'd managed to fool everyone. But he was dancing on a razor's edge, and it would take very little to push him over.

"Give me a call when you get up to your place and let me know if anyone's been there," Maggie said. "If I don't hear from you I'll be sending someone after you."

Caleb shook his head. "He won't be up there. He has no interest in killing me. Taking everything I care about, yes. Making it look like I'm responsible, of course. But he doesn't actually want to hurt me."

"Everything you care about, huh?" Maggie said. "Well, if you care so damned much about her you better find a way to explain all this to her. I've got a feeling she's not going to be listening to me. Just don't try to do it now."

Shit. "I didn't say —"

"Just shut up. Take the Volvo and get the hell out of here. And call me!" she shouted after him as he took off.

The Volvo looked pretty damned good for a car that had had a close encounter with a tree. The streets were empty at midday, and he drove too fast. Maggie was right — things had stabilized for the time being, there was no immediate danger. David thought he had gotten away with it, and Stephen Henry had even backed up his alibi. If they all played it very carefully then nothing bad would happen for the time being, and maybe they could stop David before he lost it completely. Before he hurt anyone else.

But he didn't really believe that. He knew his brother, knew the calm glint of madness in his pale blue eyes. There was no pulling back. Safety was only an illusion.

At least Sophie was safe. Rachel was another matter. He was going up to his house, taking the fastest shower on record, and grabbing the gun he'd stashed behind the mouse-eaten towels.

He knew how to use it. He had a license, which Maggie hadn't bothered to check, and he wouldn't hesitate. It would be like shooting a mad dog.

It wasn't his brother. It was the damaged creature who lived to hurt and kill. And he had to be stopped.

He drove so fast up the winding road that the tires spun, the car drifted sideways, and he ended up stuck in the mud halfway up the narrow drive that led to his house. He got out and ran, not sure why.

The house looked the same when he came around the corner. Bright blue tarp, gaping windows, rickety and ruined. There was no sign of anyone, and he started up the steps, taking them two at a time, all his senses sure of certain disaster.

The huge empty room looked the same in the shadows, the dark stain of blood a reminder. He started down the stairs that led into the room and then stopped as his eyes grew accustomed to the darkness. There was something over by the wood-stove, something small and fragile. He took another step, and saw the long blond hair, and he let out a cry, stumbling forward.

He didn't see it or hear it, but he knew it was coming. And when the blackness closed in he fought, but it was too strong, even against his rage, and he was gone.

David had won.

Rachel ran blindly, not daring to look behind her, terrified that a hand would reach out and grab her shoulder. She needed to get help, and fast, and she yanked her cell phone from her pocket as she raced down the uneven sidewalks in the heavy boots. She fumbled with the keypad, trying to dial Maggie's number, but she kept hitting the wrong buttons. She forced herself to stop, long enough to catch her breath, long enough to dial 911. Before she could hit Send the phone rang.

She stared down at the image of David's smiling face for a moment, on the phone he'd given her when she moved in, preprogrammed so that his little photo appeared anytime he called her. Tempted to smash the thing on the sidewalk, she took a deep breath and flipped it open. "Yes, David?" She spoke in a neutral voice, but her hands shook.

"Darling, where are you? I got home and the place was trashed. There were papers all over the place, and someone smashed in the window in my office. I was terrified that he'd come after you."

He sounded like David, anxious, sweet, concerned, and she wanted to believe him so badly. Not for his sake. But for hers. "Who would come after me?"

"Caleb. They didn't have enough to hold him, and he's out. They don't know where he is — I'm afraid he's gone after Sophie."

"Sophie's with the Bannisters," she said, her voice numb.

"No, she isn't. Kristen said she took off before school was over, and Sophie told her to cover for her. She stopped by my father's, but no one's seen her since. I can't bear the thought of anything happening to her."

It was so easy to believe him. "Why would she stop by Stephen Henry's? She hates him."

"I think she was trying to find Caleb. Someone must have told her he'd been arrested, and she's so blindly infatuated with him she probably thought it was all a lie. He has that effect on people."

Rachel took a deep breath. She was standing motionless in the rain, holding on to the telephone. She couldn't let him know her panic. "Have you told the police she's missing?"

"Of course I have," he said, and his voice sounded indignant, almost normal. "They'll find her before Caleb does, I'm sure of it. I don't want you to worry about it. I just want you to come back home."

That cold, empty place had never really felt like home, she could finally admit it to herself. "I don't think so, David."

"Sweetheart, I know what you're thinking. I saw the packed suitcases, the barrettes on Sophie's dresser. What I never told you is that Caleb gave me those barrettes. I was dating someone with long hair, someone Caleb used to care about, and he gave me those barrettes to give to her."

"Why didn't you?"

"She disappeared," he said, his voice, that pale version of Stephen Henry's, sounded bleak. "I know what you're thinking, and I don't know how to convince you that I haven't had anything to do with these murders. I tried to warn you that there was something wrong with Caleb, but you wouldn't listen. You almost paid for that mistake with your life. You're just lucky we got to the motel before it was too late."

He sounded so reasonable, so concerned. She wanted so much to believe him.

"Come home, Rachel," he pleaded. "We'll go see Maggie Bannister together. If I know her she'll have the entire police force out looking for Sophie, and she won't stop till she finds her. Come home, sweetheart. Don't try to go through this alone. You just need to talk to me."

"Where's Sophie?" she said, her voice raw.

"Darling, I don't know. Hiding out from me if she's believed any of Caleb's lies. Unless . . ."

"Unless what?"

"Maybe Caleb found her. Maybe she's up at his house right now, tied up, helpless." His voice had settled into a soft croon. "That's what he wanted all the time, you know. He wanted her, not you. He thought you might make him whole, but you can't do that, can you, Rachel? You're too wild, too loud. You couldn't be what he needed, and so he had to kill again."

She stood there, shivering, numb, as his awful words sank into her brain. The cracks were showing, sooner than she'd expected. "I'm so sorry," she said helplessly.

"You know that won't do any good, Rachel. She's up there, waiting for you. He wants you to come up there, Rachel. He needs you to complete the circle." His voice was eerie, calm, and she could almost believe he *was* talking about Caleb, not about himself.

"I don't have a car," she said, trying to keep her panic under control.

"You can take the BMW."

Her laugh bordered on hysteria. "You never let me drive the BMW."

"I didn't know Caleb was going to sabotage your car, now did I?" His voice was sweet. "The keys are on the counter. You'd better hurry. It's going to get dark soon, and Sophie will be frightened." There was a moment of silence. "I love you, Rachel."

Without thinking she threw the phone away from her, and it smashed against the concrete sidewalk. She wanted to sink to her knees and sob in terror. She'd put her daughter in mortal danger because she hadn't had the brains to leave this awful place. She'd fucked up, and she wasn't the one who was going to pay. Sophie was.

Not if she could help it.

She had no idea if David was home or not. All she knew was that she had to get to Sophie.

And he'd told her where she was. Up at Caleb's house.

Could she believe a word he said? If Caleb had been released then he'd be after David as well. He'd never let Sophie be taken. Unless he'd been released too late. Maybe he was already dead. Maybe Sophie was.

She had to get up there before it was too late. She looked around her, trying to control her breathing.

There were three houses on the cul-de-sac, nearly half a mile from the house she'd shared with David. She ran up to the first one, ringing the bell, banging on the door, the only answer being a very angry dog. The second one was the same. The third was double locked, but no dogs. She went around the back, picked up an ornamental planter and smashed it through the sliding-glass door.

No sound of burglar alarms, dammit. Alarms would bring the police, the only people she needed right then. People were just too damned trusting in this town. She reached past the broken glass and opened it, flipped on the nearest light switch. She could see the phone on the wall, and she grabbed it, almost sobbing at the blessed dial tone.

They put her on hold. The fucking police department put her on hold, with a Muzak version of "I Am, I Said" in the background. Neil Diamond again. She slammed it down into the cradle, wanting to scream.

She headed for the attached garage, and finally her luck had changed. Whoever lived in this spotless house had a classic 1967 Mustang, in pristine condition, parked in one of the three bays. No key, of course, but with a car like that she didn't need a key. She'd learned to hot-wire engines years ago, and it was like riding a bike. You never forgot.

She gunned the engine, searching for an automatic garage-door opener. It must have been in one of the other cars, and she got out again, frantic, looking for a button of some sort.

She was too panicky to find it. The Mustang was a muscle car, the house was a new McMansion with shoddy construction. She got back in, put the car in Reverse and floored it.

The garage door splintered as she sailed through, and a moment later she was tearing down the road, heading toward the only place she needed to be. He had her daughter up at Caleb's place. She didn't know how or why, but after his veiled conversation she was absolutely certain of it.

It couldn't be too late — she was somehow part of the equation. She was going to get there in time, and then she was going to kill David Middleton. Not for making a fool out of her. Not for making her sleep with a psychopath. But for even threatening to hurt her child. She was going to slice him to ribbons.

David surveyed his handiwork, pleased with himself. He'd been forced into this, and there was always the possibility that he wouldn't succeed, but he had faith that everything would come out the way it ought to. He'd worked too hard for it to all fall apart, and besides, with his intellect it should be simple enough for him to outsmart the police. As he had for all these years.

His father suspected, but Stephen Henry would never betray him, for the simple reason that it would take attention away from the old man himself, and he wouldn't be able to bear that. If the world discovered how very clever David had been, for all these long years, no one would care about the old man and his pretentious poetry and his overweening vanity. As long as he was the center of attention he'd turn a blind eye to his real son's real accomplishments.

He whistled beneath his breath as he finished with the ropes. He'd expected better of Caleb. His brother had walked right into his trap, taken one look at little Sophie and forgotten who he was dealing with. His skull may have been smashed in — there was blood seeping into his shirt, and David shuddered. He hated blood — it made him physically ill. Any blood but his own, that was. His body was a crisscross of scars, some old, some new, the elegant razor tracings a road map of pain. He'd made a mistake a few weeks ago, and cut too close to his testicle. He'd been unable to perform under any but the most extreme circumstances for the last few weeks, and he'd been afraid Rachel would say something.

She'd never been particularly satisfying in bed — much too active, when he wanted her to lie still. And she wanted to touch him, when he couldn't bear being touched. She'd been docile enough the first few times, and he'd really begun to believe it would work out. He could keep her until Sophie was old enough, and then a believable accident would take care of things. He hadn't wanted her to suffer — she was Sophie's mother, after all.

But right now he wanted her to suffer. He wanted to flay her flesh from her bones, he wanted to burn her alive. She'd done nothing but get in his way, and he'd seen her face when they found her in the motel with Caleb. She'd had sex with him. He could smell it on her, see it in her eyes, in Caleb's eyes. Noisy, dirty, foul sex, and she loved it.

He ought to bless her for it. Any hesitation he'd had vanished in the morning light. Any pain he could inflict, any fear he could drive into her, would only be righteous and well-deserved. He no longer had to hold back — he could do anything he wanted and it would be justified.

Not that he should need to justify his actions. He had complete faith in his preordained path.

He yanked the ropes tighter, cutting into Caleb's flesh, but his brother didn't move. Maybe he'd never regain consciousness, never feel the fire eating through his clothes, making his skin crackle and pop like pork fat in the flame. It was only a small disappointment. Rachel would be awake. Rachel would know.

He rose. The meager afternoon light was fading, and he glance at his watch, pouting. What was taking her so long? He'd told her where they were — she should have been here by now. Didn't she care about her daughter?

There was always the possibility that she'd gone to the police after all, but he didn't think she was that stupid. If he saw flashing lights or heard anything unexpected he'd kill Sophie before anyone could get close enough to stop him. He had Caleb's gun — how typical of his macho older brother, to think something as pathetic as a gun could stop him. He probably thought David didn't know how to use it. He'd always underestimated him.

No, Caleb had always thought David didn't have the stones to do what needed to be done.

David couldn't help it — he giggled. If he wasn't more careful with his beloved antique straight-edge razor he'd definitely be missing one himself. He had to watch it, but it was getting harder and harder to find areas of his skin that weren't already marked with scars. He had to be careful — Rachel had never felt the elegant tracings when she'd disobeyed him and tried to put her arms around him when they had sex. He couldn't afford to let anyone see them — it would raise too many questions with his next girl-friend.

He was going to have to get rid of Sophie, which saddened him. Because of that bitch he'd married, everything was too rushed, and Sophie knew he'd taken her. She'd fought him before he managed to knock her out with the chloroform, and he'd almost strangled her right there and then.

But he had self-control, when so many people didn't. And for Rachel, knowing that Sophie would die wouldn't be nearly as painful as seeing the girl in his control. Ca-leb and Rachel would suffer as they'd made him suffer.

He'd be gentle with Sophie, because he knew that she loved him. Oh, she pretended she didn't, because she knew her mother would be jealous, but he could see beneath her standoffishness. She was younger than the other ones, and he liked that. He liked the innocence. That silly teenager in San Francisco, the one who'd led him to Sophie, had been exciting. But nothing compared to sweet, sweet Sophie. He looked over at her. She was still unconscious. He'd forced the stuff down her throat, to keep her quiet, and he may have given her too much. Which

374

would be a shame — he wanted her awake. But if she didn't wake up, there'd be others.

He wondered how young he could safely go. He didn't want to hurt himself if they were too small. That wouldn't be very pleasant.

He heard the crash of metal on metal from a distance, and a smile wreathed his face. Caleb had left the car, his car, the one he'd bought for Rachel, halfway down the driveway. Rachel must have slammed into it.

It couldn't be the police — he would have heard the sirens. She was coming. He was really quite cross with her, the most uncooperative of women. She'd tried hard in the beginning — he could give her credit for that. But it hadn't taken her long to start rebelling, trying to change his ordered life and his ordered house.

Though she had given him Sophie, and for that he would always be grateful. She was still going to suffer — she'd know that the fire would take her and she would die screaming.

Part of him would regret that, quite sincerely.

He heard her running up the front stairs, loud and graceless, and he made a face. Sophie would never be so clumsy. Sophie would never be so rude.

He knelt down beside the young girl, pulling her limp body into his arms, stroking her long, golden hair.

And when the front door slammed open, and Rachel stood there, muddy, furious, he smiled up at her, as he stroked and he stroked her daughter.

"I was afraid you wouldn't get here in time," he said. "Close the door behind you. It's chilly. You wouldn't want our Sophie to catch a cold."

And to his utter amazement, his wife came at him, a kitchen knife in her hand.

20

Rachel froze where she was. David was sitting on the floor, her baby daughter cradled in his arms, and he was holding a gun to her head. Her silky blond hair flowed over his arm. His expression was almost genial.

"Do drop the knife, Rachel," he said. "I don't want to shoot her. I despise blood, but you'll find that I can't be pushed. Drop the knife, kick it out of the way, and then sit, right where you are."

She had no choice. She could see Caleb on the floor behind him, unconscious, bleeding, tied up, and she could only hope he was still alive. She kicked the knife out of the way and sat, cross-legged, prepared to leap if given half a chance.

But David wasn't going to do that. He lay Sophie down on the plywood floor very carefully, and she could see that her daughter was alive, seemingly undamaged, and unconscious. It was a small blessing. He rose and turned to her, the gun looking quite natural in his small, well-manicured hand. "It took you a great deal longer than I would have expected, Rachel," he said in a mild tone. "I thought you would have been up here at least an hour ago. Here I was, rushing to get Caleb properly trussed, afraid that the drugs would wear off and Sophie would start being difficult. I was really getting quite cross with you. Don't you care about your daughter?"

"I didn't have a car," she said in a dull voice. "I had to break into someone's house and steal one."

David laughed. "How enterprising of you. But I told you that I didn't mind if you drove the BMW. I trust you."

"I didn't trust you."

He laughed. "But the BMW is perfectly safe. It does still retain a hint of Melinda — I never would have guessed it would be so difficult to get the smell of putrefaction from a car trunk."

She wasn't going to throw up. "Who — *Melinda?* Then it wasn't a dead deer?"

"Don't be naïve. I kept Melinda in the trunk for weeks. I thought I'd been careful — she was wrapped in layers of plastic and I sprinkled half a dozen boxes of baking soda back there to absorb the odor, along with some of those sprays. I have to tell you that those air fresheners are useless."

"You should write the company a letter of complaint."

"You're making fun of me — but you know, I just might do that," he said, moving toward her.

She could dive for the knife, but he'd shoot her first and then there'd be no one to help Sophie.

"That's right, my love," he said. "I really don't want to shoot you. It's just a matter of personal taste. I could certainly get away with it — it's Caleb's gun, after all. He's going to be blamed for everything, and if you have a bullet in your skull it won't make any difference. But I told you, I don't like blood, and I don't like loud noises. You're a very noisy person, did you know that, Rachel? Clomping around in those boots — I thought I'd gotten rid of them. Even in bare feet you always moved around the house like a storm trooper. You rattle dishes, you sing, you close doors too noisily, you drive too fast."

"Is that why you're going to kill me?"

Sophie had moved behind him, just the slightest stirring, and Rachel silently prayed. *Get up, baby. Get away from here, fast.*

"Of course not," he said, affronted. "I

could have trained you properly. Things just got out of control. You can thank my brother for that. We were doing just fine until he came home. We could have had three good years together, waiting for Sophie to mature and take your place, if he hadn't barged in. Fortunately I'm a brilliant man, and I was prepared for any eventuality, and Caleb's always had a bad habit of interfering with my particular pleasures. I must have known subconsciously that he'd come back when I met with Jessica. I'd planned to take her out of state but I changed my mind at the last minute. I'm intuitive, you know. I must have sensed his presence."

Rachel just stared at him, sick inside. How could she have gotten her daughter into this? "But why, David?" she said, her voice desperate. "Why did you kill that girl?"

He looked at her with a pitying expression. "Because I had to. And I got away with it, time after time. I happen to be brilliant. My IQ is sixteen points higher than Ted Bundy's."

"You checked?"

"Of course I checked! He's the gold standard against which everyone is measured, but I can assure you, I'm far brighter than he ever was."

"I'm sure you are," she said, trying to keep

her voice from shaking. "Smart enough to know that this has gone too far. You're going to get caught."

"Don't be absurd. I've been setting Caleb up for years. My father will give me an alibi — he can't bear the thought of his golden son going to jail."

"But what about Caleb?"

"Oh, he'll already be dead. He chained you up, strangled and raped Sophie and threw her over the falls, and then set fire to his house in a fit of remorse. I've set it up perfectly. His ropes will burn off in the fire," he said, pulling out a pair of handcuffs, "but these will still be wrapped around your scorched corpse. You're such a horse, my dear. I had a hard time finding handcuffs that would fit you."

"Can't they trace them to you?"

He shook his head. "I told you, I'm much too careful. You may as well stop arguing. I've thought of everything. Please move back against the wall, next to that pipe."

"And if I don't?"

"Don't be tiresome. I'll put a bullet in your mouth and drag your body over there. The fire I've set will burn so hotly that no one will be able to tell that you were shot before you were burned."

She scooted back against the wall. Sophie

381

was moving a little bit more — if she could just keep David talking it might give her enough time to come to.

He took her arm and slapped the heavy manacle round her wrist, then closed the other one around the exposed pipe. "She's not going to wake up in time, Rachel. She may get a little more active, but not enough to actually get away. Consider it a blessing. She'll never know what happened to her."

"Won't that ruin all your fun?" she said in a furious tone.

"Of course not. I'm a very considerate man. I make it quick. And I make love to them afterward, so they don't have to deal with the shame beforehand."

"You're not going to touch my daughter."

"Of course I am. No one can stop me. When I'm done I'll throw her body over the falls and take the back way down to my father's house, where we'll have a nice dinner and a good bottle of pinot grigio, and when Maggie Bannister comes to tell us what happened we'll both be distraught. It's a shame you won't have a chance to see it — I'm really very good."

"I know you are, David. You fooled me completely."

"Ah, but you aren't much of a challenge," he said with a condescending smile. He rose, stepping away from her. "I could make this painless for you. I'd be willing to shoot you, despite my dislike of blood, so you won't have to deal with the pain of burning to death. After all, you did love me, and I can be generous."

"I didn't love you, David," she said, her voice flat. "I married you to provide what I thought was a safe life for Sophie. You're absolutely right, I was an idiot, but you were simply a means to an end."

She'd gotten to him. His face crumpled for a moment, and he looked like a little boy whose dog had died. Then he shook his head. "You're just saying that."

"I jumped at the chance of separate bedrooms, David. I slept with your brother the first chance I got." She glanced over at Sophie to make certain she was still unconscious. "I sucked his cock, David. He's much bigger than you, and he doesn't get limp. I fucked him and I liked it."

"Stop it!" His voice rose in distress. "You know I don't like that language."

"I was a whore, David. I did everything with Caleb that I wouldn't do with you."

"I didn't want you to do those things . . ."

"Yes, you did. Deep inside, you wanted me to do all those things with you, but you were afraid, because you knew you couldn't get it up, not often enough to even begin to please me. You can only get it up with dead girls, isn't that it?"

He hit her then, slamming the gun across her face so hard that for a moment everything turned black. When the world came back into focus again he'd managed to regain his calm.

"You're an ugly, dirty girl," he said. "And if I had time I'd show you how wrong you are. But I can only count on the idiocy of the police to last so long, and I don't want to risk all this hard work for nothing."

"David." Caleb's voice was hoarse, muffled. She hadn't even realized he was coming to.

David whirled around, momentarily startled. "My brother awakens. I was afraid I'd killed you."

"Untie me, David. You know you don't want to do this." Caleb's voice was rough, pleading.

"Of course I do. I was just explaining to your whore here how much I want to do this. I must say she hasn't expressed much interest in you — she's more concerned about her daughter."

"Let them go, David. You know this is between you and me, and always has been."

David giggled, and the sound made her

skin crawl. "Don't be naïve, Caleb. All you are is a scapegoat. I couldn't care less who gets blamed — you're just the easiest one to use. I'll find someone else once you're gone. Stephen Henry might be a good choice. He can walk, you know. He's been hiding that fact for years, just to get attention."

"And he's been covering for you for years. Do you think he'll keep covering for you if you try to frame him?"

"Yes," David said simply.

"Then just let Sophie go. She's too young — you never wanted to hurt anyone that young."

"She loves me," David said airily. "I know that she does, she just hasn't been brave enough to tell me. I owe this to her."

"Owe her death?" Rachel demanded.

"Shut up!" David shrieked in a lightning change of mood. "It's all your fault. I was going to wait until she grew up, I was going to start to train her, but you kept interfering, trying to turn her against me. If it weren't for you none of this would have happened. You're the one who's responsible for your daughter's death, not me."

"And you're batshit insane," Rachel spat back.

But David had regained his calm. "I'm finished arguing with you both." He walked back to Sophie's limp body and hoisted her into his arms effortlessly. He was much stronger than he looked. "I promise you I'll wait until after she's dead. After all, she loves me."

"She hates you. She thinks you're a disgusting creep," Rachel said, desperate.

"Don't lie. She's just shy." He started up the stairs to the front door, Sophie in his arms, her long blond hair hanging down. "You know, I'm really looking forward to this. It's been so long since I've enjoyed myself with a child." And the door closed behind him.

Caleb immediately began to move, struggling against the ropes. "We have to —" the explosion silenced him. From a distance she could hear the crackle of fire, see the sinister swirls of smoke as the house started to burn. He looked over at her, a bleak expression on his face. "I don't know how to get you loose."

"There's a knife over there. You can cut yourself free." She nodded in the direction of the kitchen knife David had made her kick away. It was an unexpected mistake. Maybe there was a chance he'd make more.

Caleb inched his way to the spot, somehow managing to pick the knife up with his hands tied behind him. He was cursing beneath his breath, and fresh red blood was running down the side of his head, and all she could do was watch, and pray, until a moment later his hands were free, and he was sawing away at the ropes that bound his ankles together. And then he looked up at her.

She forestalled him. "The only thing that matters is Sophie," she said. "Don't even think about it."

"I can't leave you here. You won't be able to get free."

"You can't stay. Get the hell out of here. If I'm supposed to die then I'm okay with it. As long as Sophie is all right."

For a moment he didn't move, looking down at her with a bleak expression.

"Get out of here!" she screamed at him, as she felt the heat coming at her from the back of the building.

He moved then, fast. He caught her chin in his hand and kissed her, hard and fast, and then he was gone.

Leaving her to die.

21

She spent precisely fifteen seconds panicking. And then she spun around and began kicking at the pipe, her heavy boots making little difference. She pulled at her wrist, trying to twist it, but her bones were too big and she couldn't slip out of the cuff. She could feel the heat from the fire, the flames getting closer, and she kicked harder, hard enough to bend the pipe, not hard enough to break it, and she kicked again, screaming with rage and frustration, and again.

She heard his voice from a distance, and for a moment she thought she was imagining things. Stephen Henry, playing to the third balcony, his voice coming through the gathering smoke, calling for David.

She had no idea whether she could trust him or not, and she had even less time to think about it. "Stephen Henry!" she screamed. "Get me out of here!"

He emerged from the smoke, walking, no,

running, straight toward her, and she half expected him to be bringing a merciful death. Instead he started yanking at the pipe that held her prisoner, and she felt it begin to give with their combined strength.

A moment later it pulled free from the framing, and she scrambled to her feet, pulling the ring of the cuffs off the end of it. "He's got Sophie," she said in a strangled voice. "He's going to kill her. And you knew it."

He shook his head, his face old and broken. "I didn't. I didn't want to. Where are they? Where's Caleb?"

"He's gone after them."

"My poor wounded boy," Stephen Henry began to intone, and Rachel shoved him aside, too panicked to slap him.

"Fuck your wounded boy. I'm going to save my daughter."

They barely made it down the rickety front steps as the flames followed, eating the water-soaked wood as if it were dry kindling. It was late afternoon — what little sun there was had already begun to set, and the shadowy darkness was all around.

"He was heading up to the falls," Rachel said. "I don't know how to get there."

"I do," Stephen Henry said, charging

ahead of her, leaving her to follow in his wake.

She had no choice but to run after him. For all she knew he was simply leading her to her death — he'd already lied for and protected his murderous son past all reasonable limits, and there was no guarantee that he was finally ready to stop. He'd just saved her life, but she'd be a fool to trust anyone. It didn't matter. She'd only been on this trail once, following behind Caleb, and she couldn't afford to waste even a moment.

"You move fast for a cripple," she said sharply, catching up with him.

He didn't even bother to glance at her. He was out of breath, moving fast, and she could barely keep up with him. All she could do was keep her head down and offer up a silent litany of prayer, of bargains, of mindless panic. *Don't let him hurt her. Don't let him touch her. Let Caleb get there in time.*

The sound of the water grew louder, drowning out even her labored breathing. She almost thought she could hear voices, and she tried to push past Stephen Henry, but he shoved her out of the way, bursting through the clearing ahead of her.

And then he was falling back, against her, before she even heard the shot, and she collapsed under his weight, trapped for a moment as she saw David dragging a now-struggling Sophie toward the falls. Rachel shoved the old man off her, hearing his grunt as he landed in the mud, and she struggled past him into the clearing, slipping in the mud as she scrambled toward them.

David had the gun in his hand, pressing it against Sophie once more, and Caleb was a few feet away, held at bay by the threat. "Don't come any closer, Rachel," David said, his eyes glinting.

"Please, David," she sobbed. "Let her go. It's gone too far — you can't get away with it. You can kill all of us, but no one will believe you."

She half expected to hear him laugh maniacally, but he simply looked at her, his tie perfect, his blond hair slightly mussed. "They'll believe me. They always do."

"You can't," she cried. "I won't let you."

At that moment Sophie moved, reaching up, her fingernails raking across his face so hard the blood spurted, and for a second he let go of her, screaming in pain.

It was enough. Rachel charged at him, slamming her body into his, and he went over the edge, toward the churning waters.

At the last minute he reached out and caught her ankle, and she followed him, hurtling downward, knowing she was going to die, knowing that Sophie would live, when an iron hand grabbed her wrist, catching her. She looked up to see Caleb, holding on to her with his last bit of strength. She looked below to see David swinging beneath her, still clinging to her ankle.

"Let go of her, David!" he shouted.

Everything suddenly seemed to move very slowly. She looked up, could see Caleb's free arm wrapped around a tree branch for support, support that wouldn't last long with both their weights pulling against him. Beneath her David thrashed, his hand burning around her ankle and he flailed.

"You love me, Rachel," he shouted at her over the roar of the water. "You always have. Let go and come with me."

She stared down at him for a long, raging moment. "Fuck . . . you," she screamed, and slammed her heavy booted foot into his face. Once, twice. With the third kick his fingers let go, and he fell, silently, spinning with the gracefulness of a diver until he disappeared into the roaring falls.

Caleb pulled her up, hoisting her onto the muddy ground, and she pushed away from him, scrambling across the dirt, breathless, until she was able to reach Sophie and pull her into her arms, sobbing. In the distance she could hear the sirens, and the flames from the burning building climbed high into the rainy sky. She buried her face in Sophie's hair and closed her eyes, letting go for the first time in days.

They were safe.

David was dead.

It was going to be all right.

22

Rachel parked her battered Volvo on the road, not in the driveway, and slowly walked up the path to the front door of the house she'd once shared with David. The apple tree in the yard had started to die, the deep ruts from her car still scarred the grass.

She hadn't been back in the two weeks since David's death. She couldn't bear to. They'd kept them in the hospital for a couple of days — she had cuts and scrapes on her arms that she'd never noticed, from jumping through broken windows, and Sophie still had the effects of David's drugs in her system.

They also wanted to do a psych evaluation. Of course Sophie passed with flying colors. She'd never had any illusions about David. She wasn't the one who'd put her own child in danger because she was so blindly certain she was doing the right thing.

But in the end they were both released,

and after ten days at the local hotel they were finally free to leave Silver Falls. Which Rachel had every intention of doing.

Stephen Henry was still in the hospital. The bullet had lodged near his heart, and he was an old man. A healthy old man and a liar, and still enough of a force in town that he probably wouldn't even be charged with obstructing justice. Rachel didn't care one way or the other. He'd been as blind as she'd been, in his own way. And he'd done his best to make up for it.

The one strange thing was Sophie's sudden affection for the Old Goat. She visited him almost every day, and they'd developed a sort of bantering rudeness that they both enjoyed tremendously, particularly once it became clear that Stephen Henry's lechery was more particularly directed toward the young male nurses than her prepubescent daughter.

Of Caleb there'd been no sign at all. At least, not for her. She had no idea where he was staying. He wasn't at the one hotel, and his own place had burned to the ground. She suspected he might be holed up at Stephen Henry's while the old man was in the hospital, but she didn't care enough to ask, she told herself. Since he didn't care enough to show his face.

Maggie was waiting for her outside the house, her broad, expressionless face the same as always. "You're really going to leave us?" she said when Rachel climbed out of the car.

"Could you even doubt it? You and Kristen can come visit with us whenever we're back in the country. Kristen could even fly overseas and join us during school vacations."

"You're forgetting how much a small-town cop makes."

"You're forgetting how much David's insurance settlement was," she replied. "I don't really want the money, but I'm more than delighted to use it for things that will make Sophie happy. She's come through this amazingly well but she'll still need her friends."

"Seems like she's come through it better than you," Maggie observed.

Rachel made a face. "Thanks for noticing. Sophie doesn't have to kick herself in the butt every day for being a gullible fool. I don't just marry a psychopath, but I nearly get us murdered because I refused to listen to . . . good advice."

Maggie had no qualms about naming names. "I don't blame you for not trusting Caleb. He's never done anything to make people trust him. I think he liked people thinking he was the crazy one. He certainly never did anything to convince people otherwise."

Rachel's smile was forced. "Well, they know now, don't they? Not that it matters. He must be long gone by now."

A slow smile lit Maggie's weathered face. "You asking me if he's still in town?"

"Of course not."

"Because he is. Man's got a boatload of guilt to deal with, and he doesn't know what the hell to do. Unlike his father, who doesn't feel a speck of responsibility for any of it. But then, anyone knows that Stephen Henry's a major asshole."

That surprised a laugh out of Rachel. "Blasphemy."

"You betcha. I brought the keys to the place. You want me to come in with you, keep you company while you pack?"

"There's no need. I don't think David's ghost is going to be bothering me."

"I doubt it. I expect he's roasting in hell right now, and they don't give day passes."

"You think he's in hell? He was a very sick man."

"Oh, screw that. He was a very bad man, and I'm just sorry I didn't get the chance to see him hang." She looked at Rachel. "At least you got to kick him in the face a couple of times."

"Three times," Rachel said. "And I feel bad about that."

"Do you really?"

She thought about it. "No. I'd do it again if I had the chance."

"Me, too. Someone threatens my daughter, they're toast."

Rachel thought about it for a moment. She'd relived those moments over and over again, the feel of her booted foot smashing into his face, and then his body falling, twisting and turning. She looked at Maggie. "Damn straight," she said.

Maggie laughed. "Good for you. Where's Sophie now?"

"Visiting the Old Goat. Which I don't understand in the slightest." Rachel shook her head. "But I think we've already established that Sophie's a better judge of character than I ever was, so there must be something good about him."

"He tried to save your life and got a bullet from his beloved son for his efforts."

"Well, there is *that*." She wasn't going to ask. She'd told herself it didn't matter — if Caleb didn't want to see her then she sure as hell didn't want to see him. She couldn't fight it anymore. "Where the fuck is he?"

"Still in the hospital, I assume."

"I didn't mean Stephen Henry."

Maggie grinned. "I know. Actually, I don't know where Caleb is. He's heading off to New Zealand in a couple of days — he's taking some time off and then he's on assignment again."

"Sophie and I are going to New Zealand," Rachel said, alarmed.

"It's a big country. You aren't going to run into him unless you want to," Maggie pointed out.

"I don't know what I want," she said, miserable.

"How's that working for you? If you don't want me to come in with you then I've got things I gotta do. Write me when you get a chance."

"I've got a cell phone, you've got a cell phone. I'll call."

"From New Zealand?"

"I'll call."

The house smelled musty, with a chemical scent to it that had to come from the armies of investigators who had gone through the place with a fine-tooth comb. David's precious BMW was long gone, evidence. There'd been a dead body in the trunk all that time. She shuddered at the thought.

She moved through the house slowly. She'd lived here for four months, and oddly enough there was no sign of her presence. Everything reflected David's sterile taste, black and white and beige, and she wondered how she'd managed to live here so long without suffocating.

She went straight for Sophie's bedroom. Her suitcase was gone, as well as the silver barrettes from the dresser, presumably taken as evidence. A stray shudder danced across Rachel's backbone.

Holding her breath, she went into her own room. No sign of her suitcase, either, and the things she'd had left to pack were gone as well. Her closet door was open, the plain clothes were still in there, and she shook her head. She hadn't remembered finishing packing, but then, that day had been such a horrific nightmare it was a surprise she remembered anything.

Maybe Maggie knew what had happened to their things. She headed out into the hallway. And then let out a shriek, as the tall shadow of a man appeared.

"For God's sake," Caleb said in a cranky tone. "It's just me."

She stared at him for a long moment. In the ill-lit hallway she couldn't see him that clearly, but there were fading bruises on his face, presumably thanks to his brother. "I thought you'd left," she mumbled.

"No, you didn't. Maggie said you asked about me."

"Maggie has a big mouth. I was just curious."

"I'm here."

"So you are."

They stared at each other, a long, tense moment. "I needed to say something to you," he said finally.

"No, you don't."

"Don't tell me what I do or don't have to do," he snapped. "I left you to die."

That was enough to startle her. "Don't be ridiculous! Do you think I care? You were trying to save my daughter. Frankly you could have slit my throat and it wouldn't have mattered. All that mattered was Sophie. You should know that."

"Sophie's not all that matters," he said in a low voice. "You matter. To me."

She didn't want to hear this. She was much too vulnerable, and the only way she'd been able to keep it together was pull a layer of ice around her heart. "Glad to hear it," she said briskly. "I'll send you a Christmas card. Now if you'll excuse me." She tried to push past him, but he put a hand on her arm.

"How will you know where to send it?"

He was too close, but somehow his presence wasn't threatening. She wanted to lean against him, put her face against his shoulder and let him hold her while she cried.

But Caleb Middleton wasn't the comforting type.

She took a deep breath. "I don't know where I'll send it. Maybe we'll all come back and spend Christmas with Stephen Henry, just one big happy family," she said sarcastically. And then realized that bizarre as it was, she wanted that. She loved the Old Goat. She loved —

Shit, that was the last thing she needed. She looked up at him. "Why are you here?"

"Sophie's in the car," he said, not answering.

"What car?"

"My car. Your suitcases are there as well."

"Are you driving us to the airport?" she asked, trying to sound cool. "We haven't booked a flight yet — I don't know exactly where we're going."

"I thought New Zealand would be nice this time of year. Hell, it's always nice. Sophie says you haven't been there yet."

"And why am I going there now?"

"Because I am," he said. "And you're coming with me."

She looked at him. "Oh, yeah? Why?"

"Because it's what Sophie wants. Don't you spend your life doing everything for Sophie, including marrying the wrong man and almost getting killed? This is a no-brainer compared to that. Sophie wants the three of us together. I've made arrangements."

She was tempted, damn she was tempted. "No," she said flatly.

"No?"

"One stupid marriage is all Sophie gets. She and I will be fine on our own. I don't have to make any more stupid sacrifices."

"Marrying me would be a stupid sacrifice?" He looked affronted.

"Why the hell are you even talking about marriage?" she countered. Her heart was hammering, and she tried to tell herself it was because she was talking to a crazy person.

He ran a hand through his long hair, uncomfortable and frustrated. "Look. I'm tired of arguing with you. The fact of the matter is, you love me —" he ignored her derisive "ha!" and went on, "— and I love you. So we're getting married and living happily ever after, whether you like it or not."

"You don't love me," she said, cursing the

fact that her voice sounded a little rough.

A wry smile lit his face. "Don't I?" He took her chin in his hand, leaned over and kissed her, very lightly, on her mouth. He brushed her eyelids, her cheekbones with his lips, then kissed her again, slow, deep, tender, and she felt her body rise into it, unable to resist.

He stepped back. "Is that settled?"

"I've already killed one man because he tried to boss me around — don't think you can get away with it."

He laughed. "I'll keep that in mind. So what do you think? New Zealand? It's lambing season."

Before she could say anything the front door slammed open, and Sophie stood there, her newly cut hair just brushing her ears. "Hasn't he talked you into it yet?" she said. "He must be doing a piss-poor job. Listen, Ma, the poor jerk is in love with you and wants to marry you, and he'll even put up with me. And I know you well enough to know you've been eating your heart over him for the last ten days. So let's get the hell out of here and you can argue on the plane."

Rachel looked at Sophie, calm and unflappable as always, one very determined young lady. She looked at Caleb. She barely knew him. She just knew he was the one, and she'd known it since she'd first looked into his dark eyes outside of Stephen Henry's kitchen.

She shrugged. "Well, at least I don't have to worry about changing my name."

Caleb grinned at her. "I like a practical woman," he said. "Let's get the hell out of here." He held out his hand, and she took it, moving forward, putting her arm around Sophie's narrow shoulders.

Sophie opened the door, and for a moment Rachel froze. For the first time in four months the sun was shining in Silver Falls, warm beams of light gilding everything.

And they stepped out into the bright sunshine, into a brave new world.